Under the Stone

Heather McConnell

First published by Belair Press, 2023

Cover by Design for Writers

ISBN: 978-1-3999-5760-1

For Gordon,
with love

Chapter 1

There would be no audience. All the better for the task ahead. Betty's daughters stood together on the rocks by the Umhlanga lighthouse. The weather had changed overnight. Banks of grey clouds sucked the colour from the sea and a fine mist cut visibility and cooled the morning air. The early hour and poor weather meant fewer people on the boardwalk.

Kate held the box that had accompanied them from Belfast to Durban, a silent companion. Ellen clutched the gerberas they had bought, their stems cut short, their heads flaming red and yellow, defying the drabness of the day.

Kate stepped closer to the water lapping the rocks, hunkered down and lifted the parchment parcel from the box. She glanced up at Ellen who nodded, then lowered the parcel into the water as if launching a toy yacht into a park pond. They watched as the water slowly stained the parchment, and the parcel with their mother's ashes slipped below the surface. Ellen tossed the dazzling flower heads onto the empty ring of water and the sisters watched them rise and fall with the swell of the waves.

Ellen turned to see tears coursing down Kate's cheeks and it startled her. The fierce self-control Kate had nurtured all her life was disintegrating in the face of that finality. Ellen rested her hand on her sister's arm, felt her body shuddering. Kate brushed away her tears and they stood staring at the sea in silence.

Ellen spoke first, in a whisper. 'It wasn't much of a send-off. No speeches. No one here but us. Have we done enough?'

Kate faced her, composure restored. 'It's exactly what Mum wanted. No fuss, no bother.'

'Best not to fling me,' Betty had said as she lay in the hospice, her eyes dancing with mischief again. 'The wind might be blowing the wrong way.'

Ellen looked across the waves, searching in vain for the flower heads. 'Feisty and funny to the end,' she murmured as they turned away.

They had the rest of the day before their flight home. A day to kill or fill. Their uncle had apologised for not being able to see them and had suggested a private tour to a kraal, a traditional African village. Ellen managed to persuade her reluctant sister and booked it. But now, as Ellen glanced back at the lighthouse, her own enthusiasm for the trip waned.

'Should we go?' she asked.

'We'd lose our money if we didn't,' Kate said, shrugging. 'I told you I could get on with emails and stuff for the exhibition but you were keen, so ...'

'Okay then, let's go,' Ellen said hurriedly. 'At least it'll be a distraction. Maybe an interesting one.' Her tentative smile was not returned.

* * *

The jeep moved through pillowed hills, criss-crossed by beaten earth tracks. Thando, the excited tour guide, told the sisters that Musa, the local sangoma, would be paying a visit. Musa hadn't wished to follow in his father's footsteps as a sangoma, Thando explained, but having been called by his ancestral spirits, he had accepted his fate as a diviner and healer.

'It's a very special visit too,' he announced as the jeep left the road and jiggled its way along a dirt track. 'Musa has offered to do a reading for you. It is truly an honour.'

Ellen beamed. Kate sighed.

The sisters, walking a cool distance apart, followed Thando to a group of beehive huts squatting in a circle of cleared ground. Hesitant children watched from dark doorways as they approached. A boy edged forward, shadowed by another, enticed by the unfamiliar. It was not the exuberant rush of South African township kids that Kate and Ellen had seen in documentaries. This was a cautious reaching out, hands slipping into their hands, turning them over, stroking their fingers, exploring their jewellery. A little unsettling, like the touch of the blind.

The children drew the sisters into the largest hut. Ellen noted with disappointment the concrete walls and two grimy latticed windows. The only furnishing was a small rush mat on the pitted concrete floor. Rubbish was piled high in a corner of the room – empty plastic bottles, rags, a battered suitcase. Thando sat down on the bare earth near the mat. Ellen and Kate took their cue from him and sat down, leaning gingerly against the blackened wall. Despite the door being wide open, the room was cell-like and claustrophobic.

Kate edged away from a child who sat beside her, his stick-thin arm touching hers. He turned to Ellen instead, who smiled at him and held out her hand. She was just drawing the boy close when he was up and rushing over to a man who had stepped into the room. Thando greeted the man in hushed tones and introduced him as Musa. The boy, he explained, was Musa's son.

While Thando talked, Musa sat calmly, languidly, on the rush mat with the boy gathered loosely in his arms. The smile he gave the child was warm and genuine. Musa was dressed in a faded t-shirt, shorts and canvas boots. His high cheekbones, wide brow and fine sculpted nose gleamed in the shafted sunlight. He appeared detached from his audience. Not rude, but nonchalant, aloof, like a lion with its fawning pride.

Snatches of Thando's explanation reached them on the hot, still air. 'The ancestors will contact him ... a messenger from his ancestors will contact yours.'

Kate shifted restlessly, cleared her throat. Musa set down his son and left the hut. Ellen looked at Thando, afraid that something was wrong or that they had somehow offended the sangoma. Thando smiled to reassure her.

'He's getting ready now. He will divine for you.' His tone was reverential.

'Let's go,' Kate mouthed at Ellen, nodding towards the door, but Ellen ignored her as Musa reappeared, padding barefoot across the floor.

He sat again on the rush mat and set a leather pouch and a flywhisk on the ground. Pulled tight over his crisp-curled hair was a leopard fur headband and draped around his shoulders and tied at the neck was a blue cotton cape. Somehow his understated appearance was more impressive than if he had entered in full ceremonial dress.

He opened the leather pouch and tumbled its contents onto the floor: fragments of bone, shells, buttons, coins, even tiny plastic toys. They were more like the turned-out contents of a boy's pockets than a spirit medium's tools. He laid the flywhisk beside them and, circling a hand over everything, began to chant. His voice was deep and resonant, the words like musical notes with soft clicks for added percussion. Thando murmured that Musa was summoning the ancestors by intoning their names. Ellen glanced at Kate who rolled her eyes.

Musa picked up a handful of the tossed items and spat on

them, then held them out towards Ellen. Thando whispered that she should spit too. Kate gasped but transformed it into a rapid-fire cough. Ellen only managed an embarrassed dry rasp of a spit. Musa offered the objects to Kate who shook her head. Unperturbed, Musa cast them onto the ground. They fanned out around him, but a little metal disc with a hole in its centre tracked its own course, a slow-motion on-its-edge trundle away from the rest, a missile seeking its target. It didn't swerve or falter until it reached its final resting place, an inch from Ellen's knee.

Ellen glanced up nervously at the sangoma. She peered down at the object again. The tyreless wheel of a toy car? A tribal pendant? A metal washer? She frowned and pulled her gaze from the disc back to Musa, willing a response. Throbbing heat and silence filled the room.

As Musa began speaking, Thando followed swiftly with the translation.

'He says you are a very lucky lady. You were born lucky, and you will have much fortune in your life.'

Kate's intake of breath was audible.

Then came Musa's voice again, low-pitched, addressing the objects at his feet while Thando translated.

'He says you are a teacher, but not of children. You are happy with your work and you are a good teacher.'

Ellen sat up straighter and smiled. She knew she wasn't supposed to give anything away but she couldn't help it. Thando grinned at her.

Musa's delivery was slow, his words soft-spoken. Thando's grin looped downwards. 'Musa says you are sad now. Someone died not long ago, someone dear to you. That is why you have come to our country, not for a holiday.'

Ellen found herself nodding. Thando returned the gesture, sympathy written on his thin mobile face. Musa's voice cut in, sharper-toned and insistent; Thando rushed to interpret.

'But here ... here is much concern.'

Musa was pointing at the little disc lying close to Ellen's leg, then stabbing his finger at Thando, uttering his words like commands. Musa was giving him no time to draw breath; the words were tumbling out of him.

'The ancestor is giving you a message. The ancestor does not rest easy. There are questions without answers. Musa says you must listen to your ancestor and obey.'

'No, this isn't right. Please, Ellen, stop this.' Kate stood up and stared at her sister, her hands clasped as if begging, but Ellen's eyes were fixed on Thando. Kate brushed past her and dashed out of the hut. Thando looked startled but Musa continued as if nothing had happened. He spoke directly to Ellen.

'If you have time tomorrow,' Thando translated, 'he will take you to the sea. He would travel with you so that you could light seven candles together. That would bring you closer to your ancestor.'

'We can't. We're flying home tonight,' Ellen said in a rush. 'But I don't understand – what questions? How can I listen and obey?'

Thando relayed Musa's answer with a reassuring nod. 'You will find out,' he said. 'Soon.'

Struggling to make sense of it all, she was ready to ask more questions, but when she looked at Musa he was scooping up the objects from the floor and dropping them into the pouch. The consultation was over. Ellen fumbled in her purse and gave the money to Thando.

Musa stood up, towering above her. The wide, lazy smile was back again and, as he held her gaze, he gestured to her to get up. She scrambled to her feet, suddenly light-headed and trembling. He steadied her, his hand on her arm.

'Are you ill?' he enquired in heavily accented English.

'No, I'm fine. It's just the heat.'

She thanked him twice, three times, a little thrown that he was speaking in English.

'Wait, please,' he said. He reached into his pouch and lifted out one of the objects he had cast across the floor. He placed it in her hand, closing her fingers around it. There was no explanation.

She thanked him again and stepped out into the shock of sunshine. A light breeze brushed her face and she gulped in the air to rid herself of the lingering, musty smell of the hut. Ellen opened her fingers; the little metal disc lay in her palm. She looked at it, quite mesmerised, then put it in her purse.

Children threaded themselves between Thando's and Ellen's legs, little hands vying to grasp their big ones, and shy smiles and giggles ushered them to the jeep. Ellen climbed in beside Kate, who remained silent, head down, studying her mobile phone, and they set off. Ellen looked back, ready to wave, but the children had vanished, their visitors forgotten already.

Thando kept silent concentration at the steering wheel. He tilted forward, like a bent twig, his face close to the windscreen as if peering through fog.

'Why did you run out of the hut?' Ellen asked in a harsh whisper.

Kate set the phone down. 'That man has no special powers, and what he said, as if Mum was sending some kind of message, was really ... disturbing. *No*,' she added with some force, 'it was sick.'

Ellen frowned. 'Well, I found it comforting, even if it was strange. When we scattered the ashes, I thought it was the final stage in Mum's life – our goodbye to her. But now I don't know. It doesn't feel like that any more.'

Kate leaned towards her. 'Trust me, Ellen, it's over. Stop looking for what's not there.'

Chapter 2

The taxi pulled up outside Ellen's flat and the driver announced his fare when her mobile began ringing in the depths of her handbag. She thrust a twenty pound note into his hand, which remained outstretched until she had scavenged for loose change in her purse. But by that time her phone had stopped ringing. She wrestled her suitcase out of the cab and was about to walk off when her phone rang again. She rooted around in her bag and tugged it out.

'Hello,' she said breathlessly.

'Ellen? Ellen Anderson?' A female voice, Northern Irish accent but posh. 'It's Jean Mason here.'

Ellen's brain worked frantically to recall the person behind the name.

'Your mother and I were work colleagues,' the caller prompted.

Ellen was still drawing a blank and remained silent.

'I was her assistant producer. I was at the funeral,' the woman said, her voice lifting at the end.

Ellen's memory conjured a tall, sixtyish, immaculately dressed woman who had taken her hand, expressed her sorrow and told her what a wonderful radio producer Betty had been.

'Oh, Mrs Mason ... Jean ... of course, yes. I remember now,' Ellen said. 'I'm sorry we didn't get a proper chance to talk then.' She dragged her suitcase along the path to the door of the flat. 'I've flown back from Durban. I'm literally just out of the taxi.' She fished the key from her bag.

'I knew you were due back today but I wasn't sure exactly when. Sorry to be ringing at an awkward time but I wanted to make sure I caught you.'

'You knew I was away?' Ellen asked, poised with her key in the lock of the door.

'Yes, I spoke to your father. He told me you'd gone to South Africa and that you'd be back in Belfast today. He gave me your number.'

'Okay,' Ellen said slowly. 'Anyway, how can I help you?' She opened the front door, bundled the suitcase into the flat and kicked the door shut behind her.

'Your mother asked me to get in touch with you as soon as you'd scattered her ashes. I know it's been a long and emotional journey for you.'

'You knew about that too?' Ellen dropped her suitcase.

'Yes, Betty mentioned it when I saw her in the hospice. The thing is, she gave me something to pass on to you.'

'Oh! What is it? Could you not have left it with my dad?'

'It's a package and, no, Betty was very definite I was to give it to you in person, so I'd like to call round with it now if that suits.'

'I'm sure it's not that urgent. I could collect it from you tomorrow If you tell me where—'

'I'm afraid I'm in meetings all day tomorrow,' Jean said quickly. 'It really suits me better to do it now. I've got your address and I won't stay, I promise.'

'Could you maybe give me half an hour?' Ellen struggled to keep her voice level.

'Well ... yes, of course,' Jean said hesitantly, then continued briskly. 'I'll see you at seven-thirty then.'

And with that she was gone.

Ellen glanced around the living room and groaned. Language books and scribbled teaching notes covered the table. Boxes of her mother's books were piled on the tiny seating area by the window. The place was a mess; she was a mess; her brain was frazzled. She swept the table of books and notes and was shoving them into an already half-filled box when her phone rang again. She punched the button without looking at the display.

'Jean?' she said sharply.

'No, Ellen, it's me. Who's Jean?'

'Oh hi, Kate. Sorry. Jean Mason rang me. You remember, she was a colleague of Mum's. Apparently she's got something for us. Something from the office, I guess. She's coming round in half an hour.'

'Oh, right. Well, I was only ringing about Dad. I know we said we'd see him tomorrow but I'll have to work late. Zoe phoned and said there's a pile of stuff to sort out for the exhibition.'

'Don't worry, he can make do with me. I bet Sophie's glad to have you home.'

'She was more interested in what present I'd brought her.' Kate laughed but Ellen could hear the tightness in her voice.

'And Alex?' she asked tentatively.

'He managed all right. Complained about juggling everything. We were only away a few days. It's Alex looking for attention as usual.'

Ellen faked a loud yawn. 'Can we talk tomorrow? I'm really tired and I need to tidy up before Jean comes.'

'No problem. I'm pretty wrecked too.'

Ellen hurried into the kitchen and opened the fridge, simply confirming what she already knew: there was nothing fresh inside. She hoped Jean meant what she said about not staying, because she had little to offer her. Half a bottle of white wine in the fridge and black coffee or herbal tea, that was it.

She stared at the bottle. Jean was in such a rush to deliver whatever it was. Why? Maybe Betty had requested a speedy delivery. It would be typical of her mother to still be playing some kind of mysterious game, frustrating Ellen's inquisitive mind as she had always done.

Ellen was the only one who had managed to prise the scant details from Betty that helped fill the gaps in their family history. Her mother had occasionally shared a few childhood memories of Durban, but the stories had been drip-fed at intervals and were insubstantial. Betty's energy had been channelled into the present; she preferred to skip over her own past. When Ellen had asked why she'd left Durban to study in the UK, Betty told her it was because she craved independence, that home life was stifling. She'd wanted to travel, to study abroad, and the UK was appealing.

But why Edinburgh? Ellen had wanted to know.

'That was my parents' choice,' Betty told her. 'Simply because my aunt lived there and could keep an eagle eye on me. I pressed for London but they threatened not to fund me, so I had to rethink. I did my research and Edinburgh turned out fine. It had a good Politics Department and a new Centre of African Studies. Anyway, when I got there I barely took the time to greet my aunt before telling her I had student accommodation in a tower block and didn't need her spare room. I got a part-time job to pay for it, so my parents couldn't really object. They never knew I worked in a bar.' She smiled and winked. 'And that was where I met your father.'

It was one of those rare times when Betty hadn't scrimped on the details and Ellen had decided to push for more.

'Why did you change your name?' she'd pressed.

'I was making a new life for myself. Liesbet was in the past. I wanted to be Betty. Simple as that.'

'Do you not want to go back to South Africa to see Uncle Hendrik? You must miss him.'

'We keep in touch.' Ellen was about to ask another question when Betty cut her short. 'That's enough, Detective Poirot. You've maths homework to do.'

Ellen, the dogged unearther of facts, frustrated yet again. Ellen, the child who liked to lift stones to investigate life underneath, and Kate the one who looked on from a safe distance.

The impatient sound of the doorbell put an end to Ellen's musing. She dashed to answer the intercom and heard Jean Mason announce herself. A moment later Ellen was welcoming her.

Jean more or less matched the hazy picture Ellen had of her from the funeral. A little taller perhaps, but as sophisticated and perfectly groomed as she had been that day. Designer jeans and jacket this time, and streaked grey hair in a sleek, styled bob. She made Ellen feel like a student in the rented flat, not the twenty-seven-year-old teacher that she was.

Jean took some persuasion to come into the living room, never mind sit down, and when she did, she perched on the edge of the sofa clutching a large bulging envelope.

'You must be worn out,' she said 'This will only take a minute.'

'Would you like tea or coffee?' Ellen asked. 'It'll have to be black, I'm afraid. I haven't had the chance to get milk yet. Or some water?'

'No, thanks. Please don't worry. Did everything go well in Durban?'

'Yes. Being there meant a lot to us, knowing it was what Mum wanted. And we met up with our uncle and aunt, and two of our cousins.' Ellen paused, but when Jean didn't say anything she blurted out, 'None of them came with us to scatter the ashes.'

Jean nodded. 'Betty talked briefly about her wishes. I got the impression she knew her relatives would let you do the ceremony alone.' She held out the envelope. It had Ellen's name written on the front. 'This is what your mother asked me to give you.'

'Is there one for Kate too?' Ellen asked, reaching out to take it.

'No, there's only this one for you.'

'Do you know what's in it?'

'Betty mentioned documents, newspaper cuttings, that sort of thing.' Jean's voice softened as she continued. 'I know how much she appreciated you coming back to care for her. Moving back here, however temporary, can't have been easy. I admired Betty greatly and it was a privilege to work with her. There was so much she still wanted to do. To be taken at sixty-four.' She glanced away, then back. 'I miss her. Now I must leave you. You need time on your own.' She held up her hand. 'Don't worry, I'll see myself out.' She leaned down and patted Ellen's shoulder, then left.

Ellen sat for a moment, listening for the sound of the front door closing and holding the envelope in both hands as if it were a precious gift. Why had Betty asked Jean to give it to her specifically?

Her phone rang. Seeing her father's name, she gently set the envelope down.

'You made it home,' he said.

'Yeah, sorry, Dad, I meant to ring you earlier.'

'I wondered if you'd had bother with the flights when I didn't hear from you. I knew Kate would be busy.'

'No, it was all straightforward. Did you get my email with the photos of Hendrik and Rosa and the family?'

'I got it, thanks.' He paused. 'All went well then.'

'Yes. I'll call round tomorrow, tell you all about it and show you more photos. Kate can't come, though.'

'It doesn't surprise me. She's got so much on her plate. I'll be home about six, so come round for half past.'

'Great. I'll pick something up on the way. What about fish and chips?'

'No, don't worry. I've plenty of chicken salad left over in the fridge.'

Ellen smiled. 'All right, but I'll bring something sweet.'

'Sounds perfect. I'll see you tomorrow, love.'

Ellen brought the envelope to the dining table. Taking a deep breath she carefully eased the sealed flap open with her thumb. She pulled out a sheaf of cuttings, paper-clipped together, with a handwritten note and two photographs attached. She set the note aside to study the photos.

One showed Kate, aged about nine, looking serious and pensive with her arm around her sister. Four-year-old Ellen, tousle-haired and sun-freckled, had a grin for the photographer. The second photo was more recent – only three years ago, the summer of 2009 – before their mother became ill. It had been taken at the opening of Kate's art gallery and shop and showed Ellen and Kate with a solemn three-year-old Sophie standing between them. Kate, a head taller than Ellen, model-slim and striking, was smiling. Ellen, with her tumbling brown shoulder-length hair, was looking down at her niece and laughing. The corners of the photos were dog-eared, signs her mother had treasured them.

Ellen unclipped the handwritten note, her heart lurching at the familiar sight of her mother's large, looped writing, but it was faint and some words were difficult to make out. Her hand shook as she read it.

> I want you to fully understand who I was, what I felt and what drove me in my life, and these documents should give you some insight. Please share them with Kate. I should have shown them to you both years ago.

As you know, when I was at Edinburgh University with Hugh in the late 60s, I joined the anti-apartheid movement and did my bit. You can read in the papers I've enclosed how we woke everybody up and achieved significant changes. I even succeeded in getting myself suspended for a while! Hugh came along to some meetings and demonstrations but he didn't share my passion.

My parents never agreed with my views. They were opposed to every stance I took. Even as a child they tried to make me see everything with blinkers on, but I was a born rebel. Once I'd taken the blinkers off, everything I saw around me seemed wrong and that awareness widened the gulf between us.

Ellen had to stop reading, upset that Betty had not felt able to share these memories with her daughters during her lifetime. She took a deep breath and read on.

We never really talked to you about our move to South Africa before you were born. It was 1982 when Hugh, Kate and I left Belfast for Durban. We were exchanging one turbulent location for another but the violence in Belfast had become personal. Hugh was receiving death threats from paramilitaries because an engineering project he was involved in was a high-security establishment, so we felt it was wiser to leave Northern Ireland. Knowing my family had a construction materials business in Durban, Hugh accepted assistance from them to secure a contract there.

He was very busy with engineering projects and away a great deal of the time. He and my parents were aware of my job as a research assistant at the university but not that it was only part-time. That gave me time to campaign in secret for the two years we were there. I knew the repercussions I might face when I joined a group of activists helping with a community newspaper, but the opportunity to be involved was irresistible. I was interviewing, taking photos at events

15

and, the task I loved best, investigating the stories. I felt motivated and so alive. That was the beginning of my career as a journalist.

As you and Kate are aware, I am and always have been a driven person, committed to my beliefs and to the people who share them. That inevitably brings challenging choices and consequences for everyone. I hope this will help you both to know and understand me better.

With my love,
Mum

Ellen's mind worked in baffled slow motion. Why had their mother not shared all this with them when she was alive? She read the note again; there was no explanation, merely regret. The chance to question Betty was gone.

Ellen set the note and clippings aside and slipped her hand into the envelope. Her fingers found a smaller envelope. Her name was on it too. She took out two handwritten sheets of paper.

My darling Ellie, it began.

For a moment Ellen could read no further than her mother's pet name for her. She wiped away the tears so she could see again the words that both comforted and pained her, and steeled herself to read on.

You and Kate have taken me back to South Africa and I thank you. I needed to go home and this was the only way possible. You asked me many times why I didn't return, except for my parents' funerals, and I'm so sorry I couldn't tell you then. Even now I'm taking the coward's way out by writing this letter. You see, I had to keep my lives – the one in South Africa and the one in Northern Ireland – completely separate. South Africa was in the past. I decided to live for the here and now.

The thing is, Ellie, my love, the father you've known all your life is not your real father. He is Kate's, but not yours.

Ellen froze. She read the two sentences again and again before reading on.

> *I can hardly bear to imagine your shock. I should be with you, holding you and explaining it all, but I can only reach you now with this letter. I understand how angry you must feel that I never told you before. Forgive me, please, Ellie. You see, I made a promise that I had to keep.*
>
> *I met the man who is your natural father (I hate the term 'biological') in Durban, not long after Hugh and I arrived. He was intelligent and caring and I fell in love with him. He believed as passionately as I did in our 'beloved country'. He was older than me and had lived through incredible times with incredible people. We were like-minded in every way and we were with others who shared our principles. The clippings accompanying this letter show what we strived for.*
>
> *When I discovered I was pregnant I had no option but to tell Hugh about the brief affair. Hugh and I had drifted apart and, due to his extensive time away on projects, he knew there was no possibility of him being the father. Your natural father was married with a family and I knew he would never leave them. I decided not to tell him I was pregnant.*

Ellen began rocking backwards and forwards, but she couldn't tear her eyes from the page.

> *To Hugh's credit, he decided to accept you as his own and we returned to Northern Ireland. Hugh loved you and was frightened that he would lose you if I ever told you that he was not your natural father. I owed him a great deal, so I promised him I would keep it a secret.*
>
> *Now, with so little time left, I am taking the step to break that promise. It is only right that you should know the truth, but I ask you, my darling, for Hugh's sake, please don't tell him that you know. Let him hold on to you as his daughter. He loved you and Kate equally.*
>
> *I never regretted for a single second having you, but I wish I had been a better mother. Ellie, my love, live your life as you*

17

have always lived it, with compassion, courage and humour.
Hold fast to your principles. I love you more than you can
ever know, and I hope with all my heart that you are able to
love and forgive me.
  Forever yours,
  Mum x

Ellen squeezed her eyes tight shut and balled her hands
into fists, her fingernails digging deep into her palms. When
she eventually stopped rocking she began to sob, loudly and
relentlessly. But it gave her no sense of release. Frustration drove
her to pace the room and harangue both Hugh and Betty aloud.
Scattering the ashes was no longer the closure, not when her
mother had opened a door to the past but hidden the key.

Kate. She would ring her. Kate would understand.

Ellen lifted her phone, then put it down. No, not yet. She
needed to be calm, not explosive. She needed time to herself.

Hunger growled in her stomach but she ignored it. She
fetched the unfinished bottle of wine and poured, steadying the
neck of the bottle against the rim of the glass, not trusting her
trembling hands. She drained the glass, letting the wine fill her
senses, seeking the effect, not the taste.

With a jolt Ellen remembered that she was going to see her
father the next day. Her *father*. Now she had two of them. How
could she face Hugh? How could she hide what she knew when
it was still so raw?

Like the nervy hour before an exam, her head was jammed
with random facts and confusing questions.

My father is not my father. My sister is my half-sister. Does
that make Sophie my half-niece? Am I South African through and
through?

And then a question that numbed her: *Who is my natural*
father and is he still alive? Her mother had written about him in
the past tense.

Ellen emptied the rest of the wine into her glass and knocked it back like medicine. She would phone Kate in the morning when she'd thought it all through.

She lay down on the bed fully clothed. Once during the night she woke from her heavy, wine-induced sleep, her mother's voice rousing her: *Ellie*. It was spoken softly but distinctly, with a questioning rise in the tone that made Ellen open her eyes and say, 'Yes?' She lay curled up in the silence, hoping for the exchange to continue, longing to ask all the questions that only her mother could answer. She wrapped her arms around herself, stifling the fury and frustration, capping the volcano within her. How could she deal with all this without her mother to help her find a way through?

Chapter 3

The next morning brought Ellen a muzzy head and no impetus to do anything but return to her mother's letter. Lifting it, she felt her fingertips tingle as if the paper was charged with electricity. She read it slowly, over and over again, forcing her tired mind to scrutinise each sentence, desperate to find out more from the scant details her mother had shared. But the answers weren't there. The only thing she knew for certain was that by writing her confession rather than face her daughter when she was alive, Betty had been intent on avoiding interrogation.

Ellen's brain buzzed. She couldn't swat away the angry swarm of accusations. She needed to focus on something without an emotional sting. The envelope with the documents her mother wanted her to read still lay on the table, Betty's handwritten comments paper-clipped to them. She spread them out.

The first one she picked up was a copy of the manifesto written by the protesting students at Edinburgh University that demanded reforms. Her mother's note simply read 'Yes!' There were also cuttings about boycotts and anti-apartheid protests against the Springboks rugby tour in Scotland. Then there were copies of South African community newspapers that, according to another of Betty's notes, 'gave ordinary people an outlet for their grievances.' There were minutes of news-gathering meetings, reports of rallies and speeches, articles from the newspapers that took an anti-government stand, all with her mother's comments.

Ellen picked up the photos of the Edinburgh rugby protests and studied each closely. Could this be a sombre, youthful Hugh looking back at her? Yes, definitely. And beside him was her mum, chin up, looking straight at the camera, defiant. Ellen couldn't help but smile. This was the Betty Ellen recognised – intensely committed and full of joy at being actively involved. And then in Durban, Ellen could imagine the delicious undercover nature of it all. What it must have meant to have someone sharing that love of furtive action. How intoxicating that must have been. How—

It suddenly occurred to her that her real father might be in a photo, standing beside her mother, just like Hugh! She frantically scanned the cuttings from South Africa, photographs taken in townships, but not a single photo of anyone white. Ellen slumped back in her chair. Even if he was mentioned in any of the articles, she didn't know his name.

She sat still for ten, maybe fifteen minutes, certain that any movement would unleash emotions she'd be unable to control. But she could not banish the memories that crept into her head of the mother she loved and thought she knew, and of all that had brought her to this flat in Belfast. Betty's cancer diagnosis two years ago had rocked the family but her mother had remained positive; breast cancer could be conquered these days, the statistics proved it. And Ellen had believed it too.

The surgery had been pronounced successful and her mother coped well with a short course of radiotherapy. She had tolerated the minimum of care and zero fuss from her family, insisting she was perfectly happy in her own apartment, convincing all of them she was fine. She even managed to return to work.

Ellen had stayed on in London, teaching English to her eager foreign students during the week but travelling back to Belfast the odd weekend and staying with her mother to confirm that all really was well. The months had slipped by and normality returned.

Then Sanjay, Ellen's boyfriend, became restless. He'd been with the same large architectural firm in London since he'd qualified but was now keen to work abroad. He began selling the idea to Ellen – what was stopping them going to work in another country? She had experience of teaching in Eastern Europe, so Ellen agreed and Sanjay had set about investigating the opportunities.

He was building up contacts when fate suddenly and cruelly intervened. Betty was told that secondary cancer had spread in every direction. No cure, only palliative care. The family wanted to be involved but Betty turned increasingly to the professionals to help her face the inevitable.

She embarked on a course of chemotherapy, which bought her some precious time but took its toll. At the beginning, Ellen increased her visits, but it became tricky to juggle work and travel. Then in the midst of it all came an irresistible offer for Sanjay: an architect's dream job in India, starting immediately. Would Ellen consider joining him if he took the job? he had asked. Forcing herself to sound upbeat, she told him to accept the job, that it was too good an opportunity for him to miss. She said she would join him when she could, even though she had doubts about securing a paid teaching position there.

So Sanjay had left for Mumbai, the city of his birth, while Ellen had moved back to Belfast to be there at the end with Betty. Her mother hadn't wanted Ellen to witness her total loss of independence with nurses coming and going, so Ellen had rented a flat close to Betty's apartment. Her mother insisted on paying for it. 'It'll be a short lease,' Betty had quipped with the smile of old, and Ellen found herself a temporary, part-time teaching job at Belfast Met.

Ellen and Sanjay spoke regularly. He was caring and understanding, and always offered a sympathetic ear. She could hear how excited he was about his job. As months rolled by, work occupied more of his time, leaving less time to chat. 'I didn't think it would take this long for you to join me,' he said during one memorable phone call, to which Ellen retorted, 'I'll tell her to hurry up and die, then, shall I?' Sanjay had been quick to apologise but the damage was done. The geographical distance that separated them was forming a gaping chasm in their relationship. Their phone calls became stilted and awkward, limited to polite discussion about Betty's health and Sanjay's work. Doubts began to creep into Ellen's mind about joining him in India.

When Betty died, Sanjay was full of regret that he wasn't able to attend the funeral. He appreciated that Ellen needed time to grieve and help Kate deal with their mother's possessions, her apartment, the legal matters. But after that, he suggested tentatively, maybe Ellen could think of making plans again. There should be no problem finding work of some sort for her, not with the contacts his family had. He told Ellen they were eager to meet her and he was looking forward to introducing her to his friends – she'd like them. Ellen's doubts grew. Would it be all about fitting into *his* life?

'I'll need to see my students through their exams and complete the last term. I can't think of anything until then,' she'd snapped, then apologised.

The strain in their long-distance relationship continued. There were no more heart-to-hearts and often no conversations at all for weeks. For the two months after her mother died, Ellen had little energy or desire to try rebuilding her bond with Sanjay, and she had experienced a surprising sense of relief at simply being on her own.

But right now, in the shabby, soulless flat, all she felt was lonely. With a sigh, she slid her mother's letter back into the envelope and shoved it across the table out of reach. She wouldn't read it again until Kate was with her. Her sister. Her *half*-sister.

She gazed at her phone. Why was she still hesitating to ring Kate? Was it the enormity of the news she had to reveal or was she worried about Kate's reaction? Maybe Kate had known and never said. Perhaps their mother had sworn her to secrecy too. Ellen shuddered, jabbed Kate's number and took a deep breath.

'Hi, this is Kate.'

Ellen started to speak, but the message continued: 'I can't take your call at the moment. Please leave your name and number and I'll get back to you as soon as I can.'

Ellen let out the breath she'd held and said, 'Kate, it's Ellen. Give me a ring. We need to— ' She jumped when she heard Kate's voice again.

'Sorry, the phone was in my bag.'

Ellen hesitated. 'Can I see you today?'

'Well, I'm at the gallery now and it's full on.'

Ellen didn't respond.

'Are you still there, Ellen? Is anything wrong?'

'Yes. I mean, no. It's okay.'

'Look, I can spare time for a quick lunch today. We could have a bite to eat across the road.'

Ellen couldn't face breaking the news to Kate in a public place. 'No, don't worry, we can do it another time.'

'No,' Kate said firmly, 'I can tell there's something bugging you, so how about coming round tomorrow morning? If you can make it early, it'll just be us. Alex is taking Sophie swimming.'

'Well, okay. Thanks.'

'Are you calling to see Dad today?' Kate asked.

'I ... maybe I'll leave it,' Ellen replied. It was such a struggle simply to speak. 'See you tomorrow,' was all she could manage.

Ellen rang her father's home number, knowing he wouldn't be there. She couldn't cope with speaking to him.

'Sorry, Dad, I can't come tonight and I'm busy tomorrow. Can we leave it till Sunday? Text me if that doesn't suit. I'm really sorry, I ...' She could say no more and hung up.

The chair scraped as she jumped up. She had to get out of this shitty flat. Grabbing her jacket, she fled.

The cool wind hitting her face came as a shock. It was a typical blustery April day in Belfast, not the warm, sunny autumn days of South Africa. Ellen let her feet take her where they wanted to go – a clockwise tour of the roads around her flat. She hoped the steady rhythm of her footsteps would calm her. And it did, but only for a while. She couldn't banish the thought of seeing Hugh, of having to put on a performance, of talking cheerily about Hendrik and Rosa and—. She stopped abruptly, then muttered apologies to the woman who had cannoned into her from behind. *Hendrik. Could he have known about his sister having an affair? Were there signs in their conversations that he knew?*

She walked on slowly, recalling their visit to Hendrik's home. Images of their living room, leached of colour, were needle-sharp. Sunlight was only allowed to enter through slatted blinds, giving tantalising glimpses of the garden beyond. The room was overstuffed with furniture and ornaments, while nondescript paintings of seascapes and mountain scenes in gilt frames and elaborate prints of fruit and flowers lined the beige walls. Ellen thought of her mother's taste: dazzling light flooding into rooms, bright, bold paintings, and slashes of colour in rugs and cushions.

Hendrik's wife, Rosa, straight-backed and straight-laced, had sat imperiously in her armchair talking to her son and Kate, while Ellen quietly quizzed Hendrik, asking how close he had been to his sister. He'd appeared startled by the question.

'Well, we were very different. I was ten years older than her, so we had little in common.'

She had nudged Hendrik further. 'Mum had her own ideas even then, I imagine. She was a strong-minded woman. Did you find that too?'

'Yes, and we had strong-minded parents who did not agree with her,' he said, glancing at his wife as if ill at ease. Ellen had followed his gaze to Rosa, who appeared to be listening to Kate's conversation with her son but was watching Hendrik intently.

'She rebelled, I conformed,' Hendrik said quietly. 'In a way, I admired, even envied her, but I didn't agree with her opinions. Or rather, her way of getting them across. She was outspoken and always defiant. The best thing for Liesbet was to go to university in Scotland. It cost a lot of money but it was the right choice. Edinburgh was where your parents met.'

He had winked at Ellen, then reddened and looked embarrassed.

'Do you know why my parents and Kate left Durban?' Ellen asked, compelled to find out more. 'They only stayed for a couple of years.'

Ellen had noticed Rosa tilting towards them, and Hendrik, too, seemed aware of her hovering presence. His voice was tight and his wording terse when he replied.

'No, I'm afraid not.'

But she had been determined not to let it go. 'Weren't there two later visits here to Durban? Didn't Mum and Dad come when her mother was ill, and then Mum came alone for her father's funeral?'

By this time Rosa was leaning over at a precarious angle.

'When your Ouma had several strokes, we thought it best to let Liesbet know. It was right for her and Hugh to come. Mother wasn't fully aware of her being here, and Father had Alzheimer's and didn't recognise her, but Liesbet spent some time with them both and was able to fulfil her duty. And yes, she came alone for your Oupa's funeral and stayed nearby. We didn't see much of her on that visit.'

At that point Rosa had clapped her hands loudly and addressed everyone in the room. 'Now let's all go out into the garden.'

And with that the conversation had ended. Ellen had wondered at the time why Hendrik looked so relieved.

She slowed to a halt. *Of course Hendrik and Rosa knew about the affair. The stilted conversation with Hendrik made perfect sense now. Rosa wasn't simply being nosy – she'd been eavesdropping, ready to prevent Hendrik from giving away any family secrets.*

Ellen pulled her coat around her and marched on against the stiff breeze. Had everyone else known about her mother's affair except her? What a fool she felt! As she turned the corner into her own street again, she felt a sudden rush of anger. She wasn't sure who she was most angry with, but it fuelled a steely resolve to find out more, whatever the cost.

Chapter 4

'Dad'll be back very soon, so you have to be ready to go.'

Sophie remained on the window seat, drumming her feet against the wooden base with increasing intensity.

'Sophie, stop that, please.'

But Sophie didn't stop.

'NOW!'

Sophie jumped down.

'Will you come and swim too, Mummy?'

'No, I have to be here. Ellen's coming.' Kate held up her hand to cut off Sophie's inevitable pleas to stay and see her aunt. 'She might still be here when you get back. Now go and get ready,' she said sharply. Then, regretting her tone, she knelt, her eyes level with Sophie's, and tweaked her daughter's nose.

Sophie giggled and Kate turned her round to put her hair in a ponytail.

'Will Ellen stay for lunch?' Sophie asked, spinning to face her mum. The nearly gathered hair sprang from Kate's grasp.

'Oh, for goodness' sake!'

'Mummy,' Sophie shook out her hair, 'will you ask her?'

'I need to be in the gallery, so not this time.'

'But it's Saturday,' Sophie looked up, her expression one of incomprehension.

Kate put her hands on Sophie's shoulders. 'I have a lot to do but I won't stay late.'

'Promise?'

'Cross my heart.' Kate smiled but got only a frown in reply. 'How about us doing something special tomorrow? We could all go to the beach. It's to be nice and sunny.'

'Daddy!' Sophie cried, spotting Alex at the door. 'We're going for a picnic tomorrow.'

Alex grinned, holding out a bag of treats for Sophie. As she reached to take it, he jerked his arm high above his head. She squealed and jumped in vain to get the treasure. She grabbed Alex's arm and swung on it, trying to pull it down.

'They're for after swimming, Sophie,' Kate said. 'Don't keep teasing her, Alex.'

He held his hands up in mock surrender.

Kate walked away, fetched the swim gear and stuffed it into the bag on the floor.

'Okay, kiddo, let's go swim.' Alex swept Sophie off her feet and hoisted her over his shoulder. Taking the swim bag from Kate, he walked out the front door.

Kate watched them from the open window walking hand-in-hand, Alex's head bowed towards Sophie's as they chatted, their words punctuated by smiles and laughs. Kate thought about knocking the window and blowing Sophie a kiss but she waited too long and the moment was gone. She remained at the window after they'd driven off, dwelling on the image of an utterly happy-looking Alex. She had to reflect back to the very beginning of their relationship to have as perfect a picture of their own happiness.

Their first meeting had been at a mutual friend's party where Kate, the art graduate, and Alex, the accountant, both ill at ease in the boisterous crowd, homed in on each other. It had been so quick and easy to fall in love.

Alex brought a new dimension to Kate's life – an intoxicating sense of fun that propelled her along the fast track to marriage at twenty-three. But they'd scarcely unpacked from the honeymoon when hairline cracks in their relationship appeared. Kate had stared at him stony-faced, the pregnancy test in her hand showing their future in double coloured lines. He had yelped with excitement and tried to hug her rigid, unresponsive body. Finally, painfully, he understood that she didn't share his unreserved joy, that Kate's tears were not happy ones. Desperately he tried to comfort her – so what if they'd had so little time alone together? They had the rest of their lives.

No, she said, it wasn't about that. It was about being driven, about having hopes and ambitions. About not being ... restricted. Not yet. She had so many plans. The art shop where she worked was giving her a good grounding, but her ultimate goal was to have her own shop and gallery.

'Whoa!' Alex had exclaimed. 'We haven't the funds for that. Those kinds of plans can go on hold, can't they?'

'But I was going to start a business course now so I'd know how to manage everything.'

Then he had lost patience with her. It was their baby, planned or not. How could she not be happy? How could she not love it?

She was hurt. Of course she would love it. It was simply the shock.

And he had softened a little, reassured her that they'd work it out. They were a team. When she later had a miscarriage, they had held each other but said little.

Then, after two years and the completion of a business course, Kate found she was pregnant again. This time they had both been happy, and when Sophie was born they came to an arrangement: Alex would work from home while Kate pursued her dream career.

Kate was still at the window staring at the space where Alex and Sophie had been when Ellen's car pulled into the vacant spot. She watched her sister walk towards the house and gave her a wave, but Ellen didn't wave back. Something was up.

In the living room Ellen perched on the edge of her seat as if not intending to stay long.

'Tea?' Kate asked, hovering over her. 'I've got any amount of herbal ones.'

'Maybe later.'

'I was talking to Dad. He said you didn't get to see him yesterday.'

'No.'

Kate decided to get straight to the point. Anything was better than this verbal tiptoeing. 'What's wrong, Ellen? Is it Sanjay?'

'No ... no, it isn't.' Ellen shook her head vigorously. 'It's about this.' She lifted a large envelope out of her bag and handed it to Kate.

'Is this what Jean Mason gave you?'

Ellen nodded. Kate pulled out the contents of the envelope and began reading the note that accompanied the cuttings.

'That can wait. The other envelope,' Ellen said abruptly.

Kate opened it and read the letter while Ellen rose and walked to the sliding door that led out to the patio. Standing close to the glass, she stared into the back garden.

'Dear God,' Kate whispered.

'Just tell me, did you know?' Ellen asked, her back to Kate.

'What? No! Did you really think that?'

Ellen turned. 'Oh, I don't know anything any more.'

31

Kate hurried to Ellen and hugged her fiercely. She waited until Ellen raised her eyes to meet her own. 'You're my sister, always were, always will be. Nothing changes that.'

'I'm sorry. I sounded as if I was accusing you. It's just ...'

Kate steered her to the sofa.

'You know those snow globes?' Ellen said. 'Well, it feels like my world's been shaken upside down but it won't ever settle back the way it was.'

Kate gave Ellen's hand a squeeze. 'I can't take this in,' she said, 'the whole thing. I mean, Mum and Dad were starting a new life in Durban. I was only two when we moved there!' Kate's voice rose. 'How could she? And never telling you. God, that's cruel. Who knows if there's more she's kept hidden.'

'She kept his name hidden. Is that not enough?' Ellen cried. She slumped suddenly, staring at the floor. Her voice dropped to a whisper. 'Those days I spent with her, the chats we had, we seemed so close. She asked about my teaching, about Sanjay, about going to India. She was encouraging me to go.' Ellen's voice pitched high again. 'But she said nothing ... nothing about her *secret*.' She spat out the word. 'I'm so angry with her, Kate. Not just with her but with Dad too. What kind of a promise was that to make Mum keep? Denying me the truth.'

'Yeah, I know. They should never have kept it from you. But thank goodness Dad was willing to accept you and keep us all together.' Kate picked up the letter again and scanned it. 'Mum doesn't sound bitter, just sorry.' She glanced up. 'It's such a mess.'

'Hendrik knew, I'm certain of it. And Rosa too.' Ellen told Kate what she'd noticed the day they had visited them. 'I'll contact Hendrik and grill him for more information,' Ellen said, but seeing Kate's alarm she added, 'I'm joking. Anyway, Rosa would kill him if he blabbed.' She gave a little sardonic laugh. 'So Musa was right after all.'

'Musa?' Kate said blankly.

'Musa, the sangoma. You know, the diviner in the village. Remember?'

'Oh, I remember that all right.' Kate sighed.

'He said I had to listen to my ancestor and obey, so I'm meant to stay quiet. Mum's message reinforced through a sangoma.' Ellen raised her hands, palms up, as if seeking a divine explanation. 'Musa said there would be questions without answers. How true is that?'

Kate said nothing. There was no point in revisiting that event. Not now.

'I'm not allowed to question Dad about it. It feels weird calling him Dad. Is he my stepfather? Adopted father? What is he to me now?' Ellen laughed again.

Kate heard the note of hysteria. 'He's been your father for nearly thirty years,' she said. 'He still is. This other man doesn't even know you exist. I think you have to play it Mum's way whether you like it or not. It would break Dad's heart if you rejected him.'

'I'm not going to reject him,' Ellen snapped. It hung in the air between them. 'I'll see him tomorrow,' she added in a softer tone. 'I'll tell him about the trip and show him our photos. That's all. I'd better go now.'

'Sophie was hoping to see you. She'll be back soon.'

'No, I'm sorry.'

'That's okay. But please, Ellen, call me, won't you, if it's all getting too much. Promise?'

'Yes, I promise. You can tell Alex if you want. I'll leave the rest of Mum's papers with you. They're all about her campaigning and stuff. I think the idea behind them was to show how much her and this other man were meant for each other.'

Kate heard the disdain in Ellen's voice. 'I can come with you to Dad's if you like,' she said. 'It's not going to be easy for you.'

'No, don't worry. I'll be fine on my own,' Ellen said. 'I'll be the soul of discretion. A new me.'

Kate could sense the tension in Ellen's body when they hugged. How long would her sister be able to keep that up, she wondered.

Chapter 5

Your father. The words shouldn't feel strange, Ellen thought, but now they do. One line in a letter and your perception of those around you is changed forever. What you took for granted, what you never gave a second thought to, is gone. Doubts arise everywhere and take up unwelcome residence in your brain.

There was now a barrier that separated her from her sister – no, her half-sister. Kate had reminded her that Hugh was the only father she knew and loved, and who loved her in return, but now Ellen could not see past him being the instigator of a secret that was never meant to be revealed.

And that sentence in her mother's letter: *he always loved you and Kate equally.* Had he really? In crept uncertainty. Growing up, Ellen had always had the impression that Kate was his favourite but she'd never said anything about it. It was the kind of accusation that tended to come at the height of a tantrum, and although Ellen had had plenty of those, she'd never wanted to risk accusing Hugh of favouring Kate in case he confirmed it. It was safer to try and find her own spot in his affections. Ellen used to wonder if it was because he'd wished for a son. He had the perfect daughter in Kate; maybe Ellen was the unalterable disappointment. She had spent many nights as a child lying awake in her bedroom, wide-eyed in the blackness, puzzling it over.

Now she had her answer. It wasn't about being another daughter. It was about being the daughter of another man.

Maybe Kate was right to doubt Ellen's ability to have an ordinary conversation with their father. It wasn't going to be easy steering away from the contents of the letter, but she had to try. She had to respect her mother's wishes.

She began downloading the photographs she had taken on the South African trip, ready to show Hugh the next day. It was a welcome distraction, interrupted by the arrival of an email from Sanjay. The tone was friendlier and more personal than his messages had been of late. He described the project he was working on and the frustrations and satisfaction it brought, and added the news that his employers wanted to extend his contract, which he was considering. He didn't ask outright about any decisions Ellen had made.

He deserved some openness from her, she thought. Once upon a time he would have been the first person she turned to. She moved away from the laptop and stretched, easing the tension in her neck and shoulders, then returned to the screen. She began her reply to him with an account of South Africa, the sights they saw and the scattering of the ashes. That was the easy bit. Then she had to tell him about her mother's revelation. She struggled with the words to capture the enormity of it. She didn't want to type 'betray' and 'torment'. Those were words to be whispered to someone next to you, someone who could comfort you, not written in black and white like some legal accusation. She couldn't do that to her mother. Instead, she gave Sanjay the bare facts and told him she was finding it hard to cope with the shock. She added how hard it was not to be able to speak openly to her father about it, not to declare 'I know'.

Her fingers rested on the keyboard as she considered telling Sanjay about the sangoma's message. He would probably react the way Kate had, so no, she'd omit that for now. She finished her email by saying she hoped he understood that, in light of this new turn of events, she needed more time to make a decision about following him to India. Then she hit *Send*.

She glanced around the room and, as usual, it depressed her. The drab curtains, the lumpy brown corduroy sofa and the matching chair with its hollowed-out seat and frayed arms that reminded her of an ancient college lecturer. The flat was always meant to be short-term, like the temporary, part-time college teaching job she'd secured. She'd never planned to stay in Belfast longer than necessary. She hadn't even tried to make the flat comfortable, to make it feel like her own place. She met up with workmates in pubs and cafés but wouldn't bring them back to the flat. The only visitors allowed in were family, and none of them lingered.

Decisions had to be made. There was little time left on her work contract and on the lease of the flat. But where would she go? To India or back to London? Enough, she told herself, snapping the lid of her laptop shut.

Ellen needed another distraction. Sinead, a fellow English language teacher, was fun to be with; her rapid-fire quips peppered every conversation. A phone call to her resulted in two other workmates joining them in the pub that evening. Sinead, along with Dave and Amy, squeezed up to make room in the booth for her. They were eager to hear how Ellen's trip had gone. In their cocooned space they listened intently. She sensed she was talking too loudly and too fast but didn't care. It wasn't only the effect of the first gin; it was also the relief of losing herself in her story. She took them with her, weaving through the crowded streets and markets of Durban, meeting her relatives for the first time. They loved it all, especially Ellen's sharp mimicry of her formidable Aunt Rosa.

'You've got the accent. I wouldn't want to cross her!' Sinead said, laughing.

The mimicry had been easy. It had been her mother's accent too, and it carried a sharp, painful memory. Still, Ellen was pleased she'd managed to skip over the moments of overwhelming grief. They were private, not for pub consumption. Sipping her second gin, Ellen told them about the visit to the village and meeting the resident sangoma. She regretted it immediately.

'Did you get a reading?' Dave asked.

'Yes,' Ellen replied slowly. Her listeners leaned forward.

'Come on, what did he say?' Sinead demanded.

'Well, he said I was a teacher but not of children, so he got that right.' Ellen's laugh was strained. 'There wasn't much else. A bit of a waste of time and money.'

'Did he not commune with your ancestors?' Amy asked. They all turned to stare at her. 'I saw a programme about it and that's what they do,' she said with a shrug.

Three heads swivelled back to Ellen. She swallowed hard. Amy saved her.

'Oh, Ellen,' she cried, colour flaring in her cheeks. 'I'm sorry, that was such an awful question with you losing your mum.'

'It's okay, we didn't stay to hear any more from him,' Ellen replied with a quivering smile. She couldn't help wondering what the response would have been if she'd announced, 'Oh, yes, he communed with my ancestor, and then I found out that my mother had an affair twenty-eight years ago and I'm the result.' She bit her lip. Alcohol was such a dangerous loosener of tongues.

The rest of the evening blurred, as did the others' chatter around the table. Ellen sat back, grinning and laughing when everyone else did, letting the murmur of their voices mingle with the background music. The warm, hazy sensation stayed with her when they said their goodbyes and she went to catch the bus at the stop beside Belfast City Hall. It was beginning to rain, a fine Irish drizzle that still managed to soak through her clothes. She found a seat downstairs and weariness swept over her. She leaned against the rain-spattered window and looked at the floodlit building with its glistening green copper dome and wedding-cake pillars. It all came back to her – another bus, a Durban tour bus, but viewing from the top deck: ornate Victorian buildings vying for attention with skyscrapers, Indian temples and mosques rubbing shoulders with African markets and bazaars. And Durban City Hall, its design inspired by their own in Belfast, almost an exact replica. It was the one building their father had told them to look out for in Durban. 'Your mother called it the link between her two homes,' he had said.

More images crowded into Ellen's head. They'd left the bus, eager to walk the streets of their mother's city and savour the heady mix of cultures. Down at street level, a hustling, bustling world; the babble of voices in a myriad of languages; suited business types zipping past street vendors, their goods piled on pavements or transported effortlessly on their heads; dazzling colours and mysterious, enticing aromas everywhere. Ellen had shadowed Kate on her mission to find Victoria Street Market, the human river sweeping them along and soon disorientating them. They had halted abruptly, causing the pedestrian river to split and flow around them as Kate fumbled with the map. Ellen was rooted to the spot. She was a child again, lost and looking for her mother. The panic was palpable. Kate had seized her hand, peering into her sister's face. No need for Ellen to explain; Kate understood. It was simply one of those moments when the searing loss caught you unawares, when the world tilted for no reason at all and you slid off into the abyss.

Ellen staggered off the Belfast bus and weaved her way back to the flat. She flung off her coat, kicked off her shoes, tumbled into bed, wrapping the duvet around her like a comfort blanket, and fell instantly asleep.

* * *

Kate hadn't mentioned Ellen's revelation to Alex yet. She needed to process it in her own time first. Anyway, he was preoccupied with his news, which he had just sprung on her: he had an interview for an accountancy job with a Belfast firm.

Kate had escaped to the gallery, glad of the extra work entailed in preparing for the exhibition. She filled her time with necessary tasks and her head with vital decisions. It helped to keep *most* of her troubled thoughts at bay. Only when she lay in bed, staring up into the darkness, did she return to Ellen's news.

What Ellen hadn't fully taken in was that it had been a huge shock to Kate too. There had never been so much as a hint, a suspicion – nothing. It prompted her to reassess her parents in every way, and she constantly switched the blame from one parent to the other before inching towards the conclusion that they were both at fault. And if *she* was struggling, what on earth must it be like for Ellen? And then the biggest concern. Would Ellen heed their mum's request not to tell their father she knew the truth? It was too much to take in in one night. She rolled onto her side, her back to Alex, willing sleep but in vain.

Chapter 6

Ellen checked the time. It was a quarter past three – too early. Hugh had asked Ellen to come at three thirty. He was both a stickler for time and a slave to routine. And he didn't like surprises. She swung the car onto the petrol station forecourt. The gauge on the dashboard had been flashing near empty so she decided to kill time by filling the tank.

Afterwards she parked the car in a side street and began walking to his house. It was about half a mile away and gave her a good chance to time her arrival better and clear her head from the night before.

'Dad's house'. Ellen still found it odd to use that phrase, or to talk of 'Mum's apartment'. Lasting family memories had not been made in either place. The house that meant most to them was the one the girls had grown up in.

The family home had been old and rambling and they'd all loved it – somewhere you could lose yourself but not get lost. Hugh liked to tell his daughters that the money he had earned in South Africa meant they could afford a far better home than their first house in Belfast. Upscaling from a street to an avenue, from a terrace house with a yard to a detached house with a garden. That mattered to Hugh.

Even after their parents had divorced, when the girls were in their teens, Kate and Ellen had continued living in the house with their mother while their dad rented a small semi-detached nearby where his daughters could stay over. Their beloved family home was sold five years later when Kate married and Ellen went to university in England. Betty bought the apartment, Hugh his current house.

Betty's decision to buy the top-floor apartment in a small complex was based mainly on two factors: the views the apartment gave her across the road to cricket grounds, the wooded hills beyond and Stormont sitting atop its parkland; and the opportunity to have all that parkland as her garden. Betty had two worlds on her doorstep – the private and the public; peaceful walks and the chance to follow the comings and goings of politicians, journalists and protesters. Living close to the political heart of Northern Ireland, she had declared, meant hearing it beat very loudly or, more commonly, not beating at all.

As Ellen headed towards Hugh's house in the east Belfast suburb, the sun struggled through the clouds, warming the day and people's moods. There was a cheery Sunday atmosphere among those around her. Most shops were closed and shuttered but restaurants and cafés were busy.

She turned into the quiet avenue and gazed up at the sentinels of hard-pruned lime trees lining the road. Their roots had forced up the pavements, splitting and cracking the stones as if the trees, tired of guard duty, were eager to desert their posts. Hugh's place was ahead of her – neat, well-turned-out, detached. A small house compared to its big neighbours, like a squeezed-in afterthought.

The apprehension Ellen had felt all morning increased with

every step. The thought of never telling Hugh that she knew about the real circumstances of her birth weighed her down. And she struggled against the desire to hear his side of the story. Kate could keep it secret; she was like their mum. Both of them could keep their cards completely out of sight, not just play them close to their chests. Ellen would have to be an actor for the afternoon. She stopped abruptly at the gate. Maybe for the rest of her life.

She walked up the path, her heart thumping. Her ring at the doorbell was answered too soon to calm herself. Hugh greeted her with a peck on the cheek.

'You've no car,' he said.

'I parked it near the shops. It's such a nice day, I wanted a walk.'

He ushered her into the living room while talking about what the weather had been like when she was away. Ellen, nodding now and again, took the chance to study him as if for the first time, knowing that she owed nothing in her own appearance to this man. He was younger looking than his sixty-five years, and had a full head of salt-and-pepper hair and a lean, paunch-free frame. He always stood tall and had the shoulders-back bearing of a military man. There was nothing in his career to justify that, but his whole demeanour was one of order and self-discipline. He kept his body and his mind fit. Full retirement was not for him, not yet. Part-time consultancy with his old engineering firm suited him perfectly.

'I want to hear how the trip went,' he said, bursting Ellen's bubble of thoughts, 'but I need to put the coffee on first. I treated myself to a fancy new coffee machine last week and I'm still getting the hang of it. Italian-made. Got excellent reviews. We'll see what you think of the results.'

Ellen, a little miffed that he'd forgotten she was a herbal tea drinker, thought about reminding him, but instead she agreed to the cappuccino he suggested.

'I haven't made one yet, so it'll be a good chance to try it out. I'll make an Americano for myself. I just need to check the instructions. I printed the main bit out. I hate the way you don't get a booklet with the things you buy nowadays.'

Ellen wandered around the living room, unable to sit at peace. It struck her how much the room reflected his personality; in the family home it had been Betty's taste that dominated. Hugh's living room was tidy and precise. There was never a picture askew or a cushion that wasn't plumped up. Bookshelves lined one wall: non-fiction to the fore, with rows of glossy books and technical manuals about engineering projects around the world. There was also a collection of cookery books. Despite being on his own since the divorce, his self-discipline wouldn't permit him to turn to convenience foods – well, only on the very odd occasion, he said – but he would never stoop to microwaved meals. Instead, he taught himself to cook efficiently.

'Come on into the kitchen. Coffee's ready,' he called out.

She walked in to find him standing proudly beside the gleaming machine like an eager salesman. 'Let's see how you rate the coffee.'

He set the mugs on the table. Ellen sliced the fruit cake he had left out. Hugh lifted the milk jug from the fridge. She relaxed a little in the harmony of their tasks. The kitchen was a pleasant place to sit in, with the large window looking out to a garden bright with spring flowers.

Her father urged her to take the first sip. The coffee was perfect, she declared, swallowing the bitterness fast. He was a true barista. Hugh beamed.

Ellen set her laptop on the table, opened the lid and found the photos. She turned the laptop round so Hugh could see and stood behind him as he looked through the images. He commented on the landmark buildings in Durban, recalling his impressions of each of them, especially the City Hall. Then Ellen scrolled through to photos of the university.

'Wasn't that where Mum worked?' she asked.

'Yes,' was all Hugh said.

Ellen moved on to photographs of the Umhlanga Rocks lighthouse.

'Were you ever there with Mum?' she asked softly.

'Once. Only the once. I was away from Durban a lot.' His eyes were fixed on the photo. 'Betty wanted to show me the beach she went to as a child.' He glanced up at Ellen. 'I'm sure you and Kate did her proud.'

'I think we did it the way Mum wanted,' Ellen said.

She clicked through to the photos of the trip to the Zulu village. She didn't mention the sangoma – that was definitely out of bounds. Hugh would have been as sceptical and scathing as Kate. Instead, she talked about the impressions the journey made on her. He mentioned the times he spent travelling in the countryside while working on a dam construction, and told her about the local workers he'd met. Their chitchat lent an air of welcome normality to the afternoon. She told him she had expected parched land, bereft of colour, but although the grasslands were dry, they were soft green and pale gold. She and Hugh shared images of skies that were stretched wider than any sky they had ever seen, with clusters of huts freckling the countryside below.

'I loved the huts with their thatched roofs,' Ellen said. 'Some were like pointed hats and others looked like berets.'

Hugh smiled and nodded. 'The countryside was so different to the city,' he remarked. 'Life was on the roads and the paths and in the fields. No one hurried in the heat. It was slow motion at the dams too.' His smile broadened.

Ellen showed him the photos of Betty's family.

Hugh's first reaction was to chuckle. 'Your Aunt Rosa has the exact same expression I remember from all those years ago.

No change there.' He scrutinised the photograph closely. 'Now, Hendrik's aged a lot. Put on a right bit of weight. Lost his hair too.'

'I liked him,' Ellen said quietly.

'So did I, very much. He was a good sort.'

'I asked Hendrik something silly.' She laughed awkwardly and Hugh smiled. 'I asked him if Mum had been adopted.' Ellen closed her eyes for a long moment. What possessed her to throw that into the mix?

Hugh frowned.

'It was when Hendrik talked about his parents,' Ellen continued. 'He said Mum was nothing like them. And he said he was ten years older than her.'

Hugh laughed. 'Well, I'm sure Hendrik put you right about that.'

'But Mum didn't get on well with her parents, did she?' Ellen recalled her mother's phrase, *the gulf between us*.

'No, she didn't. I saw that clearly when we were in Durban, though things weren't too bad at the start. I liked them well enough. They were honest and hard-working. But anything to do with politics and the three of them were at it hammer and tongs. I mean, full-scale rows. The way she argued with her parents was as if she were a teenager with no respect. Your mother surprised me when she said how much she wanted to return to South Africa, but things were happening there and she wanted to witness them. I told her it could well be out of the frying pan into the fire. Then the Troubles came close to home.'

'Is that when you got threatened?' Ellen asked.

'Yes. 1982 it was. The paramilitaries targeted some of the firm's employees, including me. We had to take it seriously. There'd been similar threats that had ended in killings. We reckoned Durban was a better option, and your mother's family were able to sort me out with work.'

'You didn't actually live with her parents though, did you? I remember years ago I asked Mum lots of questions, but she never really talked about the time you were there.' Ellen stopped dead, aware of a voice in her head saying *don't go any further.*

'We managed a week or two with them before we got a bungalow to rent and Betty got a job. She had no intention of letting her parents look after Kate. They'd "poison her mind" was her verdict, so she hired a girl to look after Kate.' Hugh drained his mug and stood up. 'You'll take a top-up.'

'No, that was plenty, thanks.'

Ellen watched him stride back to the machine and refill his mug. Suddenly, it was Kate standing there too. They had the exact same no-nonsense straight-backed stance, the same high cheekbones and slim build. It stung to no longer have any innate connection with him. She hurriedly looked away, her eyes lighting on the pinboard on the wall. Photos of Sophie with Hugh, drawings her niece had done, with 'To Papa, love from Sophie' written big and bold. Ellen was unable to hold back the tears.

Hugh, returning to the table, saw her face. 'You're upset.'

'I was ... thinking about Mum.'

He sat down, reached across the table and patted her hand. Ellen wiped away the tears and gave him a quick smile to reassure him. He gestured towards the last slice of cake. She took it even though she had no appetite.

'How's work?' she asked, relieved to be on safer ground.

'Pretty busy. Some people still want the benefit of my experience, thank goodness.'

'Garden's looking good,' Ellen said as if she were following a cue offstage.

'It still needs a bit of work. The weeds are a nightmare. But it keeps me young and fit.'

'I can give you a hand this afternoon if you like. I could do with the exercise myself,' she found herself saying.

'That would be good,' he said. 'You know, you and Kate will be able to sell or rent out your mother's apartment now.' His swift change of subject unsettled Ellen. 'It belongs to you both, so it'll be a decision for the two of you to make. Best to get some advice on that.'

'Yes, I suppose,' she said.

'And I'm sure you still have a lot of your mother's things to sort out.'

'Yes, quite a bit. Her clothes went to the charity shops and we've already parted with some of the furniture. The rest, including her paintings, are stored in Kate's attic. We're sharing out the few pieces of jewellery Mum owned, but we haven't come across her watch, the one with the turquoise strap. She loved it, wore it all the time. It's odd it's not among her stuff.'

'Sorry, I can't help you there. She must have got it after we divorced. I don't even remember it.'

'Don't worry, I'm sure it'll turn up.'

'So tell me about your plans for the future. What are you going to do now?' he asked.

'I need to get a permanent job. My contract with Belfast Met ends in June.'

'So you might stay here, or go back to London. Or follow Sanjay to India,' Hugh said.

'I don't know. Maybe I'll go back to London.'

'The kind of work you do, teaching English to foreigners, it doesn't bring in that much.'

'Not a lot, but I love it,' Ellen said. 'There's so much more I could do, especially with asylum seekers and refugees.'

'I'm sure you could get into the private sector in London or teach business English. That would pay pretty well, give you more prospects too.'

Ellen said nothing; Hugh drank his coffee. The silence became unsettling.

'Are you looking forward to Kate's grand opening on Thursday?' she asked as brightly as she could.

He leaned forward. 'Oh, yes. Kate reckons there'll be quite a crowd. She's worked so hard for this. I really hope it pays off. A first gallery exhibition is such an achievement.'

'Yeah, it's very exciting.' Ellen stood up and lifted the mugs.

'Just set them at the sink,' Hugh said. 'I'll pop them in the dishwasher.'

Her back was to him as she put the mugs on the draining board. 'Did you and Mum always want to have another child, after Kate?' she heard herself say, and instantly regretted it.

'Well, yes. We'd always hoped for at least two children.' He paused. 'I know you're worried about Kate.'

Ellen swung round. 'Kate?'

'Well, that seems to be the root of the trouble between her and Alex – whether or not to have another child. But it's really up to Kate. If she can't face risking a repeat of the awful time she went through when Sophie was born, then Alex should accept that.'

Ellen breathed a sigh of relief. 'I'm sure they'll work it out. Let's go outside, it's lovely now. Maybe I could give you a hand in the garden.'

'That would be great, and a novelty for you,' he added with a smile. 'Oh, did Jean Mason get in touch with you? She asked me for your number and wanted to know when you'd be getting back from Durban.'

Ellen steadied herself against the sink for support. 'Yes, she did. She wanted to give me some old paperwork of Mum's. You know, research stuff and outlines of programmes she'd worked on. Jean thought I'd be interested in having them.' The garbled explanation sounded lame to Ellen's ears, but it seemed to satisfy Hugh, who made no comment as he slipped on a pair of old boots and a jacket.

Ellen eased open the back door and stepped out into the sunshine. She welcomed the warmth and the scents. 'You'll have to tell me what to do, Dad,' she said. 'In the garden.'

And so she spent the afternoon pottering about, pulling weeds, cutting things back under Hugh's instructions, anything to avoid talking about what was really on her mind and the burning temptation to tell him that she knew.

Chapter 7

Thoughts of her parents and their failed marriage buzzed around Kate's head on Sunday morning as she tidied the kitchen after a cake-making session with Sophie. Were she and Alex following the same treacherous path? Already there seemed to be no turning back. Physically they were living at arm's length from each other, sharing the same bed but maintaining a strict no-go area between them. There was no tenderness, no intimacy. The last time they made love? She should have marked it on the calendar.

It took little to spark off a slanging match between them. The odd row could be excused but they were behaving like playground rivals now, constantly goading each other over the pettiest of things. They had different methods of combat: Kate was direct and sharp; Alex was all sly jibes and sarcasm.

Kate and Ellen had always believed their parents divorced simply because they were incompatible. Betty and Hugh had handled it amicably enough. At least that was what the girls had seen. Their parents explained to them that they'd grown apart,

51

that the differences in their personalities and their outlooks on life had become insurmountable hurdles. But Kate and Alex were in a very different position to her parents. Sophie was much younger than Ellen had been when Betty and Hugh divorced, and she was an only child, with no sibling for support.

The taboo topic of a second child was at the centre of Kate's and Alex's problems. 'The largest elephant in the room', as Alex put it. The ban on discussing it was Kate's decision; Alex raised it at any opportunity he could: 'Another baby, a brother or sister for Sophie. Think how wonderful that would be. I never had that, but you did.' Lately it was, 'Sophie's six. She needs a brother or sister now, before the age gap gets any bigger.' How normal it all sounded. How reasonable. But even the thought of it swept Kate back six years to the months of incomprehensible darkness that followed Sophie's birth.

She knew she could have got the understanding and help she needed if only she had asked for it. But, no, she wouldn't admit she was struggling to look after her baby, struggling to even love her. She asked herself who, other than a freak of nature, couldn't cope with or relate to her own child? Especially after having a miscarriage. She should have been ecstatic, but she wasn't and she hated herself for it. Worse still, if anyone else had known how she felt, if she'd asked for help, they would despise her for being callous and incompetent and come to hate her too. So into the black hole she had fallen, alone and desolate.

Alex had known she was unhappy. 'A natural reaction after the miscarriage,' he'd said. 'It's hard to accept that everything's turned out all right this time.' He'd tried to reassure her that she'd soon bond with Sophie, but his matter-of-factness made it sound more like a demand that she hurry up about it.

Betty had seen Kate's despair but hadn't grasped the extent of it. It was just the baby blues, Betty had said. It would settle after a week or so. And Hugh, busy with work, was oblivious to

Kate's mental state, although he could be touchingly considerate at times; a helping hand given in awkward self-conscious silence.

Only Ellen saw and understood what was going on. By that time she had moved to London and her visits home were infrequent and brief, but she could sense that all was not right with her sister. Ellen knew to skip the hand-holding and the reassuring words. She questioned Kate incessantly, constantly probing her about her state of mind, infuriating her to the point where Kate burst out with her confession. That outpouring of emotion roused the rest of the family, and Kate was finally persuaded to seek medical help.

Ellen. Without her what would have happened? Kate had made it through the worst time of her life thanks to her sister, and to the pills and counselling she was given. But she could not – would not – contemplate having another child.

Alex had tried gentle persuasion: with another pregnancy they'd know what to look out for, she would get the right medical treatment. And anyway, it wasn't a certainty that the depression would happen a second time. They should take the risk.

They? They would not be taking the risk, *she* would. Kate shuddered, remembering the ice inside her as she'd held a sleeping Sophie, and the fire that consumed her when Sophie could not be calmed. That sense of not being in control of herself had been terrifying and she swore she'd never put herself in that position again.

She wanted now to find some way to return the favour and help her sister through *her* difficulties. But at the moment it seemed that she wasn't needed, and that was hard to take. All she could do was wait for Ellen to come to her.

Kate checked on Sophie. She was lying on the living room floor absorbed in building a row of Lego houses. Alex was upstairs in his office preparing for his job interview the next morning.

She settled down on the sofa and reread the CVs of the three young artists who were exhibiting at her gallery to make sure she could talk about them and their work on the night of the opening. When she finished she went upstairs and lingered in the office doorway, watching Alex without him being aware. He was hunched over his laptop, typing furiously, stopping to read from the screen, then back to typing. He combed a hand through his hair. The familiarity of the action saddened Kate. It was the same gesture he'd made the first time they met when he was quite shy and self-conscious. His lack of self-importance along with his boyish good looks had been what had first attracted her. That and the hint of mischief in his eyes, and the way the corners of his mouth were turned up, always on the verge of a smile. How had all the things she'd loved become so irritating? How had his sense of humour become so infuriating? Had he changed or had she? Confused and close to tears, Kate turned to slip downstairs unnoticed.

Alex swung round, startled. 'How long have you been there?'

'Not long,' she said swiftly. 'I could see you were busy. I just wondered if you fancied a coffee.'

He seemed surprised, then pleased. 'Yes, thanks, I could do with one.'

He looked even more startled when she returned with two mugs. She placed his coffee on the desk, sat down facing him and began to sip her own.

'Preparations for the opening must be going well if you've time to join me,' he said.

Kate wasn't sure if he was having a go at her, but she decided to treat it as a perfectly harmless remark. 'I needed a break.'

'Where's Soph?'

'Waiting for us to go out. We all need some fresh air and exercise. I told her we'd leave in half an hour. Is that okay?'

'Should be. Listen, I haven't arranged any childcare for tomorrow yet ... you know, when I'm at the interview. Any chance you could look after her?'

'Childcare tomorrow? But it's a Monday.'

Alex rolled his eyes. 'I might have guessed you'd forget it's a teacher training day. Or rather a day when lucky teachers don't have the wee brats in and still get paid for it.'

Kate took a long deep breath. 'I can take her into the gallery for a while, but Zoe and I have a mountain of things to sort out in the afternoon and she'd be so bored. Anyway, the interview shouldn't take up too much of your time.'

'But I've got clients to see, and I'm way behind with work. Look, I had to juggle work and keep Soph entertained while you went to South Africa. And at the Easter holidays of all times. Can you not leave your precious gallery for a few hours?' Alex lowered his head to the screen again.

Kate blinked slowly and felt her jaw muscles tense. She opted to change the subject rather than get into another argument. 'Actually, there's something I wanted to tell you about Ellen.'

'Is she going back to London?' he asked, looking up.

'No ... well, I don't know yet, but it's not that.' Then Kate told him about Betty's letter and the revelation about Ellen's father. As she spoke, a train of expressions ranging from disbelief to shock raced across Alex's face.

'Poor Ellen, how on earth will she get her head around that? And she's not to tell Hugh that she knows? That's way too much to ask. And Ellen will want to find out who her real father is. She's bound to.'

Kate took a deep breath, ready to disagree with him, but changed her mind. 'Well, she knows where I am when she's ready to talk,' was all she said.

He shrugged.

'I can understand why you'd want to work in the outside world again,' Kate said to brighten the mood.

'I need to get back on the ladder, but it's not going to be easy. I've been self-employed for so long that any employer will have doubts about hiring me.'

'Then you'll have to convince them you're worth taking on.'

'Do you think I don't know that? It's what I'm working on right now,' he snapped.

'Right, I'll leave you to it. I'll give you a shout when Sophie and I are ready to go out.'

That afternoon they both spent a few hours in the park with Sophie, being excessively polite with each other and overly attentive to their daughter. Later, Alex went back to his office to do more preparation for the interview while Kate sent out reminder emails to art critics and journalists. They managed to finish work for the night at the same time and flopped onto chairs in the living room.

'Everything ready for the big exhibition opening?' Alex asked, leaning back and easing his legs out straight.

'It's all about double-checking now and keeping my fingers crossed for no disasters.' Kate tried to sound as upbeat as possible. 'How about you? Ready for your interview tomorrow?'

'Guess I can't do any more. It's all in the lap of the gods.' He stretched out his arms and Kate noticed the flick of his eyes to his watch. 'Oh, and as it was getting a bit late, I phoned Ellen. She's able to look after Soph tomorrow, so no need for you to worry.' He beamed.

'You beat me to it,' Kate replied, her voice tight with annoyance at herself for having forgotten.

'Well anyway,' he said, 'she'll pick Soph up from the gallery and take her to the park. She suggested meeting up after my interview and having a picnic if the weather stays nice.'

'I'll be too busy to leave the gallery for a picnic.'

'She meant with me and Soph. I'll have a chat with her about all this stuff with Hugh. Ellen said she'd appreciate that.'

Resentment, guilt, inadequacy – all coursed through Kate, but she suppressed them. 'I'll make you a picnic then,' was all she said.

'Perfect. Reckon I'll hit the sack. You coming?'

'I'll be there soon.' She watched him leave the room, listened to his footsteps on the stairs, imagined him running through his bedtime routine that now, inexplicably, maddened her.

Once the exhibition opening was over, she told herself, life could go back to normal. She would cope perfectly well with both family and work, and no forgetting to do things. Only a few more days. She switched off the light and climbed the stairs, leaving her laptop glowing in the dark.

* * *

Alex was pale and uncommunicative the next morning. He kept checking his notes on the company who were interviewing him and rereading his CV. Kate wished him good luck and, ushering Sophie quietly out of the house, drove to the gallery.

Only three days to go to the opening. She had an impromptu meeting with her assistant, Zoe, about the flower arrangements, the catering, the number of chairs needed, where the tables would go. Zoe reassured her on all counts, but Kate remained on edge.

It was almost a year since she'd approached the young artists straight out of art school. She was determined to prove to critics and buyers that she had an eye for spotting the talent of the future. The exhibition had to be perfect, nothing less. It was a huge gamble, but that's what gave her the biggest thrill.

While checking the captions next to paintings in the downstairs gallery, Kate watched Sophie stop to look at a picture. She studied her daughter as she gazed intently at the canvas, her head tilting from one side to the other, her hand flicking loose, untamed hair from her face. She was such a self-contained child at times. Kate found her total concentration somehow disconcerting. Suddenly she felt a desperate need to make Sophie smile. She called her name, but the tone was too sharp. Sophie jumped and swung round in alarm. Kate hurried towards her, keen to dispel her daughter's anxiety.

'Which picture do you like, Sophie? Is it the one of the children on the beach?'

They studied the large canvas with its wide, horizontal stripes of sand and sea and sky, and its vertical, primary-coloured slashes depicting the children.

'Yes,' Sophie replied, again tilting this way, then that.

'Now that would look great on your bedroom wall,' Ellen announced, stepping between Kate and Sophie, looping an arm round the little girl's shoulders and twirling her away from the picture.

Sophie gave her a hug and held on tight.

'Thanks for doing this, Ellen,' Kate said.

'No problem. The only benefits of part-time work. And it's the perfect distraction for me.'

Kate lowered her voice. 'Have you told Sanjay about everything?'

'Yes, I emailed him last night. Any news from Alex about his interview?'

'He rang and said it had been full on, with three of them grilling him. If he's got the job, he should hear by tonight. If he hasn't, he probably won't hear for a while in case the person offered the job turns it down.'

'Hope he gets it,' Ellen said. 'Right, Sophie, let's get going. We've a playground to visit, a dad to meet and a picnic to eat.'

Sophie giggled and Kate gasped. 'I forgot to make the picnic!'

'Don't worry,' Ellen said. 'We'll pick something up on the way.'

Kate watched them go. She felt angry and frustrated. She'd failed the good mother test again and she was sure she'd be reminded of that later by Alex, the one who was always keeping score.

* * *

Alex met Ellen and Sophie at the entrance to the park and the three of them, all coated-up on the cool spring day, wandered along the daffodil-edged paths, past soft budded trees. Sophie skipped ahead and Ellen relaxed, surrendering to the easy walking pace. The playground was busy with toddlers, chubby in padded coats, and older children showing off their daredevil skills to nervous parents. Sophie was easy to spot in her favourite red hat, her long hair streaming out from under it. She was threading herself in and out the bars of a climbing frame, a needle stitching its own design. Alex and Ellen sat on a bench nearby.

'Kate told me about the letter from your mother,' Alex said quietly.

Tears welled up and threatened to spill down Ellen's cheeks. She shook her head to dispel them. Tentatively she began to tell him what had happened but it quickly escalated into a fast flow of explanations and barely controlled emotions.

When she fell silent, Alex asked, 'Did you ever have a hint of any of this?'

'No, never.'

'How did you manage to keep quiet about it when you saw Hugh?'

'I've no idea. It was so hard.'

They sat quietly for a moment, watching Sophie on the climbing frame. She waved at them and Alex waved back.

'Would you ever want to try and find your natural father?' he asked.

The question triggered a bittersweet smile. 'I'd like to find out *about* him first,' she said. 'Just ask Kate. She'll tell you I'm the nosy one, always asking questions. But how can I get anywhere with no name? It's torture. I studied all the cuttings Mum gave me, searching for a photo of her and imagining every man beside her was him.' Her laugh was high-pitched. 'Isn't that crazy?'

'Sounds perfectly natural to me,' Alex replied.

Ellen gave him a weak smile. 'I don't think Kate would like it if I went looking for him.'

'It's got to be your choice, not Kate's.'

'And even if I did discover his name, I doubt I'd be able to stop there. I'd have to try to find him and contact him. And I can't do that.'

'Why not?'

'If we met, I don't think I could keep it a secret from my dad … I mean Hugh. I don't like secrets and I'm no good at keeping them. I'd be going against Mum's wishes and the sangoma told me to *obey* her.'

Alex gave Ellen a quizzical look. 'Is that the tribal guy you went to see in South Africa?'

She nodded.

'Kate told me a bit about him but she didn't go into details. She dismissed it as a tourist gimmick.'

Ellen rolled her eyes. 'Yes, she walked out halfway through. I know it's not for everyone but I'm certain he wasn't trying to fool us.'

'It's not my kind of thing,' Alex said, 'but if you got something from it, that's all that matters. Kate shouldn't rubbish it.'

'He said a couple of things that he couldn't have known about – that I teach adults, for a start, and that someone had died not long ago, someone dear to me, and that was why we'd come to South Africa. He said my ancestor did not rest easy. Those were his words. I know he meant Mum. He said I must listen to my ancestor and obey.'

Alex said nothing for a moment. 'I don't think you should feel bound by that. Saying "obey" – maybe that was just *his* choice of words.'

'Now you mention it, in her letter Mum only *asked* me not to tell my father that I knew,' Ellen said, her eyes lighting up. 'I've read the letter so often I remember every word.'

'There you are then. She *asked*. There was no "you must obey" about it.' Alex flashed her a confident smile.

'That's a good way to look at it,' Ellen said. 'But I'll not do anything about it now. Maybe never.' Her voice quivered and she quickly turned towards the playground to beckon Sophie over.

'I'm hungry!' Sophie shouted as she hurried towards them.

'You're always hungry.' Alex tweaked her nose. He turned to Ellen. 'Did Kate give you the picnic?'

'She forgot about it,' Ellen replied.

'Typical Kate,' Alex muttered. 'Her precious exhibition coming first again.'

'It's no problem,' Ellen said hastily. 'Sophie and I got some sandwiches and fruit on the way here. But do you know what we forgot?' Ellen hunkered down to Sophie. 'We forgot to buy drinks!' She rolled her eyes and grimaced.

Sophie giggled.

'I don't know about you, but I need a coffee fix,' Alex said. 'There's usually a coffee van near the bandstand.'

'I want a hot chocolate with marshmallows and I want to feed the ducks,' Sophie piped up.

'I definitely want a hot drink.' Ellen wrapped her arms round herself and shivered dramatically. 'Hot chocolate for me too, please.'

They found a seat near the van and sat together eating, drinking and chatting. Then Ellen gave Sophie the few bits of bread left over from their sandwiches to feed to the ducks.

'Kate told me you got a real grilling at your interview,' Ellen said to Alex as they watched Sophie at the pond.

'I started nervously and it just got worse and worse. I totally messed it up.' Alex swallowed hard. 'A couple of curveball questions threw me and I dried up.' He began gathering up the used cups and containers.

'You never know, you might have done better than you imagined,' Ellen said. 'To get to the interview stage your CV must have impressed them. But if it turns out you haven't got this job, then go for the next one.' She ignored the shake of his head and kept talking. 'What kind of tricky questions did they ask you?'

'Well, one was what would you do if you overheard a colleague releasing confidential client information? I've been working on my own for so long now, it's a situation that never arises.'

'Maybe I can help. I'm used to helping my students with interviews. We could do some practice ones, a bit of role play. I'll shine lights in your eyes and interrogate you.'

He managed a smile. 'I hope it doesn't come to that. It's really good of you, but you must have other things to do. And anyway, your students need different kinds of help.'

'Yes, I know they're having to cope with a different language, but it's still all about preparation and practice and that's where I come in. At least let me try.'

'Yes then, thanks. But can we keep it to ourselves?'

'You mean not tell Kate?'

'Yes.'

Ellen took a deep breath; another secret to be kept. 'If you want, but I'm sure she'd understand.'

'It's male pride, I guess,' he said.

Ellen looked at her watch. 'Listen, I'll have to head home now.'

'Yeah, we'd better go too.' Alex called Sophie over.

Sophie begged her aunt to come home with them.

'Next time, I promise,' Ellen said. She crouched down in front of Sophie. 'I'll be seeing you in a few days when your mummy opens her exhibition. I can collect you and your dad and we can go together.' She took Sophie's hand and they hooked their little fingers together.

'Now it's official,' Ellen said, smiling.

They set off through the park, pointing out things they noticed on the way and giggling at the bottom-up ducks in the pond. As they headed to Alex's car Sophie slipped her hand into Ellen's. A memory of Ellen holding her mother's hand seared through her and almost made her cry out. She was back walking with Betty through woodlands and parks, her mum filling Ellen's head with unusual facts about whatever world they were walking through – bizarre names for toadstools, like Witches' Butter and Powdery Piggyback, or titbits of random information, like that swifts can sleep on the wing, or that a group of giraffes was called a tower and a group of elephants a parade. They were always things that Ellen found hard to believe at first but came to trust. Her mum didn't lie about facts.

So what was she to make of her mother's uncharacteristic deceit about her father? The sense of betrayal was almost overwhelming.

'You're squeezing my hand,' Sophie whispered.

'Oh, I'm sorry, Sophie,' Ellen said. 'I was miles away.'

And as they walked to the car, Ellen told her about the toadstools and the swifts, the giraffes and the elephants, and smiled.

Chapter 8

Ellen parked across the driveway at Kate and Alex's and waited. After a few minutes the front door of the house was flung open and Sophie and Alex raced each other out to the car and tumbled into the back seats, laughing. Ellen was about to ask why they were both sitting in the back when Sophie said with a giggle, 'We're pretending this is a taxi and that you tooted your horn.'

'Well, where would you two passengers like to go?'

'The gallery,' Alex drawled, sounding like an old Chicago gangster, 'and step on the gas, honey!'

Ellen responded with a quick getaway, while Sophie shrieked and Alex shouted, 'They're after us!' as he mock machine-gunned through the rear windscreen. Sophie went into hysterics. Ellen chuckled.

After the gangsters had settled down, Ellen said over her shoulder, 'Sorry to hear you didn't get the job, Alex.'

'Did Kate tell you? I wasn't really surprised,' Alex replied. 'I've been on my own for too long.'

'I bet everyone's telling you there'll be lots of other opportunities.'

'That was the first thing Kate said.'

'But instead of waiting for the jobs to appear,' Ellen said, 'how about letting me help you look at what you actually gained from being self-employed, as well as those other tricky questions, so you're ready for next time.'

'Yeah, okay. Thanks.'

'How's Kate feeling today?'

'On edge, as expected. Total micromanage mode. My assigned role is childminder so she can lap up all the attention,' Alex added.

'Daddy!' Sophie tugged at Alex's sleeve. 'They're shooting at us again.'

Alex swung round to fire his pretend gun while Ellen was left to ponder Alex's sarcastic tone.

It was certainly a hard-pressed Kate they found in the gallery. She was a whirlwind of activity but always in control, busy with the caterers, checking and re-checking they had the right amount of finger-food and reminding them to offer top-ups of wine at every opportunity, except to those who were guzzling it.

A guitarist was setting up in the downstairs gallery and the three artists were already at their posts. Ellen had met them the day before when Kate had contacted her, frantically pleading for help. Some of the artwork had been delivered late, so Ellen joined Zoe to set up the rooms, all under Kate's eagle-eyed supervision. Ellen tried to calm her sister who kept repeating that the opening must be a success; everything rested on it.

Ellen had the chance now to wander through the two gallery rooms and offer words of encouragement to the artists. She returned to Kate.

'It looks fantastic,' she remarked, 'and so do you. Love the dress. Can I do anything to help?'

'Thanks, but I think – I hope – everything's ready. You could always keep Dad and Malcolm company when they come.'

Ellen laughed. 'Malcolm needs no help mixing at parties. He'll be doing all the mingling and chatting you need, as well as propping up the bar. I'll make sure he doesn't drink away your profits. Just try to relax and enjoy it all.'

'I know I'm stressing too much, but I have to get everything right.'

'Everything you do is perfection,' Ellen countered. 'Unlike me, you don't have to prove yourself to anyone.'

There was a short awkward silence.

'Maybe not to others,' Kate said, 'but I have something to prove to myself. I don't want to depend on people propping me up.' The words tumbled out at speed, an urgent confession. 'I know this exhibition has taken over my life. I've neglected everybody, especially you. I'm really sorry. I'll make it up to you, I promise.'

Ellen shook her head. 'We'll have plenty of time.'

About to add more reassurance, Ellen was distracted by the sight of Hugh walking towards them followed by Malcolm. For a moment she considered hurrying away on the pretext of looking for Sophie, but she waited a little too long. Hugh was already standing in front of them. He glanced over his shoulder.

'Malcolm's disappeared,' Hugh muttered.

'There he is.' Kate pointed to a man, shorter and broader than Hugh with a shock of grey hair that could not be tamed and matching wild eyebrows. He had veered off course and was standing at the counter, holding a bottle of wine and speaking to one of the catering staff.

'I bet you any money he's checking the label,' Hugh said.

Malcolm, wearing mustard-coloured trousers and sporting a cravat, strode towards them and headed straight to Kate with his arms outstretched. He hugged her warmly and boomed, 'Sorry,

Kate, I just had to check you got in good wine, and you have indeed. Lovely to be here. A pity Carol had one of her dos to go to. Anyway, Hugh insisted we got here ahead of the crowd. It'll give me a chance to see the works of art without being elbowed out of the way.' He laughed loudly, then turned to Ellen and embraced her.

'Ellen, my dear, lovely to see you.' His voice dropped to a conspiratorial whisper. 'Did all go well in Durban?'

'Yes, Malcolm, we did as Mum asked and it was very special.'

'Get your father out there too. Do him good. And have you plans to go to India?' Malcolm was back to full volume. 'I'm sure that young man of yours is desperate for you to join him.' His smile stretched across his face.

Ellen stiffened.

Kate quickly took Malcolm's arm. 'Malcolm,' she purred, 'can I show you around? You too, Dad.'

'Oh ... yes, I'd be delighted, my dear,' Malcolm said. 'Lead the way.'

Ellen watched them go with relief. Hugh and Malcolm's friendship was one of opposites. Where Hugh was measured and self-controlled, Malcolm was ebullient and unrestrained – he said what he thought and he said it with gusto. His gaffes were legendary. They had first worked together in a major engineering firm in Belfast and renewed their friendship when Hugh returned from South Africa. Betty had found Malcolm overbearing, especially when holding views she was strongly opposed to, and his wife, Carol, too much of a socialite, so the two couples never mixed much socially. After Hugh and Betty's divorce, the two men spent more time together, out for an occasional drink or a rugby match.

Such different men, Ellen mused, but then her parents had always seemed mismatched. Or was it the differences that had drawn Betty and Hugh together, each finding in the other person the characteristics they didn't possess but needed? Did they think those contrasting traits would meld and give them completeness? Maybe for a time they did, but in the end those differences became the emotional wedges that prised them apart and drove her mother to look elsewhere. Each time Ellen tried to understand her parents' subsequent actions she felt overwhelmed. She hurriedly rummaged in her bag for her phone and, trying to look preoccupied, pressed buttons randomly, giving her time to let the turmoil inside her subside.

She was aware of a murmur of voices and looked up to see Kate, confident and self-assured, meeting and greeting people as they arrived before handing them on to Zoe, who directed them towards the drinks and nibbles, the catalogues and the gallery rooms.

Ellen took time to speak briefly to the few people she recognised while reporters interviewed Kate, by this time flush-faced and bright-eyed. Photographers roamed the gallery herding people into groups for photos. Alex now looked pleased – even smug, Ellen thought – to be photographed with his beautiful, successful wife. Meanwhile Ellen and Sophie played a game of eluding the cameras but were eventually hunted down and snapped. Ellen didn't begrudge her sister her moment in the limelight, but there was a sneaking envy of her having success in something so tangible.

By eight o'clock the gallery rooms were buzzing. Ellen spotted several red dots on picture frames, hopefully enough to please Kate and the artists, and with a bit of eavesdropping she heard plenty of positive comments to pass on to her sister. Occasionally she passed Hugh and Malcolm, usually positioned at the refreshments table. They raised their glasses to her, and Malcolm would turn to engage someone in conversation, encouraging them with a grin to 'go on ahead, treat yourself to the picture I saw you admiring.' Most smiled in reply and even lingered a little longer over the artwork. Malcolm glowed with satisfaction. The twinge of envy for Kate that Ellen had harboured faded. She acknowledged that Kate deserved the success. After all, it hadn't been handed to her on a plate; she'd earned it.

Sophie was settled happily at a small table with a glass of juice and nibbles, a colouring book and felt-tips, snacking and working with her usual concentration.

Ellen drifted pleasantly through the evening feeling a little detached from proceedings, as if she'd drunk more than the small glass of wine she actually had. The journalists and photographers had done their work and left and, as the end of the evening approached, people glanced at their watches, emptied their plates of food, downed their wine and took their leave. The caterers cleared everything, the guitarist packed up and the three artists gave and received hugs and handshakes. They disappeared into the gathering darkness leaving only the family members and Zoe and Malcolm in the now echoey gallery.

'There's nearly a full bottle of Prosecco under the counter and a few canapés left,' Kate announced. 'We've got some glass tumblers in the kitchen if anyone fancies some.'

'Well, I think we need to make a toast, anyway,' Hugh replied.

Zoe fetched the remaining clean glasses, supplemented by a few mugs, and poured the wine, tipping a spoonful into a tumbler for Sophie who was already giggling. They all gathered around the counter.

'Well done, Kate, the whole evening has been a triumph,' Hugh declared, raising his glass and causing a ripple effect around the circle.

'Thanks, Dad, but I couldn't have done all this without Zoe, so please raise your glasses to her too.'

Zoe blushed.

They remarked on the music and the atmosphere and, with the glasses and mugs drained, made moves to go.

Malcolm raised his hand to get attention. 'May I just say, as a bit of an outsider I feel proud to have been included in your inner circle, Kate. It's been a marvellous opening night and, on behalf of everyone, I'd like to give you our best wishes for what I'm certain will be a most successful exhibition.'

Everyone muttered their agreement and began to shift away from the counter.

'Hugh', Malcolm said, turning to address his friend at the same volume he had used for his little speech, 'seeing this wonderful gallery and the obvious success Kate has made of it, well, all I can say is, it was the best investment you could have made in your daughter. Twenty thousand pounds well spent!'

The others were caught in a freeze-frame photo, transfixed for several seconds, their shock tangible. Oblivious to the reaction he'd caused, Malcolm went to fetch his coat. Kate's face flared red as she walked briskly away. Zoe murmured her goodbyes and scurried after her. Hugh paled visibly, his whole face tightening under the struggle to control his fury as he too strode off. Alex and Ellen were left alone, wide-eyed and silent, as if someone had slapped them both, leaving them too stunned to react.

It was Alex who recovered first. 'What the bloody hell was that all about? Twenty thousand pounds? Did you know about it?' he stormed, pitching each question higher and higher.

Sophie ran off towards where the coats were stored.

Ellen grabbed his arm. 'Not here, not now, Alex. Look, Sophie's upset.'

Alex hurried to his daughter standing in the archway. He swept her up in his arms, switching on a smile and trying to steady his voice as he told her it was nothing, they were all tired after the opening and he'd just lost his temper.

'Like a tantrum?' Sophie asked, babyness creeping into her voice.

'Yes, Soph,' Alex said, stroking her hair. 'Ellen, could you take us home please?'

She nodded, not trusting herself to speak.

* * *

Kate parked outside the house and switched off the engine. The curtains were pulled in the living room but there was a glow from within. The front door was in darkness. Alex hadn't remembered, or hadn't bothered, to switch on the outside light.

She let herself into the house. Alex was at the foot of the stairs. She brushed past him and walked into the kitchen. She could smell whiskey on his breath. He followed her and stood in the doorway as she took her time drinking a glass of water, staring out the window into the darkness.

'So?' he said, the single word loaded with aggression.

Kate put the glass into the sink and turned slowly to face him. 'I'm going to bed, I'm shattered. I'm really not up to talking tonight,' she said and headed towards the door. 'Let me through please.'

Alex didn't move. His jaw was set tight, thrust forward. Kate was not alarmed; she'd seen this harmless posturing before.

'You can't leave it like that,' he shouted. 'I want an explanation. Now.' In the midst of it all Kate could see the child he must have been, petulant in his tantrums but all bluster.

'I really am exhausted,' she said quietly, determined to sound calm but firm. 'We'll talk tomorrow, I promise. I'm sorry about all this. Please, let me go.'

He stared at her with unfocused eyes, then stepped aside.

* * *

Back in her flat Ellen's mobile chimed, but it didn't herald the message she'd been hoping for – an abject apology from Hugh or Kate. It was a rather formal email from Sanjay. He was shocked at Ellen's news about her *real* father. He offered to come over if she wanted him to, but she didn't welcome his advice to think carefully about searching for her natural father and its implications for everyone. He went on to remind her of the decision she had to make about joining him in India. His impatience for her answer irked her. Only in signing off did he write the word *love*.

That certainly wasn't enough to prompt her to move halfway across the world for him. She sent a curt reply telling him not to think of coming over to Belfast and that she hadn't had a chance yet to give any thought to India; it was up to him whether he stayed there or left. She signed it *Ellen x*, just as she did with all her friends.

The anger and hurt at what Malcolm had divulged at the gallery churned inside her. Why had her father and Kate never told her about the money? Her own family! But of course, she quickly reminded herself, there was no flesh and blood connection to Hugh, and only a diluted one to Kate. And that old niggle about Kate being his favourite? Well, now it was confirmed, and in public too. Her father had some explaining to do. Enough of meek acceptance, it was time to challenge him. She had never done it before and she knew it wouldn't be easy.

She hunted under a pile of books at the end of the sofa and unearthed a photo album, its *Family Photos* sticky label losing its grip on the front cover. Time slipped past as she sat with the book unopened, absent-mindedly stroking the label back into place. It would surely contain evidence that Kate had always been their father's favourite. She steeled herself and began turning the pages, trying to look at the photographs the way a stranger would and gauging her reaction with clinical impartiality. Without lingering on the photos of her mother, she searched for photos of father and daughters, especially ones she'd never taken much notice of before. She sat absorbed, her free hand twirling a long strand of hair behind her ear.

First was Kate, cradled in Hugh's arms, then lifted high, or sitting on his knee, or walking towards him while he smiled in encouragement. Then Ellen in similar circumstances, but with Kate alongside too. There was hardly a photo of Ellen and Hugh without Kate in it. She leafed through the pages until she found one – Ellen as a toddler with Hugh. But what she saw was the indifference in his expression, the yawning space between them, a loose hand-hold to bridge the gap, her tiny face upturned to her father, her gaze not returned.

Ellen closed the album and sat with it on her knee. It gave her the confidence to face Hugh, and she resolved to see him at the weekend. But there was more. The gratitude she had felt for him loving and accepting her, gratitude that until only a few days ago had transcended any painful inkling of being second best, was slipping away. Had she spent all these years trying to earn the same unconditional love he showed Kate? Well, no longer. There was another father in her story now, if only she could discover him.

Chapter 9

Kate slipped out of the house early the next morning. It wasn't just about avoiding Alex and delaying the inevitable argument about Hugh's gift. It was about letting him have time to think about it rationally and to acknowledge that the benefits the gift brought far outweighed his frustration at not being told.

The neighbouring businesses were still closed as she opened the gallery shutter and went in. Everything from the night before – the buzz of talk and laughter, the euphoria of the opening's success, even the moment of Malcolm's unguarded comment – was lost in the stillness that enveloped her. She savoured its comfort, letting minutes pass. It was cut short by her phone ringing.

'Kate, it's me.'

'Yes, Dad.'

'I'm heading out to a site in a few minutes but I need to speak to you first ... Maybe this is a bad time to ring.' He sounded anxious.

'No, I'm at work but we haven't opened yet. I'm on my own.'

'Good. I wanted you to know I took Malcolm to task last night for ...' Hugh paused. 'Anyway, he's apologised, profusely.

He knows he shouldn't have mentioned the money.'

'He shouldn't have been *told* about it,' Kate replied dryly.

'He was the only one I spoke to. I swore him to secrecy, but I forgot he tends to speak before he thinks, especially after a glass or two. I'm sorry. It should have stayed between us.'

'Thank you for the apology, Dad, but you're wrong. We should have told Ellen.'

Hugh said nothing.

Kate sighed. 'I'd better open the shop. Zoe will be here any minute.'

'Give me a ring sometime. Soon,' he added hurriedly. 'Take care.'

As she prepared to open up, she replayed the conversation in her mind. Her father hadn't said he would contact Ellen and explain. Was he leaving that to her? She was going to talk to her sister to smooth things over between them, but she wasn't going to shoulder her father's responsibility too.

When Zoe arrived, Kate avoided any small talk and slipped upstairs. She rang Ellen's number and felt both relief and anxiety when Ellen answered.

'I'm so sorry. That must have been such a shock to you last night,' Kate said.

'Yes, it was.'

'Dad should have told you about it as soon as he gave it to me,' Kate said.

'He should have but he didn't. *You* could have told me though.' Ellen's voice was tight. 'You had how long to tell me?'

'Three years,' Kate said quietly.

'Three years,' Ellen repeated. 'It hurts, Kate.'

'Let's meet. It's not the same talking on the phone. Please.'

'Okay, but it'll have to wait. I need to speak to Dad. I can't imagine he's going to get in touch with me.'

'Well, I've just spoken to him. He's heading to a site.'

'Great, he'll phone you but not me,' Ellen muttered.

'How about coming to us for lunch on Sunday?'

'I'll let you know if it suits,' Ellen answered briskly. 'I've things to do.'

Kate went downstairs, feeling as if she already had a day's work behind her. Zoe called her into the office.

'Some emails from people last night. They were very impressed,' she said. 'Do you want to read them?'

'Yes, I do,' Kate said. 'I need cheering up.'

* * *

'You did what?' Kate demanded. She banged her bag and keys down on the kitchen table.

'I rang Rachel's mum and asked if Sophie could stay over tonight,' Alex replied, emphasising each word as if Kate was hard of hearing.

'How did you explain that?'

'I told her we'd got this last-minute invitation to go out with friends and had no babysitter. Don't worry, I didn't pressurise her. Give me some credit. It's just a sleepover, like all the others she's had.' Alex accentuated every phrase. 'I did it so we could talk. It's not good for her to overhear us arguing, like we're doing now.'

'We could talk tonight when Sophie's in bed,' Kate countered, 'but you obviously assume we're going to have a row.' She shook her head in disbelief.

'Yes, well, we're having that row right now because I want to hear why the hell you never bothered to tell me your father gave you twenty grand. You told me you'd taken out a loan and you were paying it back. You were determined to look after your own accounts and said the gallery was doing really well. And there was me trying to get clients, working my socks off to help you pay off the loan.' He laughed bitterly. 'Your father gave you twenty thousand pounds. A gift, not a loan. And you ...' He paused to catch his breath. '... you lied to me.'

Kate struggled to stay calm. 'It was Dad's idea to keep it secret.' She saw him flinch. 'He wanted it to be a father-daughter thing, just between the two of us. He didn't want you to think he was propping us up financially.'

'Come on, Kate, that's bullshit.' Alex leaned over the table, jabbing his finger at her. 'I'd have been delighted to accept the money from your father. Plenty of our friends got help from the bank of Mum and Dad when the recession hit and are quite happy to admit it. Hugh had – and still has – plenty to spare and we don't. The real reason he didn't want me to be a part of your special arrangement is because he doesn't think I'm good enough for his beloved daughter.'

Kate bristled. 'Without the money I'd never have got the gallery,' she retorted. 'It's an investment in our future. You have so little faith in me. Dad knows what it's taken for me to get to this stage. He's proud of me. Why can't you be the same?'

'In your eyes your father can do no wrong. He has you under his thumb,' Alex said, slapping the table. 'You know we could have spent the money on extending the house. Even better, we'd have had enough to extend our family. What a gift that would be for Sophie.' He stood up and faced Kate. She took a step back.

'You're right. It seems we can't stop arguing,' Kate murmured, breaking the silence. 'Sophie shouldn't hear our rows. My mother's apartment is empty. Ellen and I will either sell it or rent it out. Until then, you're welcome to stay there.'

Alex glared at her, slack-jawed. 'No way,' he shouted. 'I'm not leaving Sophie. Never. You go if you want. She'd hardly miss you.'

Kate felt as if she'd been punched in the stomach. Her eyes filled with tears.

'I didn't mean that,' Alex said quickly, raising his hands. 'Kate? ... Kate?'

But he was talking to her back as she walked out of the room.

Chapter 10

Hugh was a creature of habit at the weekends, so Ellen reckoned he would be back home from the supermarket by ten that morning. When he opened the door to her, she registered the ripple of surprise, then confusion on his face. He hurried to replace it with a smile that didn't quite reach his eyes.

'Ellen,' he said, beckoning her in. 'I didn't know you were coming. Did I miss a phone call or a text?'

'I don't always need to call ahead, do I?'

Her father looked taken aback at the snapped answer. 'No ... no, of course not. Come on in. I'm not long home from the supermarket.'

She followed him down the hallway and into the kitchen.

'I'll just put these bits and pieces away, ' he said as he unpacked his shopping bags, taking time to put a spice jar in its appropriate space alphabetically. 'Can you get out a couple of mugs? We'll have coffee ... or tea. There's fresh orange juice in the fridge if you prefer. Now, have I got enough milk?' He opened the fridge and peered inside, then gave a nervous laugh. 'What am I like? Didn't I just buy some. Here it is.' Grinning foolishly, he held up the container as if it were a prize.

This was not her father. The self-assured, organised man she knew had been replaced by a faltering stranger. It shocked her. She poured herself a glass of orange juice, left out a mug for Hugh and put some biscuits on a plate. Her father delivered a monologue on the frustrations of supermarket checkouts while he made the coffee. Ellen didn't interrupt. At last he took a seat opposite her, drinking his coffee. Ellen noticed a slight shake in his hand as it gripped the mug. When she finished her orange juice, Hugh offered to refill her glass and reached out to take it.

'You know why I've come,' Ellen said, touching his outstretched hand. 'Please, Dad.' The 'Dad' sounded unnatural to her ears, like a word that had been repeated until it lost all meaning.

He sighed. 'Kate needed the money for the gallery, simple as that,' he said in his usual measured way. 'She didn't ask for it, I offered ... well, insisted. I saw the problems she and Alex were having. Not simply financial problems.' Hugh looked intently at Ellen. 'I thought it was important to give Kate the opportunity to make something of herself,' he continued, a note of annoyance creeping into his voice. 'And she has. You can see what it means to her, can't you?'

Ellen gave him a single nod of the head.

'You must have been as proud of her as I was at the opening to see what she's achieved,' he went on. Ellen didn't respond. 'Anyway, I'm glad you'll be inheriting a fair bit from your mother. It shouldn't take long to come through.'

Ellen thought of the times she had struggled financially, when she and Sanjay couldn't afford anywhere to rent together in London, having to live in shared houses. What a difference it would have made with a gift like Kate's. Why had he not done that for her?

'Kate's cross with me,' Hugh went on. 'She said I should have told you about the money I gave her. I'm sorry, I don't know why I didn't.'

'I do,' Ellen answered quietly, coldly.

'What do you mean?'

'Kate's always been your favourite.'

'That's not true. I love you both equally.'

Ellen was startled. *Loves you both equally*: her mother's words in the letter. 'Maybe you didn't mean to treat us differently but you did. You never even thought of giving me a gift of twenty thousand pounds.'

'We financed you at university in England. Kate stayed here and there were far fewer expenses.' Hugh stood up. 'But obviously I hurt you, so I'll give you the same as I gave Kate. I'll write you a cheque now.'

Ellen leapt to her feet. 'Forget about it.'

'No, I can see how much it matters to you.' He brushed past her.

She grabbed his arm, pulled him back. Her voice trembled a little when she spoke. 'You said you loved us equally, but you didn't. You couldn't.'

'What do you mean?' he asked, frowning.

'I can understand how hard it must have been for you.' Her voice was a whisper.

'What was hard?' he demanded. 'Tell me.'

'I know I'm not your daughter.'

Ellen watched the colour drain from Hugh's face. A stab of remorse caught her unawares, but it was too late.

'What makes you say that?'

'It's the truth,' Ellen said, her voice cracking. 'You've always known it. I found out last week. Mum left me a letter telling me I was not your child. She said you chose to accept me but were frightened you'd lose me if I discovered I wasn't yours. She asked me not to let on I knew, but it's too much for me to keep secret.' The blood was pulsing in her head. 'I need to hear about it from you. I can't ask Mum. She's denied me the chance.'

Hugh sat down again slowly and closed his eyes.

She waited, clasping her hands together, trying to stop them shaking. Eventually he opened his eyes, sat up soldier-straight in his chair and gave her a long look, pinning her like a caught bird.

'She broke her promise.'

Ellen shuddered at his words and sank back into her chair. 'Is that all that really matters to you?'

'No, of course not. I suppose I shouldn't be surprised, though. With her life ending ...' He studied Ellen long enough to make her feel unnerved. 'Does Kate know?'

'Yes.'

He bit his lower lip. 'You must have been devastated when you found out. Honestly, I'd no idea you thought that Kate was my favourite. You are, and always have been, my daughter. I made ... I asked your mother to keep it a secret because, yes, I was scared – terrified – I'd lose your trust and your love. That was my biggest worry. It seems I was right to be afraid.'

Ellen said nothing. All she felt was another searing bereavement. The relationship she'd had with her father was over and now she would have to forge a new one. Suddenly the enormity of it hit her. The kitchen was closing in on her. She needed air. Her father began talking again: he and Betty had thought they were doing the right thing. They'd had their reasons; maybe they were the wrong reasons but they'd done it for the best.

'NO!' She was shocked by the vehemence in her own voice. 'No more.'

She hurried to the French doors and struggled with the catch, desperate to open them. Then she was out into the garden, alone.

She shivered violently despite the warmth of the day and paced the lawn, seeing nothing but a blur of colour in the flowerbeds. Eventually her breathing slowed; the plants gradually found their shape again and came back into focus. Sitting on the garden bench near the cherry tree, she glanced back towards the kitchen. Hugh was loading the dishwasher. Even now, he couldn't help but be practical. That hurt.

A light breeze touched her face, bringing with it a sweet scent of blossom. Bird song and the muffled sound of traffic drifted through the garden. It should have brought her calm but didn't. She caught movement out of the corner of her eye. Her father was walking towards her. Without a word he sat beside her. Her heart was pounding. She gripped the seat of the bench.

'When I first met your mother, she was so ... so alive,' Hugh began. 'I'd never met anyone like her. I'd no idea what she saw in me. Maybe it was the old saying – you know, opposites attract. I think she took me on as a challenge. Being with her was exciting, unpredictable. She would suddenly decide to do something and sweep you along with her, like going to protests at university. Even us getting married. Betty wanted just the two of us at the registry office in Edinburgh and said "let's do it", so we did.'

Ellen glanced sideways at him. There was a hint of a smile on his face, and he gave a little shake of his head as if marvelling at what he'd done and enjoying the fact that he'd done it. This was a Hugh Ellen had never known. She wished she had.

When he spoke again, the lightness of tone had gone. 'You knew about your mum and me living in Scotland after we graduated, then coming to Northern Ireland for my project manager job. But you wouldn't have known how much she missed her radio work in Edinburgh, news stuff, behind the scenes. She never spoke about it, did she?'

'No,' Ellen said quietly.

'When anything came to an end, Betty would seal it up and move on. That's the way she was. Anyway, she found it hard getting work here. She did some freelance writing, mostly articles. Her interest was always in current affairs, but the Northern Irish public weren't keen to hear an outsider's point of view. And she didn't have any contacts. It was a challenging time for her. Then along came Kate, and Betty became frustrated being at home with a baby.' Hugh swung round to face Ellen. 'Don't get me wrong,' he said in a rush, 'she loved Kate. She was a good mother.' He rubbed the back of his neck. 'She came alive again when we moved to Durban and she started work at the university as a research assistant.'

'Mum said she loved it,' was all Ellen could manage.

'Well, she spent a lot of time there. She got all fired up with ideals and causes too, as if she hadn't left her student days behind.'

It took no effort for Ellen to imagine her parents at that time – her father absorbed in his work and away a lot, Betty loving her job and her secret activism, and Kate probably growing closer to the childminder than to her own mother. The start of a three-way split.

'Then Betty started going off on research assignments,' Hugh said, bringing her back to his story. 'And I got really worried about her safety. I was angry too. It was dangerous to be active in the anti-apartheid movement and she was putting everyone at risk, especially Kate. But she wouldn't let it go.'

He sighed. ' I was convinced that our problems stemmed from me being away so much and my anxiety about what she might be getting involved in politically. But I was so naïve.' He laughed bitterly. 'I never thought Betty would do anything to jeopardise our marriage, or to hurt Kate.'

He slumped suddenly. Ellen reached out her hand but quickly withdrew it.

'Our arguments weren't just about her principles and my lack of them,' he continued. 'She didn't need me any more. That's what I felt. She had this other life away from Kate and me, and it was becoming much more important to her. She'd drifted away from us.' He sat silent for a few moments, then drew himself up straight.

'When Betty told me she was pregnant for a second time, I knew it wasn't mine. I'd been away on a project for months. And anyway, we hadn't been ... close for a long time. She'd had a fling with someone at the university and hadn't told him about the pregnancy. It was never going to be a relationship, she said.' He spoke in a rush, punching out his words, his hands gripping his knees. 'She was frightened. She didn't know how I'd react, but there was nowhere else for her to turn. She couldn't face an abortion. Anyway, they were illegal in South Africa at the time.'

Ellen shuddered. Resentment rose inside her like bile.

'I had to get out of the house the night she told me. I wouldn't have harmed her, but all the anger, all the hurt ... I had to find a way to deal with it. I still loved her and wanted to stay with her, even though I knew she didn't feel that way about me. So I came up with a plan. If she wasn't going to get rid of the baby' – Hugh glanced at Ellen – 'then we'd head back to Northern Ireland, I'd bring it up as my own and she had to promise never to tell anyone. She knew she had no choice. As far as anyone was concerned, the baby was mine. It was the only way we could all stay together. I didn't want to risk her disappearing with Kate. Betty agreed to it. She could see no alternative at the time.'

The reality of her mother's position shocked Ellen. It was nothing less than a prison sentence.

Hugh turned to face her, his back ramrod straight again. 'I did what I thought was best for everyone. Not many men in that position would do it.'

Ellen held her head up, her unflinching gaze meeting her father's. He was first to lower his eyes.

'I admit it was hard at times,' he said softly, his shoulders sagging. 'You were another man's child, but I grew to love you very quickly, Ellen. I'd never have rejected you. All I wanted was to be your father. I could never let you know about Fraser. I couldn't face the prospect of losing you to him.' He reached out his hand. 'Please understand.'

She turned away and closed her eyes, shutting him out. Yes, he had taken in another man's child and accepted his wife back. Those were the facts, but Ellen struggled to summon any compassion for him, any sense of forgiveness. To never tell her the truth? Did he have any idea what that meant to her?

Ellen stood up. He moved towards her, but she turned and made her way back across the garden. He made no attempt to speak or to stop her as she went into the house. She lifted her bag and walked through to the front door, then closed it quietly behind her and walked down the driveway. She did not look back.

Her head was spinning as she drove off, but two pieces of information stood out sharp and strong and she clung to them. The place where her mother and her natural father met: the university; and his name: *Fraser*. She gave thanks for those precious gifts from Hugh, her prayer unwittingly answered.

Chapter 11

Ellen remembered little of the journey back to her flat or the call from Kate that followed. Hugh had phoned Kate to tell her about Ellen's revelation and Kate called Ellen to scold her for not honouring Betty's request to say nothing. They arranged to meet the next day to talk instead of bickering on the phone.

Ellen's life had changed in the shortest space of time. Her connections to her father and her sister felt tenuous now, as if someone was tugging her away from them. Her closest friends were in London. She had never felt so isolated and alone. Sanjay would have been the first she'd have talked it over with had he been there. Could she confide in him now after the dismissive email she had sent? Could she apologise? Should she?

Those questions jostled in her mind with her exchange with Hugh and the guilty reminders that she had gone against her mother's wishes. She craved a distraction and there was one task she knew would be all-consuming: to look for information about her natural father. Just a bit of research, gather a few facts, nothing else. She would keep it to herself; no one need ever know.

Had Hugh realised the gift he had handed her when he'd mentioned her natural father's name? The key to unlock everything; far better than any sum of money. At the table in the living room she rummaged through her mother's newspaper clippings, searching for the name 'Fraser'. But they yielded nothing. She flipped open the lid of her laptop and began typing.

Without knowing his date of birth, the field he worked in or his full name, a Google search proved useless. The number of Frasers in South Africa was overwhelming. She checked the KwaZulu-Natal University website and typed in his name and 'staff'. If he hadn't retired and was still working there – two ifs which struck her as doubtful – he should be listed somewhere. Nothing. Remember, she told herself, he could be dead. He was older than her mum. She had to go back in time. She entered the dates '1982 to 1984', which covered the time Betty, Hugh and Kate were in Durban, only to discover that in those years the university was known as the University of Natal. She searched its site and learned that staff as well as students had been very active politically in the Durban campus. Significant, but not what she was after. There was no list available of past staff members.

She hammered the table in frustration. And then came another exasperating thought. Fraser. Was it his first name or his surname? She tried to remember the actual words Hugh had used. Something about not wanting – no, it was worded more strongly than that: 'I could never let you know about Fraser. I couldn't face the prospect of losing you to him.' Would Hugh have used his first name or his surname? She assumed the latter, but if it was his first name, where could she even begin?

A text from Alex interrupted her thoughts.

Hi. At my parents with Soph. Hope you're ok after Thurs night. Can I take up offer of interview help? Want to be prepared for next job. A

Ellen had forgotten that she'd offered to help him with interview techniques. She had some work to do for a Chinese student she had taken on privately but she could find some time for Alex too. It would be good to channel her feelings into the role of interviewer or, even better, interrogator. They could try out some role play and pressurised questioning. It would be good, too, to step away from the futile search for a while. But her resolution remained intact. She would not give up. She would find a way somehow.

* * *

Ellen spotted Kate inside the restaurant. 'Have you been here long?' she asked when she got to the corner table.

'No, I've just arrived. I booked a table, but it doesn't seem too busy.'

Ellen slid along the high-backed bench seat opposite Kate. 'Have you been here before?'

'Once or twice.'

The small talk eased the awkwardness between them. Ellen took in the trendy industrial decor with exposed pipes and brick walls with huge aluminium lampshades hanging low over stripped-wood tables. Ellen preferred shabby chic.

They spent a few tense minutes studying the menu.

'Anything you'd recommend?' Ellen said, breaking the silence.

'Well, the chowder's good, and the Caesar salad.'

The waitress appeared beside them, hovering with a pen poised over a pad. Kate ordered the Caesar salad and mineral water and questioned Ellen with a raised eyebrow. Ellen nodded.

'Make that two,' Kate said.

Here was Kate taking command, happy organising life and the people around her. So like Hugh. 'I'm hungry,' Ellen said. 'I haven't eaten much since I saw Dad yesterday.'

Kate glanced up. 'I'm sorry, really sorry about the way you found out about Dad's gift to me. That must have been awful for you. It should never have been a secret in the first place.'

Ellen was taken aback that her revelation to Hugh hadn't been raised first.

'Yeah, it was upsetting,' Ellen replied. 'I thought we told each other everything.'

'Dad asked me to keep it to myself. I didn't feel right about that and I shouldn't have agreed to it. I don't know why he wanted it like that.'

'Well, I know why.'

Kate leaned forward to speak but the waitress arrived at the same time with cutlery and napkins. They said nothing as the girl arranged the settings, giving them a smile that was not returned.

'I assumed you seeing Dad was only about the money,' Kate whispered fiercely when the waitress left. 'Why on earth did you tell him everything?'

'I should have guessed he'd go running straight to you,' Ellen retorted. 'It's simple. I couldn't face the thought that I'd have to keep this big secret every time I saw him. I hate secrets. Obviously you, Dad and Mum can keep them, but I can't.' Tears pooled in her eyes. Kate reached out across the table, but Ellen raised her hand to stop her. 'I told him he treated us differently. I never felt I matched up to you in his eyes and I always believed it was my fault.'

'I don't think Dad treated us differently,' Kate said in a low voice.

The waitress arrived with the bottle of water and set it down without comment.

Ellen leaned forward, glaring at Kate. 'Well, he did. And that's why he gave you the money. It was one more thing I wasn't to know about. Let's keep Ellen in the dark.'

Kate sat back abruptly.

'He said he never meant to show you any favouritism. *Never meant to.*' Ellen paused. 'You see? He knew you were his favourite, intentionally or not.' Her hands were gripped into fists. 'Do you know what his first words were when I told him I knew he wasn't my father?'

Kate didn't respond.

'*She broke her promise*,' Ellen hissed. 'That's what he said. The first thing he thought of was that Mum broke her promise.'

Kate poured water into her glass and cradled it with both hands. She took a sip and set it down gently. 'Dad explained things to me too,' she said. 'He rang again last night. He's so distressed, especially at the thought of you rejecting him.'

'I bet he didn't tell you everything,' Ellen snapped. 'You'd have got the edited version. For once, would you stop taking his side.'

The waitress set their salads down and rushed off. They stared at their plates, then began to eat in mirrored slow motion, not speaking or savouring the food. But gradually the charged atmosphere between them lost a little of its energy.

Kate reached across the table again and placed her hand on Ellen's. 'I can only imagine how awful this has been for you. I've never seen you like this. Please let's not argue. It's the last thing we should do.'

Ellen nodded and slipped her hand out from under Kate's. The storm inside her had abated, but she wasn't done yet. 'I'm going to find out about my natural father. I have his name now – well, one of his names. *Fraser.* Dad let it slip.'

Kate pushed the last few pieces of chicken to the side of her plate and looked up, frowning. 'Everything's been so sudden. Would you not let it all settle in your head for a while?'

'Are you serious?' Ellen asked with a sharp laugh.

'Dad's so scared he'll lose you. He assumes Mum told you his name and that you'll try and find him.'

Ellen grabbed Kate's wrist. 'Did he tell you his name, his full name?' she demanded.

'No,' Kate said sharply, pulling her arm away. 'You've already started looking, haven't you?'

'Yes, but it's going nowhere. I haven't enough information.' Ellen stood up. 'I'd like you to wish me luck with my search. That would mean a lot to me.'

'I can see how important it is to you, but please, you and Dad mustn't fall out.'

Ellen said nothing. She set the money for her lunch on the table and left.

* * *

Back at home that afternoon, Kate couldn't get Ellen's words out of her head. Lunch with her sister had been deeply unsettling. She hadn't been prepared for all that bitterness, and she was alarmed by Ellen's unwavering determination to find out about her natural father. She knew Ellen wouldn't stop there, either.

Maybe she and her father *had* been closer than Ellen and Hugh, Kate thought, but the idea that she was his favourite had never occurred to her. She tried to find something in Hugh's and Betty's attitude to the girls that revealed a difference but could think of nothing significant. Then she tried to recall any unguarded remarks Betty and Hugh might have made in the heat of the moment, but nothing surfaced. There had certainly been some tension between headstrong Betty and frosty Hugh, but nothing to suggest it had any connection to the two girls. Any preferential treatment was a figment of Ellen's imagination, Kate decided.

Much more disturbing was the way Ellen had confronted Hugh. He had told Kate all about it. Hearing his voice breaking on the phone, Kate knew the state he was in. He could deal with facts but was ill at ease with open displays of emotion. He wasn't angry with Betty for writing the letter; he was simply terrified of Ellen rejecting him. The triangle of Hugh, Kate and Ellen was being wrenched apart and Kate felt powerless to mend it.

Sophie wandered into the kitchen and perched on a high stool, putting an end to Kate's brooding. Kate prepared Sophie's packed lunch for school the next day while Sophie swung her legs backwards and forwards.

'Mummy, can we get a dog like Granny and Grandad's? Daddy says maybe. I played with Mac all day.'

'I don't know. It's not a good time right now.'

'I really want a sister ... or a brother,' Sophie declared, still swinging her legs. 'Rachel has two brothers.'

Kate focused on packing the lunch box.

'Daddy says I might get one,' Sophie said.

Kate looked up, ready to put an end to the conversation.

'If I can't,' Sophie went on, her head tilted to one side, 'then I want a dog.'

Kate took a deep breath. 'You can always see Mac and play with him,' she said, snapping the lunch box closed.

'But they live soooo far away,' Sophie said. 'Mummy?'

'Yes?'

'Will Granny die like Nana did?'

Kate set the lunch box aside. Why did children never do lead-ins to really big questions? She sat on a stool beside her daughter.

'Nana was very ill,' she said. 'She was never going to get better. But Granny is fine. You saw how well she was, didn't you?'

'But Granny said she wasn't up to running about when I wanted her to play with me and Mac,' Sophie said, her eyes as big as saucers. 'I miss Nana,' she whispered. 'I liked when she came on the swings with me and down the slides. She got stuck.' She giggled. 'And in the shops with music, she danced with me. Everyone laughed at us.' Her lower lip trembled. 'I forget what she looks like, Mummy.'

Sadness enveloped Kate as she hugged her daughter, rocking her gently. 'We'll look at photos of Nana on my iPad, then you'll remember.'

As Kate spoke, memories came flooding back of the times when her mother was ill but still able to respond to her granddaughter. Betty sitting on the sofa propped up with cushions, Sophie tucked in beside her, sharing the book they both loved best, the one with the funny drawings of naughty toddlers and exasperated parents, while Kate stood unnoticed in the doorway, listening to them chatting and laughing at the pictures.

Betty hadn't been the most reliable of grandparents. Kate couldn't depend on her for any set child-minding arrangements, but Betty was the kind of grandmother children loved, funny, imaginative, rebellious and more than happy to flout the parents' rules. It had driven Kate mad at times. But now, with Sophie wrapped in her arms, Kate vowed to bring some of that outrageous fun back into her daughter's life.

Chapter 12

After the weekend she'd had, Ellen was glad to go to work on Monday, to mix with the students and other teachers and catch up on their news. Teaching made life seem normal and her efforts were rewarded with smiles and grateful comments in reasonable English from her students. She managed to ease some of the anxiety in the room over exams in early June with reassurance and coping strategies, and plenty of thumbs-up gestures.

Low cloud and mizzle greeted her when she left the college after her morning's work, but it didn't dampen her mood. Her phone started ringing and she hurried back inside, struggling with a half-opened umbrella. A quick glance at the screen told her it was Hugh and she hesitated to answer it.

'It's me. I've caught you at a bad time,' he said when she eventually did.

'I'm at the college. Are you at work?'

'Lunch break. I wondered if we could talk, sort things out.'

'I'm hard at work with my students right now. It's the busiest time of the year, helping them prepare for exams. I've lots to do and I've got my other private student too.' Ellen was aware of how irritated she sounded, but she didn't care.

'Of course, I understand. I'm sorry, I just don't want to ...' Hugh paused.

'What do you not want?'

'I don't want us to drift apart, and I think that's what's happening already.' His voice was so quiet she had to strain to catch his words. 'You still there?' he asked when she didn't respond.

'Yes, I'm here. Look, I need some space. Can we talk another time?' And without waiting to hear Hugh's response she ended the call.

The sound of a text message made her jump. It was Alex. *Free tomorrow or Wed? Possible job. Appreciate help*

Ellen typed her reply: *Free tomorrow before 10am at my place*

9 after school run ok? Alex replied. *Have a call nearby after*

She sent a thumbs-up and headed back out into the rain.

* * *

The gallery was Kate's haven. Zoe didn't work on Mondays and Kate was perfectly happy to have the place to herself. She read the note Zoe had left on Saturday: quite a bit of interest in the young artists' work and some sales, and busy enough in the art shop. Kate had still hoped for more.

Kate wandered into the gallery space. It had been quite a while since she'd had the luxury of time to appreciate the artwork on the walls. Caught up in the day-to-day running of the business left her with few opportunities to stand and stare. She remembered when, soon after she'd set up her gallery three years ago, she and her mother had stood together looking at the paintings and drawings on display at the time.

Betty's verdicts were worth listening to, and on that day she had expressed her views on every piece of art, not holding back with either criticism or praise. She judged each picture for technique and interpretation, and whether it pleased her or not. She kept returning to two particular paintings: one, an oil with bold, primary-coloured rays radiating from a thickly painted centre, like a giant flower exploding; the other, a crowded African market scene in gouache, fussy with colour and stylised people. They were not quiet, reflective works of art; they were bursting with life and energy, demanding a reaction from the viewer. Stepping close, then stepping back, she pressed her fingers to her lips, then clasped her hands in delight.

'I'll have them both,' she eventually proclaimed. 'Wrap them, Kate, they're coming with me. You and Ellen will get them when I'm gone, but in the meantime, I'm going to enjoy them,' she added as a light throwaway.

'Well, then you'll get to enjoy them for a long time, Mum.'

Betty had smiled, linked her arm through Kate's and steered her to another painting.

'Now as for this one' – she indicated it with a sweep of her free hand – 'it belongs on a biscuit tin, not gracing these walls.'

Betty had proudly displayed the two paintings in her apartment. Every time Kate came to see her, Betty would remark on what a great purchase they were and how much happiness they gave her. But when cancer struck, she prompted the girls to choose which one they wanted. Without hesitation, Kate had opted for the abstract, Ellen for the market scene. It was as if their mother had chosen the two pictures with the girls in mind rather than for herself. Now both pictures were hanging in Kate's house until Ellen found a more permanent home for hers.

Her mother would have loved the exhibition in the gallery now, Kate mused. And if she was here, she would tell her to start planning the next. Kate thought about that for a moment. Yes, that's what she would do. She had the experience, and Zoe was a real asset. There was an artist she had in mind and, with the moderate success of the first exhibition, she might be able to tempt him to agree. It would be quite a coup if she got him as he was already creating a lot of interest. Kate felt energised by the decision. It would take her mind off the collapsing relationships in her life and give her something she could control. That was what she badly needed – a sense of control.

When she got home she told Alex what had happened between Ellen and Hugh at the weekend. 'Dad's really upset that Ellen knows he's not her biological father, so I've invited him here for dinner tomorrow.'

'Ellen must be pretty upset too,' Alex said.

'Well yes, she's still in shock. I just don't think she should have told Dad. She went against Mum's wishes. And now she wants to find out about her biological father. But she won't be able to stop there. I know what she's like. She'll want to contact this man. She needs to give herself time to take it all in and consider the consequences. She should—'

'*This man?*' Alex shouted. 'Ellen has every right to find her real father. She needs your support, not a lecture.'

'I can't sit back and watch my family fall apart.'

'Which family?' retorted Alex. 'If you paid as much attention to *our* family we'd all be a lot happier.'

'And what's that supposed to mean?' Kate said in a low voice.

'Your dad and Ellen can sort themselves out, so why don't you try to fix what's wrong in *our* family instead. You bury your head in work all the time. If you slowed down a bit, took some time off—'

'We wouldn't be able to pay the bills,' Kate finished sharply. She picked up her phone and walked towards the hallway.

Chapter 13

Ellen was running late the next morning. It was almost nine o'clock and she was still typing and rethinking and typing again when the doorbell rang. She was feeling decidedly flustered as she greeted Alex.

'Anything wrong?' he asked as he stepped inside the flat.

'I meant to have everything ready for our mock interview but, well, a late night got in the way.' She smiled ruefully.

'Ah ha,' he said giving her a wink. 'Say no more.'

She flushed deeply. 'No, nothing like that,' she said, 'just out with workmates for drinks, that's all.'

'Those were the days. Long gone for me now. No workmates to go drinking with when you're self-employed.'

'You'll get a job soon,' she said, 'and you'll be back among work colleagues again. You must feel cut off at home. I know how much I need to be out working.'

'I wish it was just that.' He was suddenly glum. 'Life at home's not great either, to be honest. Kate—'

'Come and sit down,' Ellen interrupted breezily, gesturing

towards a chair at the table. There was no way she was going to venture into McCandless family territory. She disappeared into the tiny kitchen. 'You're coffee, aren't you?' she called out as she reached up to one of the cupboards.

'Yes, a strong one,' he replied, standing right behind her.

Ellen yelped. 'God, you made me jump. I thought you were in the other room.'

He laughed and apologised, backing out of the kitchen. 'You're a bundle of nerves,' he said. 'Maybe some camomile tea for you.'

A few minutes later, Ellen brought two steaming mugs into the living room and set Alex's coffee on the table in front of him.

'This job you mentioned. When's the interview likely to be?' Ellen asked as she sat down.

'Actually' – he spun out the word – 'it hasn't been advertised yet. Jack, an accountant mate of mine, said there might be an opening in the firm he works for. All a bit vague at the moment but he says he'll keep me posted. Good to have someone on the inside.'

'Yes, I'm sure,' she said, a little irritated that he had made this prep seem so urgent. 'I suppose we can do a bit of work on interview techniques. Then you'll be ready if something comes along.'

Alex peered at her like a concerned doctor. She tried to smile but it felt like a grimace.

'Maybe we should talk about something else first,' he said.

'What?' asked Ellen, a little startled.

'Kate told me you'd been to see Hugh,' he said, raising an eyebrow.

Ellen lifted the lid of her laptop and the screen lit up. 'Yeah, I told him I knew he wasn't my father.'

'Well, what else could you do, especially after hearing about the pot of gold he'd given to Kate that you were never to know about.'

She sighed. 'It's such a relief to hear that someone understands why I told him.'

'So are you going to try and find out about your real father?' Alex asked.

'I've already tried. His name's Fraser. Dad accidentally told me his name. They met at the university where Mum worked. I knew the dates Mum was in Durban so I thought it would be easy to track him down, but without any other details, I got nowhere.' Ellen paused. 'I want to keep trying but don't know what to do next.'

'If I can help at all,' Alex lifted both eyebrows this time.

'Got any suggestions where I should look?' Ellen asked.

Alex pursed his lips. 'If you've got nothing to show that a Fraser was working there in the eighties, what about him working there now?'

'I checked. Nothing.'

'Hmm ... could I have a top-up? I always work best fuelled up on coffee,' Alex said.

Ellen went to get it, leaving Alex staring at the blank screen of Ellen's laptop. When she came back with the mug full to the brim, Alex had pulled the laptop closer and had his hands poised over the keyboard.

'I'm wondering if he was actually working at the university at that time,' Alex said before taking a long slow drink of his coffee.

'But it's where he and Mum met. She was definite about that.'

'Did Hugh say if Fraser was a lecturer or a professor?'

'No,' Ellen said slowly. 'He only said, "someone in the university".'

'So what if he wasn't working there, but studying?'

'But Mum wrote that he was older than her and she would have been in her early thirties by then, so it's not likely.'

'Not necessarily,' Alex said, looking smug. 'He could have been a mature student doing, say, a master's or a PhD. Or another degree in a different subject even. How about we check his name among the past students?'

Ellen wrested the laptop away from Alex and began typing, Alex craning his neck to see. She found the website but any enquiries about former students or staff went no further than the signing-in page. She slumped over the keyboard with a heavy sigh.

'Don't give up so easily,' Alex said. He swivelled the laptop round. 'What do you call it when someone has made their name in a particular field? He might have gone on to do something special if he was still getting further degrees in, say, his mid or late thirties?'

'Notable alumni?'

'Okay then, let's try Google. The answer to everything,' Alex said with a grin.

A few minutes later Ellen cried out, 'There it is – Notable Alumni, University of Natal! Let's have a look.'

Alex clicked on the link and up came an alphabetical list. Ellen moved closer to peer at the screen. He scrolled down to F. There was one Fraser – Peter Fraser. Alex beamed and raised his hand for a high five.

'But hold on,' Ellen said.

'What's wrong?'

'We're galloping ahead. We can't be certain this is him. Fraser could be his first name. Let's check the whole list.'

They scrolled up and down. There were no other Frasers.

Ellen swung the laptop round towards her again. Her fingers trembled over the keys. 'I need to be absolutely sure it's him. I can have a look at the university alumni page, check the info there. Then try Wikipedia. He might have his own page.'

'Good idea,' Alex said. 'I'll see if he's on LinkedIn.' He reached down for the bag at his feet and lifted out his own laptop. 'Two laptops, as well as two heads, are better than one,' he said with a grin.

'No, Alex,' Ellen said quietly, putting her hand on his wrist. 'I need to do this on my own.'

Alex looked like a child that had been refused its most cherished wish.

'I'm sorry, but it has to be this way,' she said.

'Of course,' he said, rising to his feet. 'I'll wait in the kitchen.'

'I meant when I'm on my own.' Ellen smiled to soften the let-down. She glanced at her watch. 'I have to head to college. I'm sorry we didn't get doing your interview prep. Anyway, haven't you got an appointment?'

He looked puzzled.

'You said you had a call nearby.'

'Yes, sorry, I forgot. I'll head there now.' Flustered, he lifted his mug, then set it down again. 'Will you let me know how you get on?'

'Of course. And thanks, I wouldn't have got this far without you. We'll organise another time to do the interview practice. I'll give you a ring.'

'Yes, right,' Alex said, and he lifted his bag and left the flat.

Ellen's eagerness to search was briefly replaced by worries about what the next step might bring. Was Peter Fraser still alive? And would there be a photograph? Was she ready for any of this? There was no turning back. She hovered over his name on the list of alumni, then clicked it and let out the breath she'd been holding.

There was no photograph, only text. Frantically she scanned the page, found 'born in Johannesburg' and his date of birth, 3 February 1944. She did a quick mental calculation: sixty-eight. There was no 'died'. A surge of relief. But when had the site last been updated? There was other information and it drew her in.

He had 'Doctor' as his title. He was an epidemiologist. Wasn't that to do with insects? Science subjects had never been her strength. Or was it about infectious diseases? She read on and came across references to HIV prevention.

She leaned in close to the screen. He had attended the University of the Witwatersrand in Johannesburg and gained his degree in medicine. Focused on epidemiology. Spent time at Columbia University in the States, then back to South Africa, this time to the university in Durban where he did his PhD.

'Yes!' she exclaimed and punched the air. He had received his doctorate the year after Betty and Hugh left Durban. It had to be him.

She scanned the rest of the information. He'd returned to Johannesburg and specialised in HIV/AIDS in Chris Hani Baragwanath Hospital. Received copious awards. Had a lengthy list of published work, academic fellowships and boards he'd served on. Co-founder and director of a non-profit AIDS organisation called APTO based in Johannesburg. There was no mention of anything to do with his personal life or of any family.

He had obviously made his mark in life, although it was in a field of work that was alien to her. Her father, worthy and acclaimed. It seemed unreal.

She desperately wanted to see what he looked like. She harboured a natural hope that he would be good-looking in a rugged, older movie-star way. Would she feel a connection with him? What if she didn't?

She left the alumni page, googled his title, full name and Johannesburg. She didn't want any confusion. It had to be him and him alone. And there he was in front of her: a small photo alongside a short introduction on a Wikipedia page. She clicked on the photo to get a bigger version of it. She could imagine her mother loving this man. He was looking directly at the camera and commanded the screen, not aggressively but almost hypnotically. A confident man, relaxed and at ease with himself.

She peered closer, eager to find familiar features, anything that linked father to daughter. He wasn't what she would have called handsome – no high cheekbones or chiselled features, apart from a strong, aquiline nose. His silver-grey hair, brushed back, was thick and wavy, like her own, and he sported a neat silvery beard. His eyes, full of humour and intelligence, were hazel, more green than brown. But it was his slightly lopsided smile that delighted her the most. She beamed back, knowing it was exactly the same as hers.

She found more images. In some he was a thinner, younger version of the man in the first photo, his hair quite dark, his face clean-shaven, but he was still recognisable. The same compelling, easy, generous smile was in almost every picture.

Ellen glanced at her watch and swore. She had to leave to get to her class in time. A quick look at the summary information below his photo: beside 'Spouse' was 'Diane Fraser-Allen', and beside 'Children', the number two.

'You have three!' she shouted as she grabbed an apple from the fruit bowl and scurried out of the flat, leaving her laptop open with the photograph of Peter Fraser glowing brightly on the screen.

Chapter 14

Kate registered the tension in Hugh as soon as he arrived for dinner on Tuesday evening and it escalated as the evening wore on. She read it in his fingers tapping the arm of the chair and his feet tapping the floor. There was none of the usual banter with Sophie, and the discussion among the adults was mundane; a civil if somewhat strained exchange of trivia. Alex was more subdued than usual too and Kate made up for him by talking rather too much and avoiding silences with repeated offers of more food. It was only when Alex took Sophie up to bed that Hugh began speaking about Ellen.

'She said she wanted time and space,' he said in a breathy whisper. 'Those were her words. But how much time and space? I need to sort things out with her right now. I don't want this gap between us to widen any further.'

'Ellen has had quite a shock and it'll take her time to process it,' Kate said. 'I'm sure she wasn't rejecting you. She's just overwhelmed. She'll come round.'

'Can you remember times when I favoured you over Ellen?' Hugh asked. 'I can't. Nothing that special or important, anyway. A sibling always thinks he or she is hard done by. Your Uncle Stuart and I were often at loggerheads with each other. Mind you, he got away with a lot more than I did.' Kate hid her smile as her father continued. 'It's all because of the money. She saw it as me giving you preferential treatment.' He paused. 'I know you think I should have told her.'

'We both should have,' Kate said. 'And I should have told Alex.'

'I want to apologise to Ellen, but she's pulling away from me.' He glanced away, then back to Kate; a haunted look. 'She'll find some way to trace Fraser, I'm sure of it. And she won't stop there. She's going to walk away from us all. I know she will.'

Kate was seeing her father unguarded with his emotions for the first time. So this was what lay hidden behind the usual unruffled facade. When Betty had died, Kate saw his fight to conceal his sorrow. But this with Ellen was something different, something he wasn't able to hide. Ellen had to be made aware of the depth of his feelings and Kate had to tell her.

'I'll make sure she won't,' she said with conviction as she kissed him goodnight and waved him off from the front door.

'I'm going to get Ellen and Dad together at the weekend, give them the chance to sort things out,' Kate announced to Alex later that evening.

'And what if Ellen doesn't want to do that?' Alex said.

'She won't have much choice. She'll not know I've invited Dad too. We can leave them alone, or I can act as referee if necessary.'

'For God's sake, you're always bloody meddling!'

Kate sat stunned as Alex marched out of the room and stomped upstairs to his office like a petulant teenager.

* * *

There was a folded sheet of paper lying on the floor under the letterbox when Ellen returned home from college that evening.

Hi, sorry not to catch you in. Hope you got somewhere checking out our friend Peter. I found quite a bit of info in LinkedIn and some other sources. Give me a ring and I'll tell you all. Alex

So Alex had taken the step to do his own investigating, despite her saying that she wanted to do it on her own. What were the 'other sources'? And calling her new-found father 'our friend Peter'. Well, that rankled. Hadn't he grasped how deeply personal and sensitive this search was to her? It was all some kind of a game to him.

But he did have information. She picked up her phone, ran her fingers slowly over the contacts, then set it down. She was desperate to know everything about Peter Fraser and his family, but she decided to do her own search first. If Alex could add to it, then that would be a bonus. The evening ahead of Ellen was settled and she relished it.

She tapped a key on her laptop and her father's face sprung into life on the screen, his eyes looking directly at her. She returned his smile with a shiver of excitement. She opened her browser and typed 'Diane Fraser-Allen' in the search box. The first photo she came across was of Peter and Diane standing together. His wife almost matched him for height. It appeared to have been taken at a formal occasion. He was in a dress suit, looking quite comfortable, she in an elegant dress and shawl. Their names appeared below the picture: *Peter and Diane Fraser-Allen.*

Ellen instinctively drew comparisons between her mother and Diane. His wife was more strikingly attractive; it could not be denied. Her arm was linked through her husband's, her head inclined towards him, making her seem overly coy in Ellen's opinion. Had he stayed faithful to his wife in all the years after his affair with Betty ended? Or was he a serial adulterer while acting the part of the loyal husband? Isn't that what many powerful men did, as if it was their right or what was expected of them? Ellen wondered if he still loved his wife.

Diane's looks were far more artificial than Betty's, Ellen decided. Her hair was shoulder length and undoubtedly mahogany-enhanced, and she seemed to have applied a huge amount of make-up. Betty always made do with very little help from cosmetics; just a dab of this and a dab of that. 'What you see is what you get,' she used to say.

It wasn't the only photo of the two of them together. Ellen came across several more, taken at other functions, mostly fundraisers for his work, but a caption under one revealed that Diane was an attorney. Ellen studied each photo avidly but her eyes were always drawn back to Peter. All the images from various sources added up to the man she had first encountered. There were no obvious contradictions to that impression of him.

She trawled through the next page or two of identical pictures, but her heart lurched when she came across a photo of the entire Fraser family.

The parents, again dressed for a function, occupied the centre of the image and their grown-up children flanked them. In their hands they had glasses, presumably filled with champagne, raised in celebration. Ellen focused on the daughter and son, scrutinising their features, their hair, the expressions on their faces. She tried to guess their ages. The daughter was maybe around Kate's age. The son might be younger than Ellen, but not by much.

Ellen enlarged the image. The daughter had hazel eyes, like her father, and his long, aquiline nose, which suited him but rather dominated her face. She had Peter's confident, direct look at the camera, but her smile appeared more contrived. Her hair was straight, the same length and colour as her mother's. More likely it was Diane who was attempting to be a reproduction of her daughter, Ellen thought.

The son looked uncomfortable. His shoulders were hunched, his head lowered; there wasn't even so much as a hint of a smile, as if he wanted to be doing something – anything – other than posing for this photograph. Ellen identified with his apparent discomfort. She hated formality and the necessity to conform. She immediately recalled her graduation ceremony when she'd refused an official photograph and returned the hired gown as fast as she could after the ceremony.

She studied the son closely, looking for any similarities to her. He was shorter than his father, not by much, but Ellen could imagine his displeasure at that. He had neat, regular features like his mother, but his hair was dark and unruly.

'My brother,' she whispered. 'My father, my sister and my brother.' No need for *half*-sister, *half*-brother. The words came naturally and they delighted her.

She was getting close to them, but not close enough. She was greedy for more. Now that she'd started work on the jigsaw of her other family's life, she wanted to fill in the gaps, finding the missing pieces, but she had no names or ages for her siblings.

She clicked on the family photo and got more information about it. The image was from a Johannesburg newspaper, dated the end of the previous year, and there was a caption: *Dr Peter Fraser with his wife, Diane Fraser-Allen, and children Kirsten and Benjamin at the AIDS Prevention and Treatment Organisation Gala Dinner honouring his recent retirement.*

At last she had their names. She said them out loud, over and over again, laughing with pleasure at the sound. 'Thank you for being famous!' she shouted.

But there was even more to digest: a short paragraph about her father having retired as director of the charity but still supporting it. 'It is imperative,' he said, 'to inform the young of the still ever-present threat of HIV/AIDS and I will direct my efforts towards that.' His wife Diane was, according to her husband, 'the greatest help in this latest venture of mine.' He went on to say that his work over the past decades had demanded a huge commitment and, at times, personal sacrifice, but he felt privileged to have made a difference to people's lives and was forever grateful for his family's wholehearted support.

Ellen leaned back in her chair. A very pleasant jigsaw picture was taking shape faster than she had ever imagined. Here was a man right in the public eye, a man she could be proud to call her father. She was both humbled and inspired by his dedication to working solely for the benefit of others. He was even finding new avenues of work at a time when he could have eased himself into retirement.

Checking out the APTO charity website, she saw the stock photo of Peter that had already appeared in her searches. There were no new personal details. She tried to trace the family members through Facebook, but had no luck. Had they all avoided social media?

It was hunger that finally pulled her away from the search, but she brought the laptop with her into the kitchen, and even while stir-frying whatever ingredients she had in her fridge, she glanced often at his photograph on the screen. She stared at it as she ate, picking absent-mindedly at her food but devouring every detail of the picture, imagining him sitting with her at the tiny kitchen table.

A text message from Alex startled her back to reality.

How's it going? Do you want my info? Next step, contact him!

It felt as if he were in the room, leaning over her shoulder, anxious to hear back from her. Yes, she did want his info, but she wasn't ready to reply just yet. She wanted to keep it all to herself for a bit longer; she wanted to stay in control. She didn't want Alex to pressurise her or jump ahead. Contacting Peter Fraser would be her decision, and if she chose to do it, it would be on her terms, her timing, not Alex's.

But she was terrified that Peter Fraser would ignore her or, worse still, reject her. Be calm and level-headed; no knee-jerk response. That would be Kate's advice, and Ellen felt she had heeded it so far by doing all the research to make sure she had found the right Peter Fraser. But her mother's advice would have been to follow her gut instinct. That was what Ellen preferred to do. So yes, she would try to make contact. Decision made.

But how to do that? There was little chance of him having a personal email address available online, so Ellen went back to the APTO charity website and got the business addresses. Sending an email would surely carry a high risk of it being opened and read by someone else, as would sending a letter by post. He probably had a secretary who took care of his email and correspondence.

She decided to send an email but word it in such a way that no one would have any idea of her real intent. She grabbed a piece of paper and a pen to jot down some ideas. Half an hour slipped by without her having written anything. This next step of reaching out and making contact had seemed easy by comparison to searching for him. Now it appeared to be far beyond her. She couldn't think clearly or objectively; she was too emotionally involved.

She texted Alex: *Search going well. Meet here to get your info?*

She didn't have to wait long for a reply.

Friday pm ok? BTW, Kate's going to try and get you and Hugh together at the weekend.

Chapter 15

The next day, Kate sent Ellen a text inviting her for lunch at the weekend. A chance to catch up, she said. No mention of Hugh.

Later that evening, standing in the open kitchen door, Kate watched Alex and Sophie in the garden as the daylight slipped away. The still evening air was a degree or two short of cold, and the moon was a perfect slice of lemon. It was a frustratingly small garden patch as far as Kate was concerned. The tiny lawn was fringed by a narrow row of shrubs on three sides with high, light-blocking hedges behind them. A range of colourful, flower-filled pots and a small table and chairs were squeezed into the only sunny spot.

Sophie was sitting cross-legged on the top platform of her climbing frame, which occupied the entire lawn. It was her favourite retreat and gave her the perfect spying vantage. As she talked to her dad, her arms were moving like rotor blades, her fingers jabbing at whatever was in sight. Kate couldn't make out the words, but she could see Alex mouthing replies.

It had a calming effect on Kate and made her want to capture the moment: the evident happiness in Sophie's laugh, her head thrown back, mouth open, eyes closed, like a clip from a silent comedy. Unexpectedly it brought tears to Kate's eyes.

The ping of her phone broke the mood. It was a text from Ellen.

Thanks. Happy to come so long as there's no set-up with Dad.

Kate scowled at the screen, then rang her.

'What made you think it might be a set-up?' she asked.

'It's the kind of thing you'd do.'

'Well, I have asked him round but it's not a set-up.'

'Were you going to tell me you'd invited him?'

'No, but I knew if I told you, you wouldn't come.'

'That's a set-up,' Ellen said abruptly.

'He's desperate to sort things out with you. I had to do something.' Kate sighed. 'Did Alex warn you about the lunch?'

'Yes. He's been helping me.'

'What do you mean he's been helping you?'

'Alex has been helping me look for my natural father.'

Kate was stunned into silence for a moment. 'And you never thought to tell me?'

'I assumed Alex would.' Ellen paused. 'I didn't set out to keep it a secret from you.'

Kate could hear the sneer in her voice. 'Oh, grow up, Ellen!'

'I've found out so much about my real father,' Ellen began, and she launched into a recital of his career and achievements.

Kate cut her off. 'You're going to contact him, aren't you?'

'Well, yes. I need to.'

'He knows nothing about you,' Kate said. 'You don't exist as far as he's concerned. What kind of a reception do you think you'll get? Are you expecting him to welcome you into his family with outstretched arms?'

All Kate could hear was silence.

'Ellen? ... Ellen?' but there was no reply. Kate looked at her screen. Ellen had ended the call.

* * *

'I think it's for the best,' Alex said.

He had sprung his change of heart on Kate in the driveway as soon as she got home from the gallery. He had decided to move into Betty's empty apartment after all; no coercion needed. His composure rocked Kate. She assumed that was his intention. Calm and rational. No mention of the bitter argument they'd had the evening before when she'd tackled him for helping with Ellen's search and tipping Ellen off about the lunch plans. He had called Kate a manipulator, a control freak.

'Does Sophie know you're moving out?' Kate asked now, her voice tight.

'Yes. I told her that I'm going to guard the apartment because it's empty,' Alex said. 'I took her there this afternoon when I brought a few of my things round. I made it into a little adventure for her, but she did get upset before we left. I told her I wouldn't be away for long. That is right, isn't it?' His smile unnerved Kate.

'Well, it'll take time,' she replied curtly. 'We'll play it by ear.'

'I need to see Sophie at weekends as well as after school, and some evenings of course. No discussion.' Alex's face was set hard.

'We need to do things sensibly, set up a proper rota,' Kate said, keeping her voice level. 'You can't just walk in any time you want to. We need to give each other space. That's the whole point of the exercise.'

'Oh, and Soph wants a dog,' Alex said as if he hadn't heard her. 'I told her it would be good for us all.'

'You can't keep doing this.'

'Doing what?' he asked, eyes wide and hands raised.

'Making promises to Sophie without talking it over with me. We're not competing to win her affection. We'll do what parents in this situation should do. We'll give our daughter equal time and attention, and we'll keep life as normal as possible.' Kate was finding it hard to disguise the tremor in her voice.

Alex took a step towards her. 'But guess what Soph really wants? She said she'd rather have a sister or a brother.' He gave a short, sharp laugh.

'Not this again.'

He glared at her. 'Your precious gallery is your second baby!'

Kate felt her face burn as Alex stormed back into the house. She waited for the sound of the front door slamming, then she leaned against the car as the tears flowed. How had it come to this? She struggled to recall the times when she had found Alex attentive and entertaining, when they'd laughed together. Those times were over, that was clear. Now there was a sting in their every remark, and the pain caused was intentional. When exactly had things turned sour? Back in the days after Sophie's birth, everything had changed, those black days when she felt she couldn't turn to Alex for help or understanding. Later, jibing at each other had become the nastiest of habits, an addiction of the cruellest kind.

The sadness weighed her down, exhausting her mentally and physically, like the stone that had crushed her six years before. She had hated herself for not loving her baby and she couldn't bear that again. There would be no more children, and if that was the deal-breaker between her and Alex, then so be it.

Kate blew her nose and checked her mascara in the wing mirror of the car. She didn't want Sophie to see she was upset. Then she picked up her laptop case and bag and let herself into the house.

Chapter 16

Ellen was baffled. She'd received a text from Alex at breakfast time on Friday changing their arrangement to meet at Ellen's flat and inviting her to Betty's apartment instead. It took two more texts to drag out of him a few more clarifying details and they alarmed her: he had moved into the apartment for a while; he would explain everything when he saw her.

The apartment had been where Betty lived but not where she died. How brave her mother had been, Ellen reflected, choosing to leave the home she loved and go into the hospice for her last few weeks. Maybe *brave* wasn't the right word. Betty wouldn't have approved of it. *Pragmatic* was better. Definitely not *resigned*; her mother was never negative. Ellen smiled.

Tensions between Alex and Kate must have escalated. Ellen would hear Alex's side of the story today, but what about Kate's? Her sister hadn't mentioned it; maybe there was a reason. Maybe she shouldn't press Alex for details; better to wait for Kate to open up. But she needed help with writing the email to Peter Fraser. That much was certain.

There was a crispness in the air which made Ellen button her jacket as she left the car to walk to the block of apartments. The sun peeped in and out of the clouds, not lingering long enough to warm her. She shivered. Going to see Alex felt wrong, underhand. Meeting up with him in her mother's apartment for a start, and also the probability that Kate didn't know about it. She should turn back right now and go home. And yet ... her feet carried her along the path to the front door. Should she press the buzzer or use her key? She pressed the buzzer.

'Hi, Ellen, come in.'

There was Alex standing in the doorway, welcoming her into her own mother's apartment.

'This must feel really strange.' He grimaced.

Ellen nodded.

'I'm just making myself a coffee. Would you like some tea? I haven't any herbal. Sorry,' Alex said.

It was like a first teenage date. That absurd thought made Ellen relax a little. 'I'm fine,' she said. 'You go on ahead.'

She was relieved to have a few moments alone in the living room. The need to feel her mother's presence gripped her, but the room gave nothing back. Betty's furniture had been removed and all trace of colour in the apartment had vanished. The sisters had reluctantly agreed that their mother's bold colours should be neutralised and the rooms left empty so the apartment would have wider appeal for buyers. A blank canvas. Her mother had been erased from her own home and Ellen felt bereft.

Betty had such confidence with colour: cool turquoise met hot orange, splashes of zingy yellow hit steely grey. It always worked. Now all Ellen sensed, with the keenest of pain, was her mother's absence. She moved slowly to the sliding door and stepped onto the tiny balcony where her mother loved to sit with her coffee, newspaper and radio. Her pen would be on the table ready for the crossword, and binoculars handy to spot birds and politicians. Ellen stepped back into the room and slid the door shut.

'I've got two fold-up chairs if you want to grab one, or I have a bean bag,' Alex said as he walked back into the living room. 'There's no comfort, but they'll have to do.'

He'd also installed a small picnic table, and his laptop lay open on it. In one corner of the room sat several piles of boxes which Ellen assumed contained most of what he needed for work. There were still blinds and lights, but the room looked bleak.

'What's brought you to this?' Ellen asked quietly, sitting down on one of the chairs.

'I knew the apartment was empty and Kate said I was welcome to it,' Alex said, taking the other chair. 'Sorry, I should have checked with you before moving in.'

'*Kate* should have checked with me. It's a bit of a shock, but you must have your reasons.'

'Well, you know we've been arguing a lot,' Alex said.

'Eh, not really,' Ellen mumbled, shaking her head.

His eyebrows shot upwards. 'She hasn't mentioned it? Kate said we needed space from each other. I wasn't convinced, but you know Kate. What she wants, she gets.'

'I'm sure you'll work things out between you,' Ellen said briskly. 'You said you had some more information about Peter Fraser.'

He turned to his laptop and brought up the LinkedIn page. He showed it to Ellen and sat back, grinning broadly. Ellen scanned the web page.

'Thanks, Alex. I got most of that when I came across articles about his work but it's good to have the extra bits about his career.'

'We seem to have covered the same sources,' Alex said with a shrug. 'I can still try and dig out more though.'

'Yes, I'll be doing that too.'

Then, with growing excitement, she went on to tell him about discovering Peter's family and the joy at seeing their photos. She was eager to discover more about her new siblings. 'I tried Facebook, but no luck,' she said. 'I was also thinking of emailing Peter. I have an address.'

'Oh wow, you have been busy!' Alex exclaimed.

Ellen shrugged. 'Yes, but how on earth does a daughter introduce herself to a father who knows nothing of her existence?'

'That *is* going to be tricky.' He drummed his fingers on the table, then jumped up. 'Let me get another refill and try and get my head around this.'

It didn't take him long and when he returned he was buzzing. 'I've got it!' he said, grinning. 'Well, it's not foolproof, but I reckon it's the best we can do. Okay, so we can rule out any kind of *Dear Peter, I'm your daughter* approach. But how about this? You write that your mother has recently died and, as she'd spent some time back in South Africa, you want to contact people who would have known her to tell them the news. We can slip in a bit about when you and Kate were born. That would hopefully bring a reply from him. He would probably put two and two together and you could take it from there.' He beamed and waited for her response.

'Sounds great. But wait,' Ellen said, 'he's going to wonder how I knew about him.'

Alex thought for a moment, then clicked his fingers. 'You can say your mother left you cuttings and articles about her political involvement in Durban and—'

'That would work,' Ellen burst in excitedly. 'I could add she'd mentioned people who were friends and colleagues with her at the time, and that's how I got his name.'

'You did a bit of Googling and, bingo, you found him!' Alex cried.

Ellen grasped Alex's hand in delight. 'Perfect.'

Alex blushed and Ellen immediately lifted her hand away.

'Let's do it now before we forget,' he said.

'As long as you have time,' she replied. She pulled her own laptop from her bag.

It took half an hour for Ellen to write a draft email. She agonised over every sentence, but Alex offered her reassurance and advice when she faltered.

'Right,' she announced, 'I'll read it out loud and you can say if it's all right.'

'No pressure then,' Alex said, laughing. 'Off you go.'

Ellen took a deep breath. *'Dear Mr Fraser,'* she read, *'my name is Ellen Anderson. I am writing to let you know of the sad death of my mother, Betty Anderson. I am contacting friends and colleagues she knew from her home city, Durban. I understand, from documents she left to me, that you would have known her when she worked at the University of Natal from 1982 to 1984. The political stance she took and those who stood with her were of huge importance to her throughout her life. I wasn't born until several months after Betty, Hugh and my sister Kate returned to Northern Ireland, so I would be very grateful to hear any recollections of Betty during her time in Durban which you and others may have. Please do not hesitate to contact me. Yours sincerely, Ellen Anderson.'*

Ellen's eyes were fixed on the screen.

'That's great, Ellen. It doesn't need any changes. It's perfect the way it is. Now press *Send*,' Alex said quietly.

She looked at him as if not understanding the words he spoke.

'Press *Send*,' he repeated gently.

Her finger lay on the key. She pressed it and the tears flowed unheeded. Alex came round to her chair and patted her arm. She struggled to her feet and laid her head on his shoulder, sobbing. He did not put his arms around her; he just said her name: 'Ellie.'

It was the name only her mother had used. For a moment she clung to him.

'Oh God, I'm sorry, Alex, I didn't mean to do that,' Ellen gasped, stepping back from him. She wiped her eyes hurriedly with the back of her hand.

'Don't worry about it,' Alex said with a grin.

The sound of her phone ringing was a welcome diversion but it involved too much effort to deal with.

'I'll ring them back,' she said hurriedly. The ringing continued, filling the apartment with its irritating sound.

'Sure go ahead and answer it.' Alex said, still smiling.

His constant smiling felt patronising, but she went ahead and hit the button on her phone without checking the caller's name or number.

'Hello,' she said sharply.

'Hi, Ellen.'

'Sanjay?'

'Yes. How are you?'

Ellen glanced at Alex. He hadn't moved, but his smile had disappeared. Her glance became a stare and he eventually turned and walked into the kitchen.

'Sorry, I wasn't expecting it to be you,' she said quietly. 'But I'm pleased you rang,' she added, swiftly and genuinely. 'Where are you ringing from?'

'I'm in London. We need to talk. No more emails. Can I come and see you? Or if you want to come here, that's fine. Please, Ellen.'

'You're in England? Can I ring you back? I'm out at the moment. In about an hour?'

'No problem. Don't forget now.'

'No, I won't,' Ellen said, suddenly weary. 'I'll ring you later, I promise.'

She put her phone and laptop in her bag and slipped her

jacket on before she called out to Alex. He hurried into the room, looking worried.

'Are you all right?' he asked. 'You could probably do with tea now, or something stronger.'

'No, I'll head on. Thanks for your help. I've lots of things to catch up on. Sorry I got so emotional earlier.'

'Let me know if you hear from Peter, won't you?'

Ellen stepped into the hallway. 'Of course.'

'And never worry about getting emotional,' he called out as she hurried away.

She had intended driving straight back to her flat, but instead she found herself heading in the opposite direction, towards the pathway along a disused railway line. She parked and joined the trickle of dog walkers and cyclists.

Her pace was slow, as images of all that had happened flowed through her mind. She managed, with relief, to block out the memory of clinging like a limpet to her brother-in-law and replaced it with the sound of Sanjay's voice. He was right. The emails were faceless; too easy a way to send mixed messages and unwittingly inflict pain. She remembered how she had dismissed him before and shuddered. Sanjay wanted to see her and she wanted to see him. She stopped suddenly in the middle of the path. It was a no-brainer. Of course they should meet; in London or in Belfast, it didn't really matter.

She walked briskly back to her car. The breeze, unnoticed when it had been behind her, now struck her face with a chilly rebuke.

When she got home she rang Sanjay. He answered immediately.

'Hello there.' The familiar lilting rhythm of his voice.

They laughed when they said each other's names at the same time. Then they said 'You first' in unison and laughed again.

'I'm sorry about my email, Sanjay. It was a bit abrupt.'

'Well, I was going to apologise for putting pressure on you at the worst of moments. I … Can we Skype? This doesn't feel right.'

'Yes, please.'

A few moments later they were looking at each other face to face. It had been weeks since they'd done that. They kept on staring, like tongue-tied teenagers.

Ellen ended the silence. 'You look well, though I'm not so sure about the beard.'

'It's only experimental,' he quipped, stroking his face, grinning.

'Is this just a visit to London?' she asked.

'I hope it's more than that. The project in Mumbai is finished and I've done a lot of thinking. I don't see any future for me in India. It was a great experience and I wouldn't have missed it but, I don't know, maybe being with my family and old friends made me feel I was going back in time instead of moving forward. And I think it would have been too hard for you,' he added.

Ellen, too emotional to speak, could only nod.

'I did some checking on jobs in London and one came up which excites me.'

'Tell me more,' she said.

The architects firm he was keen to join was based in South London. He talked with passion about their innovative social housing projects.

'I know it's exactly what I want to do. I've never felt this keen before. I've just applied for it. So while I'm waiting to hear back, can I come over?'

Ellen hesitated. 'It would be great to see you, but things have got really complicated here. Could you maybe leave it for a week or two?' She could see the disappointment in his face. 'I've fallen out with my dad and Kate,' she explained in a rush.

'Both of them? What happened?'

'I told him I knew the truth about my paternity and Kate's angry with me.' She lowered her head.

'Didn't your mum tell you not to say anything to Hugh?'

'She only asked. It wasn't an order,' Ellen countered, looking straight at Sanjay. 'Anyway, I had good reason to tell him,' she added, and she explained about Hugh's gift of money to Kate and her belief that Hugh had always favoured her sister, which Hugh had denied.

'Wow,' Sanjay said after a long silence. 'That's traumatic.'

Ellen nodded, trying hard not to cry.

'But why is Kate so angry?' he asked.

'Oh, because it's upset Dad. He thinks he's lost me,' Ellen replied with a dismissive wave of her hand. 'He's scared I'll find my real dad and Kate's worried about him. '

'And is he right to be scared?'

That wasn't the response she'd been hoping for. He sounded like he was questioning her actions, not supporting them.

'I've found out lots about Peter,' she said boldly. 'He's very impressive. I'll send you the links.'

'I'm worried about you, Ellen,' Sanjay said quietly. 'Please, let's meet soon.'

She forced a smile, her lips quivering. 'I'm fine, really.'

They said their goodnights, and once the image of Sanjay disappeared from her screen, Ellen sat on in the room, wondering why she hadn't told him that she'd already contacted Peter.

Chapter 17

Kate awoke to a strong sense of relief on Monday morning. The absence of the usual tension and bickering was sweet. The only thing that surprised her was that she had no inclination to occupy any part of Alex's vacant side of the double bed. Not even a desire to stretch her legs across the expanse. Old habits die hard, she thought.

As she drove to the gallery, she wondered how her mother would have reacted to what was happening between her and Alex. Betty had see-sawed in her opinions of her son-in-law over the years. At the beginning of their relationship she said she found him pleasant enough but perhaps rather immature, shallow even. Kate, still in that early heady romantic phase, had been affronted, and her mother's comment, rather than prompt her to reassess the man she was about to marry, merely spurred her on. Later, when Alex decided to work from home, Betty was full of praise. He was letting Kate pursue her dream and move on from her depression. Bonus points galore. But years later, when Betty received the diagnosis that her cancer had spread, she offered some words of warning to Kate, this time delivered with a little more sensitivity.

'Just be aware,' she'd said, taking hold of her daughter's hand. 'Alex has given you great support, but he envies you. He's not achieving anything for himself and he'll come to resent you and any success you have. Yes, he's a good father and Sophie worships him, but that's all he has to show for it and he knows it.'

The message had had little impact at the time, for Kate had been consumed with the knowledge that Betty was dying, but now she could see the wisdom in her mother's words.

Zoe arrived at the gallery looking ill and miserable, but when the sneezing and coughing started and she began to burn up, Kate chased her home.

Without Zoe for the next few days, Kate struggled to run the gallery and shop single-handedly and stay on top of the paperwork. The argument with Ellen the previous Wednesday still upset her and she was getting phone calls from an increasingly distraught Hugh, which brought alternating pangs of guilt and frustration. The last call had ended with Kate asking Hugh not to ring Ellen just yet and promising to let him know any news.

These were the times she usually would have turned to Ellen for support. But Ellen was no longer the sister she knew, the one who would have been on her doorstep, willing and eager to help. They were running on very different tracks now, parallel ones that seemed unlikely to ever join again.

* * *

Ellen struggled to summon any enthusiasm for preparing her students for exams. She was too easily distracted. She'd already cleaned the whole flat and tidied the living room, housework she normally loathed doing.

She had heard nothing from Peter Fraser, and she killed time obsessively searching the internet for more information on his family, but there was nothing new to find. It had been three days since she had emailed him. She kept checking her inbox, and her junk folder, always in vain. Every time her phone signalled a new email, there was the rush of edgy excitement, then the dip into disappointment, followed by the hard climb back up to hope again. He dominated her every thought, elbowing out all others, even Sanjay. And when memories of her conversations with Hugh surfaced, she pushed them back down into the depths. Kate and her troubles with Alex? Surely Kate knew all she needed to do was ask and Ellen would give her whatever support she needed.

She had chatted with Sanjay over the weekend, ahead of his job interview, and they had been more relaxed with each other. They'd talked about fairly mundane things, which made it easier. She told him about her work and how much she enjoyed her students; she made him laugh at some of the unintentionally funny comments they made. He talked about the things in India he missed: the fabulous food, the heat and the bustle of the streets; and the things he now didn't miss: the constant spicy food, the over-powering heat and the chaos and deafening sounds of the streets. His honesty made her laugh. He was getting used to and enjoying London life again, he said, and looking forward to his interview. His experimental beard had gone. 'Without it, the job's yours,' she had quipped.

They had eased themselves back into a relationship of some sort, whether that was friendship or something more. But she couldn't get rid of a small grain of frustration. She had forwarded links to Sanjay about Peter and asked what he thought. But Sanjay had fobbed her off, saying that he wanted to wait until he saw her so they could talk about it in person.

Ellen was struck by the different ways Sanjay and Alex dealt with the topic of Peter. While Sanjay didn't quiz Ellen about her research, Alex continually pestered her for updates. He had begun phoning instead of texting, and that evening, just as Ellen had finally settled down to do some exam prep, he called again. Once the inevitable question about Peter was out of the way, he asked if she had found out any more about Kirsten and Benjamin.

'Nothing yet,' she said with a sigh.

'I'm still searching too,' he said. 'It takes my mind off the fact that I'm sitting in my dead mother-in-law's – sorry, that was insensitive – in Betty's empty flat and not at home with Sophie and Kate. The novelty's wearing off. It's getting too hard to deal with.'

'How's Sophie coping?' Ellen asked, skipping the sympathy.

'We're trying to keep things normal for her, but she's always asking when I'm coming home and I can't keep saying "soon".'

'How about I pick her up from school tomorrow?' Ellen suggested. 'I could take her out for a while, cheer her up. We could go to the museum. It's nice and handy to school.'

'She'd love it, and it would help me too, as long as your students can cope without you.'

'They're revising hard,' Ellen said.

'Great, I could fit in a visit to one of my clients. I can pick her up from your flat when I'm finished.'

After she'd spoken to Alex, Ellen accepted the need to work on exam prep. A couple of hours later she slumped onto the sofa and let herself drift into an imagined life with Sanjay in London. They had been apart now for over six months, and she wasn't sure she had the same feelings for him as she'd had before. Could their relationship be patched up?

She switched to thinking about more practical considerations, which were easier to work through. If, and it was a big if, they got together again, would they try to find a flat together? Could they afford it? If she and Kate were able to sell Betty's apartment, it would certainly help. But it would all take time. And she would have to find work in London. Maybe she'd give her London flatmates a ring, see if there was any chance of reclaiming her room for a while. Just until, or rather if, she and Sanjay found their own place. She took a deep breath. She needed something to stop her from overthinking everything. From the back of a cupboard she unearthed a box set of an American drama she and Sanjay used to watch together in London. He had given it to her when she returned to Belfast to help take her mind off her mum's illness, but it had seemed disrespectful somehow to watch them then. Now it felt right.

* * *

Sophie clutched Ellen's hand and the two of them raced along the path through the park and up the broad flight of steps to the Ulster Museum. Ellen paused at the top and gasped for air dramatically.

'I'm getting too old for this, Sophie,' she cried.

'No, you're not,' replied her niece defiantly.

Ellen hugged her tight. 'I'm not fit, that's all. Your mum's far fitter than me.'

'But she won't run with me,' Sophie said with a tiny pout of the lips.

'Right, well let's head up to the art room. Then we'll make our way down in the lift, stopping at each floor to see whatever you want.'

'I don't like the lift.'

'Well, we can walk then,' Ellen declared, setting off in the lead. 'Race you!'

After climbing to the fifth floor, Ellen settled beside Sophie in the Art activity room. They got absorbed in studying and drawing the objects that had been left out to sketch. When Sophie finished her drawing, she shyly held it up for Ellen to see.

'It's super,' Ellen said. 'Are you going to give it to Mummy and Daddy?'

'I'll give it to Daddy. He's in Nana's apartment and it's not very nice. He can put it on the wall.'

Ellen put her arm around her. 'I don't think your daddy will stay there for much longer.'

'But someone might still break in. Daddy says so.'

'Well, then he'll be glad to have your picture on his wall. How about us heading down to the Nature room? The last time we were there, they had a dinosaur's egg you could touch. Do you remember?'

'Yes,' said Sophie excitedly. 'And there was a real dead turtle to stroke.'

Ellen laughed and pulled Sophie to her feet. 'Come on, slowcoach.'

'What's a slowcoach?' Sophie asked, forgetting all about her drawing as they set off to explore the other rooms in the museum.

An hour or so later, they were sitting in the café on the ground floor, sipping drinks and gazing out at the park. Suddenly Sophie squealed and pointed out the window.

'Daddy!'

Alex was standing near the entrance, head down, phone in one hand and a document case in the other. Sophie shrieked with laughter and started knocking the window. A bubble of annoyance rose inside Ellen. Just then, her mobile rang. It was Alex.

'Hi Ellen, I'm outside the museum,' he announced.

Sophie held out her hand for Ellen's phone and Ellen gave it to her gladly.

'We're inside, Daddy,' Sophie shouted into the phone. 'I can see you. We're over here.' She was waving now.

Ellen watched him glance around, then do a comical double-take when he saw them behind the glass. A few minutes later he joined them in the café but didn't order anything.

All at once Sophie's face crumpled in despair. 'I left my picture for you upstairs,' she announced.

Ellen explained to Alex about the Art activity room and offered to fetch it.

'No, don't worry, we can get it in a minute. That's okay, isn't it?' Alex said, turning to Sophie. 'I've something to show Ellen first.'

While Sophie sulked, Alex took a folded sheet of paper from his case and slid it across the table to Ellen. She reached out to take it, but he kept a finger on one end of it. He gave her a tight, self-satisfied smile. 'I think this will make you happy.'

He lifted his finger and she picked up the sheet. At the top was the title *Kirsten* followed by two neatly typed paragraphs of text. Ellen resisted the overwhelming desire to devour every detail and slipped the paper into her bag.

'That's great, thanks.'

'Don't you want to read it now?' Alex asked, his smile vanishing.

'No, I'll read it later.' She turned to her niece. 'Sophie, you stay here with your dad and I'll nip up in the lift and get your drawing.'

Alex opened his mouth to protest, but Ellen hurried off.

As soon as the lift doors closed, Ellen took the sheet from her bag and read it at speed. Kirsten was a paediatrician, specialising in neonatal care and working at the same hospital in Johannesburg as her father. Alex had added an exclamation mark after the hospital's impressively long name. The next paragraph was from a newspaper article giving Kirsten's reaction to the gift of six neonatal breathing units to the hospital she worked in. She thanked donors for their generosity and explained the enormous benefits for the babies. A wave of inadequacy swept over Ellen all of a sudden.

She retrieved Sophie's drawing, sitting exactly where she'd left it earlier, and took her time returning to the café, reading the sheet again and again on the way down.

When the three of them were making their way through the park later, Sophie skipping ahead, Ellen thanked Alex for the information about Kirsten and asked how he'd got it. He glowed with pride and was only too happy to explain in great detail how he'd trawled through lots of references to Peter, eventually coming across one mentioning his daughter who also had a medical career under her married name, Gregg.

'And Benjamin?' Ellen asked.

'No luck at all. There's really nothing to go on, sorry.'

Ellen waved Alex and Sophie off, then sat in her own car without starting the engine. She glanced out of the window. Pedestrians passed her in a muffled migration from the university, everyone intent on moving on, everyone but her. So her new-found sister was a *baby-saver*.

Peter must be very proud of her. How could Ellen compete with that?

Chapter 18

'I was really tense going in for the interview. I didn't realise until then how much it meant to me.'

Ellen was curled up in the corner of the ancient, lumpy sofa in her flat with Sanjay's animated face looking out at her from the screen. It was good to see him so fired up.

'But when I got into my stride, I actually enjoyed it. I think they could tell how impressed I was with their work and tuned-in to their concepts, so let's see what happens.' He paused. 'Listen, how would it be if I came over this weekend instead of next? Things could get busy for me if I land this job and I'd really like to see you.'

Ellen sat back a little. She had had a mental time slot for Sanjay's visit and suddenly it had shot forward to a few days' time.

'Do you not need to stay there in case they offer you the job?' she asked.

'They'll let me know tomorrow if the job's mine.'

'So soon?'

'I know. It took me by surprise too. That's why I'm suggesting this weekend. They want to fill the post as soon as possible and I was the final candidate to be interviewed.'

'But a last-minute flight, it'll be a wild price.'

'That's okay. It'll be worth it. We really need to talk, Ellen, face to face sitting in the same room.' He sighed. 'Look, if you don't want me to come over, just tell me.'

'No, of course I want you to come.' She felt her face burn. 'It's just ... well, I'm nervous about seeing you again. Isn't that crazy?'

'No.' He gave her a rueful smile. 'I am too. But it'll only get harder the longer we leave it.'

'Then come.'

'I can find a hotel. It'll just be for the one night.'

'Don't be daft, you can stay here. I've got a bed settee.' She winced. Why did she have to say that? 'Let's play it by ear,' she added.

But he was chuckling. 'That's great. I'll book the flight now.'

* * *

Kate was preoccupied with the visit she'd just made to Hugh. The warmth of his greeting had moved her, but his desperation to renew contact with Ellen had been alarming.

'I've left two voicemails, but she hasn't got back to me,' he'd complained.

Kate had tried to reassure him, explaining that it was a busy time of year for Ellen at the college, but Hugh was unconvinced.

'Let things play out in their own time, Dad, please,' she eventually said. 'Just be patient with her.'

Hugh's shoulders had slumped. 'What choice do I have?'

The hazy awareness that Sophie was still talking about her trip to the museum that afternoon brought Kate abruptly away from her thoughts. She closed the kitchen door so Alex, in the living room, wouldn't overhear and kept her tone light.

'Did Daddy come to the museum too?'

'I already told you that, Mummy,' Sophie said indignantly.

Kate could envisage Sophie, the petulant teenager. 'Ellen took you there and Daddy collected you?' she said.

'Yes, and he gave Ellen a bit of paper. I wanted him to get my drawing, but Ellen got it for me in the lift and I gave it to him.'

Kate struggled in vain to make sense of Sophie's account; it was easier to dismiss it, but what was the bit of paper about? She felt as if everything was being done behind her back. The fact that Ellen had made the offer of the museum visit to Alex, not her, and that Alex let Kate presume it was a father and daughter outing riled her.

She propelled Sophie into the living room, asked Alex to put his daughter to bed, then disappeared back to the kitchen to phone Ellen, after taking a few deep breaths.

'Thanks for taking Sophie to the museum today,' Kate said when Ellen picked up. 'She really enjoyed it.'

'So did I,' Ellen said. 'It was great to spend some time with her.'

'I knew nothing about it until Sophie told me just now.'

'Really? Did Alex not tell you?'

'No, he didn't,' Kate answered coolly. 'And Alex joined you there, according to Sophie.'

'Yeah, he popped in for a few minutes. Listen, I've some news,' Ellen said quickly. 'Sanjay's back in London and he had an interview today for a job. He's coming to Belfast on Saturday morning and flying back on Sunday night.'

'Oh,' Kate replied, relieved the news wasn't about Peter Fraser. 'That's nice. You must be looking forward to seeing him again. When will he hear about the job?'

'Maybe tomorrow. Yeah, he wants to talk things over. It's making me a bit nervous, to be honest.'

'Well, why don't you both come round for lunch on Sunday?'

Kate suggested with little enthusiasm. 'It would be lovely to see him again.'

Ellen hesitated. 'Leave it this time. I'm sure Sanjay will come over again.'

'No, lunch is fine. There's stuff in the freezer. Nothing fancy.'

'Well, thanks then. Just ...'

'Just what?'

'Just us for lunch, please.'

Kate knew exactly what Ellen was getting at. No Hugh. 'Make it twelve thirty,' she said brusquely.

* * *

Sanjay called Ellen on Wednesday to tell her he had got the job and they made arrangements for Saturday. Then Ellen made a quick dash to the supermarket to buy some bed linen, a couple of fluffy towels to replace the washed-out ones, a decent bottle of wine and some fresh food to supplement the bare essentials in the fridge. Saturday morning arrived with anxious anticipation for her.

She decided to spend an extortionate amount of money to park the car at the airport and was in the arrivals hall far too early, nervously waiting for the sliding doors to open.

Eventually the flight landed and the passengers started to appear. Sanjay came straight towards her with his familiar light, bouncing walk, as if struggling not to break into a run. He greeted her with a surprisingly shy smile and they hugged, touching cheek to cheek like strangers. They made small talk about the flight, the weather and what he wanted to eat for brunch.

The café they chose was busier than Ellen had expected, but somehow less intimidating than a quiet place where their words and silences would carry an uncomfortable weight. They shuffled their chairs closer to each other to be heard, and that move brought a more relaxed intimacy. Ellen listened eagerly as Sanjay described what his new job entailed.

'They're working on social housing schemes but want to create places where anyone can be happy and proud to live. It's not simply about being affordable. The houses and apartments are to be as eco-friendly as possible with proper community spaces. It's so exciting. I can't wait to get stuck in.'

He was full of enthusiasm about his new job and Ellen loved seeing him so animated. Even his language was different, a world away from the jargon he'd used when talking about the high-end projects he'd worked on in London and Mumbai.

As she listened, nodding in all the right places, she studied him, searching for any changes after the months apart. Physically he was the same, especially now the beard had gone. But there were subtle differences that were hard to pinpoint.

In their early months together, Sanjay had tried hard to impress her, arriving at her flat with oversized bunches of flowers or expensive boxes of chocolates. It all became a bit embarrassing. The confidence he showed in his working life and socially with their friends was missing at times in their personal relationship. It was as if he felt he was on probation, overly careful, and the impression persisted. Ellen had challenged him once about it and he admitted that he'd never been in a long-term relationship before. He wanted this one to last, but he was scared of doing the wrong thing.

But here, before her, was a Sanjay with no pretence, and the thrill of that made her happy. She became swept along by his eagerness as she listened to him talking about what lay ahead.

'Okay, enough about me,' he said abruptly. 'Fill me in about Peter Fraser. I'd rather hear it from you than from reading emails.'

Taken unawares, Ellen wasn't sure where to begin. 'I've found out some ... well, quite a bit of information about him and his family. It wasn't easy to uncover.'

'I'm sure.'

'I wouldn't have got anywhere without Alex's help though,' Ellen said and immediately regretted it when she saw Sanjay looking baffled. 'He ... it only got me started. That's all I needed.' She knew she was babbling but seemed powerless to stop it.

'So what have you found out?'

And sitting on in the café over refills, Ellen told him all she knew. She referred to Peter as her father and his children as her siblings, which brought a quizzical look from Sanjay but no comment. She spoke warmly and excitedly about Peter's achievements.

'Does Hugh know you've found out all this stuff about Peter Fraser?' Sanjay asked.

'I've no idea. Anyway, it's got nothing to do with him.'

Sanjay took a deep breath. 'Do you really think that?' Ellen said nothing. 'Well, Kate then? What's her reaction?'

Ellen struggled to keep her voice even. 'Oh, she still thinks I'm wrong to go looking for my father, that it'll tear the family apart.'

'Wait a minute,' Sanjay said, his eyes narrowing. '*Go looking?* This has already gone beyond getting information, hasn't it? Have you contacted him?'

'Yes, I have. Nobody understands what it means to me. This is what I have to do.' Ellen's voice was close to breaking. 'I wasn't stupid. I didn't tell him in my email that he was my father. Give me some credit.'

'I know it's important to you,' Sanjay said softly, 'but you're trying to make it happen too fast. You're not giving yourself time to think things through. It sounds like you've turned your back on your family and you believe a whole new one is there waiting for you.' He leaned forward, staring at her. 'That's a dream, Ellen, an unrealistic one.'

She met his eyes with denial and defiance, her eyes flooded with tears.

'You've never knowingly hurt the people you love,' he added quietly.

Ellen shook her head, too choked to reply. Sanjay reached across the table and touched her hand. Motionless, she stared down at it.

The tension between them remained as they drove to the flat. Once inside, Ellen began apologising for the condition of her temporary home. Sanjay dismissed her concerns, trying hard to reassure her. But she kept on apologising, as if unable to stop herself, and Sanjay soon fell silent.

It was all going wrong. The image of a cosy dinner in, of them sharing a bottle of good wine and even a bed had vanished completely. How could she have let herself jump that far ahead? It was a bad habit.

Ellen suggested having a meal out and Sanjay agreed without hesitation. So they had dinner in an Italian restaurant in a trendy Belfast suburb and toasted Sanjay's job success. The noisy clamour and clatter around them prevented any chat, cosy or otherwise, and the food was good but not memorable. The movie they went to afterwards was all action, which suited Ellen just fine. At least it wasn't a rom-com or a weepie about an adopted child.

Back in the flat they busied themselves making up the sofa bed and their joint attempts at it gave them a few giggles until Sanjay convinced Ellen he could accomplish the task on his own. Their goodnight parting was a self-conscious exchange of 'sleep wells'.

The atmosphere over breakfast was more relaxed, and the morning sunshine enticed them out for a walk afterwards. Sanjay asked if they could go to the seaside. He missed the sea air and the pleasure of strolling along a beach.

The soft sand at Crawfordsburn yielded beneath their feet, slowing their pace. They wandered down along the shoreline where the sand was firmer and the waves washed towards them, swooshing the pebbles. Ellen, stooping now and again, was unable to resist the desire to fill her pockets full of stones and shells, treasure that she only ever intended to keep until it was time to go home and common sense kicked in. Betty had loved beaches too. In an instant Ellen was back on Umhlanga beach, scattering Betty's ashes. Just over three weeks ago. And here she was now, her life reshuffled, unrecognisable.

She dropped the shell she was holding as if it burned her. Sanjay took her hand and together they walked slowly along the beach. Dogs hurtled past them, bounding into the sea, people greeted them on their walk, making Sanjay smile with surprise and say hello back.

At one point he hunkered down on the sand and turned over the pebbles lying there. Ellen watched him with rapt attention. He lifted a stone, slim and flat and glistening, and cradled it in the palm of his hand. Then, finger and thumb wrapped round it, he crouched low at the water's edge, drew his arm back, snapped it forward and, with a flick of his wrist, sent the tiny missile skimming across the water – one, two, three, four, five skips.

She whooped with delight. 'Wow, you're an expert.'

'First time. Beginner's luck,' he answered with a grin.

'No way, I don't believe it,' she shouted.

He laughed. 'I can't fool you. You know me too well.'

He faced her, his expression turning serious, and pulled her close to his chest, wrapping his arms around her as if shielding her from harm. He stroked her hair and she relaxed against his body, oblivious to others on *their* beach. He kissed her softly, briefly, then gave her a longer kiss which she returned hungrily.

She was safe and wanted, and maybe even loved again. But it suddenly felt too quick. Ellen eased herself away and he lowered his arms.

'Are you okay with this?' he asked.

'Yes, yes, it's just a bit ... public.'

'You never worried about that before.'

She forced a laugh. 'I'm out of practice. Anyway, I think we'd better head back now. Kate's expecting us at twelve thirty.'

'Fine.' He swung away from her, then turned back. 'Just for the record I'd like to do that again sometime soon.' He smiled and raised his eyebrows; she smiled in return. 'You're not the only one who tries to make things happen too fast,' he said.

She sighed and they walked back to the car holding hands loosely.

When they arrived punctually for lunch, Kate greeted Sanjay effusively while Sophie stood behind her father's legs as the two men shook hands. The niceties over, Kate ushered everyone to the table, straight into eating and a question and answer session with Sanjay conducted exclusively by Kate. Alex was intent on eating his lunch and spoke only to Ellen and Sophie.

The atmosphere disturbed Ellen, but Sanjay didn't seem to notice the domestic ploys and counter-ploys going on around him and was more than happy to chat to Kate about his time spent in Mumbai and his new job in London.

'Is Papa coming?' Sophie's question silenced everyone at the table. She repeated it directly to Kate.

'Not this time,' Kate answered briskly. She immediately stood up and started to clear the table of dinner plates.

Ellen caught her eye and decided to come to her defence. 'Actually, I asked Kate if it was okay not to invite him today,' she said. 'I didn't want to overwhelm Sanjay with us all.'

Kate turned to Sophie. 'I'll make sure Papa comes to see us soon, darling. Or maybe we could go out with him. Have a treat. Would you like that?'

'But he promised to help me build a Lego bridge,' Sophie said, her voice quavering. 'We drawed it all on paper.'

'It's *drew*. We *drew* it all on paper. I know you're disappointed but—'

Alex cut in. 'Daddy to the rescue, Soph. When we've finished eating, we'll get out the Lego and start building. Okay?' He reached across the table, hand up for a high five. Sophie hesitated, then reached forward and lightly touched his palm with hers.

Ellen helped Kate clear the table, shuttling in and out of the kitchen, avoiding conversation. Alex brought in the Lego box and Sophie fetched the plans she and Hugh had drawn and set them out on a table. Sanjay leaned against the door frame, watching them.

'Do you want to see my drawing?' Sophie asked him.

'I'd love to,' he said, walking to the table.

'Mummy said you draw pictures like mine and you build things too. Do you want to help build my bridge?'

'Sanjay's an architect, not an engineer,' Alex said, reaching across the table for bricks. 'But he could make the fancy wee towers. Couldn't you, Sanjay?'

Sanjay faced Sophie. 'I'll have a go at the towers and make them extra fancy. Your dad can tackle the bridge and your Papa can always fix it the next time he's here.'

Sophie scooped up most of the Lego bricks from the table and spread them over the floor, babbling away to Sanjay who had hunkered down beside her. Alex began constructing the bridge on his own at the table.

While the men helped Sophie build the Lego bridge, Kate and Ellen made polite conversation, Kate quickly filling any lapses with small talk, even discussing the weather in detail. Alex told her she sounded like a TV forecaster. Kate laughed off his remark, but Ellen heard the tension in her laughter.

When Sanjay announced that it was time for him to head to the airport, it immediately brought a new energy into the room. Kate and Sophie escorted Ellen and Sanjay to the front door while Alex tidied away the excess Lego bricks. Sophie insisted on giving Sanjay one of her drawings, so the two of them hurried back to the living room to choose from her collection.

Kate touched Ellen's arm. 'Will you go and see Dad?'

Ellen didn't answer.

'At least think of ringing him. Please.'

'I'll see,' Ellen said. But the concern written on Kate's face made her remember Sanjay's warning about pushing her family away. Here was another person she loved who she was hurting. As Sophie and Sanjay dashed towards them, Ellen gave Kate an urgent hug.

Ellen appreciated the absence of a post-lunch inquest as she drove Sanjay to the airport. He wasn't that sort of person, something she had always liked about him. Instead, he talked about his new job and finding somewhere to live in London, and she talked about her students and some wonderful classroom moments.

She was frightened of the parting ahead of them, shocked at how close they had got to breaking what they had only started to mend. She decided not to mention Peter Fraser again, but not being able to share the thrill of finding her biological father with Sanjay was agonising. Don't jump ahead, Ellen told herself firmly; deal with the here and now.

She parked the car in the short-stay car park, wincing at the cost, and walked with him into the airport.

'Do you think you'll come over to London?' Sanjay asked.

'Would you like me to?' Ellen replied shyly.

'You know I would.'

'Well then, I'll come over soon, I promise.'

Sanjay's face lit up. 'I'll stay on at Joel's place for a while. He says it's no problem.'

'And I'll check with Tanya and Kim to see if I can stay in the flat.'

'Great.'

'You know, if you sprint back to the car, you won't need to pay.' He winked at her and they both laughed.

They gazed at each other, suddenly a little self-conscious. Ellen reached up to give him a kiss on the cheek but he turned his face so their lips met. She wrapped her arms around his neck and he pulled her close.

'I'll see you soon then,' he whispered softly in her ear, then he turned and walked through the departure gate.

Chapter 19

The first week of living apart had been tense but manageable as far as Kate was concerned, but tempers soon began to fray again. On Tuesday of the second week, Alex brought Sophie home from school and they were both in foul moods; Kate had to ask Sophie three times to go upstairs and get changed. As soon as she stomped off, Alex started complaining. He hadn't realised the amount of extra travelling he would be doing every day to and from the apartment for the school runs. It was taking him away from work too much and he had to tackle the backlog every night. And the apartment, yes it was pleasant enough, but it was soulless, like a hotel room. It was all a stupid waste of time.

'It's not working,' he went on, his voice raised and his face red. 'Soph feels the same. Look at her. She's turning into a stroppy teenager at six. She hates me not being here at breakfast time and she doesn't want to stay overnight with me because it's where her dead Nana used to live. All she wants is her dad at home the way things used to be. Is that too much to ask?'

Kate didn't feel ready to end the arrangement yet, but the effect on Sophie worried her.

'Did you hear a single word I said?' Alex demanded.

'Let's give it to the end of the week,' she answered, and seeing Alex throw his hands up in despair added, 'okay, two days.'

'I'll be counting the hours.'

Over the evening meal, they struggled to maintain some sense of normality in front of Sophie and resorted to forced, light-hearted chat about the weather and uplifting news events. Sophie interrupted them to ask why Nana's flat still needed a guard, and when Alex and Kate paused in their efforts to distract her, their daughter's face suddenly brightened.

'You can get an alarm for Nana's flat,' Sophie announced with the pure logic of a six-year-old. 'Rachel's house has an alarm.' She looked expectantly at Alex.

'Hey, that's a great idea, Soph,' he exclaimed over-enthusiastically. 'I'll get one as soon as I can.' He suddenly switched on a serious expression. 'But the thing is I'll have to get someone to fit it. It might take a couple of days.'

Sophie looked crestfallen.

On Thursday, Alex reminded Kate that the two days were up. Coping with an increasingly troubled child was becoming unbearable, he said. When he was collecting Sophie from school, her teacher had told him that Sophie had been upset about forgetting her PE clothes. She then became very distressed, which the teacher said was out of character, and asked Alex if there might be anything else worrying her.

'I lied to the teacher,' Alex told Kate, his eyes narrowing. 'I said that Sophie had been out of sorts recently, maybe coming down with something, that's all. Nothing to worry about. But we know the truth, don't we?'

'Yes,' Kate replied, taking Alex by surprise. 'It's getting us nowhere. We've been acting the happy parents for Sophie and now it's turned into a farce.'

'This arrangement has to end,' Alex said. 'All Soph wants is for me to be at home. And so do I. Surely we can make this work, even if it's only for her sake.'

'Not if it means us quarrelling all the time,' Kate said. 'The atmosphere has been terrible. I know what it's like to have parents heading for a divorce and I honestly wish mine hadn't waited until I was eighteen to do it. Ellen and I might have had a chance to get to know them better separately without their forced play-acting. Because that's what they did, consciously or not. And it's exactly what we're doing too. We know what we have to do.' She let the sentence hang in the air for a moment. 'We have to consider separating more formally.'

Alex was stunned into silence, but it didn't last long. 'You mean let's divorce, don't you? Can you imagine explaining that to Sophie? I hate to think what effect that'll have on her.' The accusation in Alex's words was outweighed by the sadness in the tone of his voice.

Kate said nothing.

'We're not in the same boat as your parents,' Alex continued more quietly. 'We haven't any skeletons in the cupboard.'

Kate bristled at his reference to her mother's affair.

'How they managed to live together at all, with your dad having to raise Ellen as his own, I don't know. Big secrets like that would put a strain on any relationship. But we're not like them. We're just finding it a struggle to get on with each other. We've got into bad habits, that's all. You wind me up, I wind you up. It's like a game we can't stop playing.' His tentative smile vanished. 'We're not heading for divorce. No way. We'll work at this. And if we need help to sort ourselves out, we can do that too. But for now, let's be under the same roof. For— '

'—Sophie's sake,' Kate added.

She was taken aback by Alex's acceptance of help. It was so out of character for him. He was being surprisingly mature and showing a sense of responsibility where she would have expected him to be all bluster and demanding to be allowed to live in his own house. She had always preferred to rely on herself and find her own way through any setbacks. She had shied away from outside support when she had her post-natal depression. But she would never have climbed out of that deepest of holes if she hadn't taken Ellen's advice to seek professional help. Maybe Alex was right. A separation was still what she wanted, but if there was someone who could help them find a way of at least being civil to each other, it would be worth it. It would give Sophie the chance to have parents who could at least cooperate with each other. They all needed a truce.

'Yes,' Kate said, then seeing his look of surprise, she repeated 'yes' louder.

'So can I move back?' he asked.

She nodded. 'The bed's made up in the office.'

'I'll go get my things now,' he said brightly and dashed off.

Chapter 20

It was almost two weeks since Ellen had sent the email to Peter, but she still hadn't heard back from him. Maybe it had gone into his junk folder. Or he had deleted it without checking it. Or she'd sent it to the wrong email address. Maybe he was ill or away on holiday. She couldn't bear to think that he'd read it and had no interest in replying.

Little helped to ward off the constant disappointment of no word from Peter. Sanjay had phoned, which distracted her for a while. He liked the people he was working with in his new job and enthused about the housing project in South London. It was easy to listen and respond, but she was reluctant to talk about her own issues. When Sanjay asked her if she'd done anything about coming over to London to see him, or if she'd heard from Peter Fraser, she replied 'not yet' to both questions. When it came to saying goodbye, Sanjay said he hoped that would change to 'yes' very soon.

Hugh phoned her one day.

'How are you?' he'd asked.

She hadn't expected that. 'I've been very busy with exams at college and trying to decide what to do next. My contract will be up soon.'

'And Sanjay?'

Kate had obviously told Hugh that Sanjay had been over. 'Yes, he was here for a last-minute visit at the weekend.' She paused. 'I should have phoned you ... I'm sorry.'

'It doesn't matter. We're in touch now. I was worried you wouldn't speak to me at all.' Hugh gave a nervous laugh. 'Maybe we could go for a coffee, wherever you fancy, whenever suits you. Please.'

Had she done this to Hugh? Made the strong, assertive father-figure she had known become this timid, insecure man?

'Can we leave it this week? I'll let you know when things settle down.'

'Oh, well ... I understand.'

She heard the disappointment in his voice, and the effort to disguise it. 'Are you keeping all right?' she asked.

'I worry, Ellen. I worry that we'll drift—'

'Sorry, there's someone at the door. I have to go. We'll speak again soon. Bye.' She had to get off the phone; she didn't want him to hear her crying.

Ellen kept herself busy at work, devoting more hours than necessary to exam preparation for her students. Evenings at home she spent trawling through her mother's papers and putting them in labelled folders. When sleep at night didn't come easily, she got up, made camomile tea and sat in bed reading them all again.

Alex texted her twice during the week, each one asking if there was any news from South Africa. Ellen didn't respond. But the need to check her phone had become a compulsion and nothing but the longed-for email mattered. When it was switched to silent while she was at work, she would surreptitiously peep at the screen under her desk, the very thing she chastised her students for.

Ellen accepted Sinead's suggestion to go out one evening for a bite to eat. She found herself opening up a bit about Sanjay and was partly relieved by Sinead's directness; her friend wasn't one for pussyfooting around. When pressed about moving to London and her future with Sanjay, Ellen discovered that she was clearer about what she wanted to do than she'd thought.

'I'll go for a visit anyway,' she said. 'It was really good to see him again.'

'And?' Sinead asked with an amused gleam in her eye.

Ellen felt shy all of a sudden. 'Maybe we'll get back together again.'

'You want to, I can tell,' Sinead said, raising a glass and grinning.

She arrived home after the night out, tired and longing for a soak in a hot bath. But just as she opened the front door, she heard the familiar ping of an email arriving. She pulled savagely at the key to remove it from the lock, slammed the door shut behind her and groped in her pocket for her phone. The screen lit up: it was an email from an address with the suffix .za. She tapped on the email. At last! It was from him. Sinking into the nearest chair, she read it eagerly.

> *Dear Ellen,*
>
> *A sincere thank you for your email. Please accept my deepest condolences to you and your family for the loss of your dear mother. I greatly appreciate you taking the time and trouble to find her friends and colleagues and letting us know the very sad news of her death. It must have been very difficult for you to undertake such a task while still grieving.*
>
> *I was privileged to have been both a colleague and a close friend of Betty's. She was an inspiration to all who knew and loved her. Her passionate commitment to the causes*

she supported was her driving force and we, who shared her principles of equality and fairness for all, followed in her wake. She believed in always 'doing the right thing' and she put that principle into action. I remember her too for her wonderful sense of humour which was razor-sharp but never cruel.

I can imagine that any daughter of hers must have inherited at least some of those fine qualities and it is obvious to me that, with your awareness of duty towards your mother and the tenacity you have shown in contacting me, you have indeed a nature very similar to hers.

Betty was taken at far too young an age. I only hope she felt she had accomplished enough in her life to satisfy her and that she found happiness.

I would be very keen to learn more about Betty's life after she left Durban, and to discover more about you and your sister. Would you by any chance consider continuing this correspondence? As you see I have used my personal email address and if you do want to contact me, this would be the one to use.

However, if you feel unable or unwilling to commit to such an arrangement at this tragic time, I fully understand.

With my warmest regards to you,
Peter

Hands clasped prayer-like, fingertips pressed to her lips, Ellen stared at the screen. Just *Peter*, no *Fraser*. *My warmest regards*, not simply *regards*. And to think he had asked if she would consider continuing the correspondence. Ellen laughed out loud. She had hoped for an answer from him. Any kind of acknowledgement would have meant a lot, but this ... this was eloquent, beautiful. His carefully chosen words revealed his admiration and affection for her mother.

She read the email again, the second time thrilling her as much as the first. She had to reply immediately. He wanted to know all about her, and her mother, and Kate too, of course. It was as if he already wanted to be a part of their family. How should she tell him that she wasn't merely his dear friend's daughter?

She couldn't wait to get started. Pulling a notebook and pen from her bag, she scribbled down ideas as they came to her. It was easy to sketch out her life and Kate's, but when it came to the details of her mother's life, she knew she didn't have much to go on.

The basic outline was there: Betty worked first as a radio programme researcher and then became a producer, concentrating on news and current affairs and short documentaries. And she'd won awards. But that was more or less the extent of Ellen's information. How could she not know more about what had mattered so much in Betty's life? Had she been too busy living her own life? But that's what children do. They leave their parents and set off on their own paths. They assume their parents will always be there in the background, until suddenly they're not.

Jean Mason could tell her more about Betty's career, but that would take too long. This email was really about telling Peter the truth. That took priority. But breaking that kind of news needed subtlety as well as tact. How were these kinds of situations handled in TV programmes where families were reunited? They got someone else to do it. She googled 'how to tell a stranger you're his daughter' but got no matches. She would pay anything to get sample sentences.

Peter's email was still on the screen. She hit *Reply* and up popped an email window, the cursor blinking in the empty space. She sat transfixed. Minutes passed. This was worse than breaking the news of her mother's death to friends and relations. Most people had been prepared to hear that news. They knew how ill she had been.

Ellen was burning with the urgency of it. Concentrate, she told herself as she put her fingers on the keyboard.

My mother left me a letter telling me you are my father.

She imagined him looking over her shoulder. That kind of bold-faced statement could easily scare him off. It needed to be couched in terms that wouldn't alarm him.

I just wondered if there was a possibility I might be your daughter.

No, too cringe-making.

How about one short line? *Am I your daughter, yes or no?* Putting a metaphorical gun to his head. Surely some actor had said that in a movie.

But what if Peter asked if she was sure he was her father? Was she? Her mother was. Betty had described him as her 'natural father'. And so was Hugh.

She was getting nowhere, so she leapt up and went into the bathroom, stripped off and jumped under the shower at full-strength. No relaxing bath this time. She tilted her head back, letting the water pound her scalp and face, and stood like that for a few minutes, imagining all her angst and frustration being washed down the plughole. After she'd dried herself she checked her phone. There was a text she'd missed. It was from Alex, ending with an exclamation mark, telling her he had moved back home. The news barely registered, but it made her think. She had to get this email right. Perhaps she could bounce some ideas off Alex. She replied to his text, asking for his help, just one last time.

Chapter 21

Ellen phoned Jean early the next morning. Jean sounded anxious and asked if there was anything wrong.

'No, nothing at all. I'm trying to document all my mum's papers which were in the package you gave me.'

'Ah, yes those,' Jean said. 'Betty showed them to me. Fascinating.'

Ellen hesitated. Had her mother told Jean about the personal letter in the package? She doubted it. Betty wasn't one to share her secrets, even with her closest colleague.

'There's nothing about my mother's radio work in Belfast,' Ellen said. 'I didn't ask her much about what she did. I should have, but ...' An unexpected stab of grief stopped Ellen in her tracks.

'Are you all right, Ellen?' Jean asked quietly.

'Yes, sorry, Jean. I was about to say it's too late to ask her.'

'Well, I can tell you plenty about your mother's work if it would help. Do you want to come and see me?'

Ellen hesitated. 'I've a lot on at college at the moment. It's coming up to exam time. Could you give me a rough idea of what she did now? Just to start me off.'

'Yes, of course. I can give you the short version,' Jean replied.

'That would be great, thank you.'

Ellen made notes as Jean spoke of some of the programmes Betty was involved in. Hers had been a fast, if not quite meteoric, climb up the ranks.

'I was happy to stay as an assistant producer, especially when I could continue working with your mother when she became a producer,' Jean added. 'We both loved radio work and we were the best of teams. They were wonderful times, inspirational, and your mother was rightly recognised for her work. Betty always made sure I got my share of the credit.'

'You must miss my mum a lot,' Ellen said gently.

'All the time. She was an absolute joy to work with. Strong-willed, of course. The stories I could tell you—'

'I'd love to hear them, Jean, but I have to get to work now. Let's get together soon. You can give me the long version then.'

'Yes, that would be lovely.' Jean's reply was muted, her tone wistful. 'The tapes, Ellen, I forgot to tell you,' she added with an excited rush of words. 'I have tape recordings of some of her early documentaries, mostly investigative, the kind Betty loved.'

'That's wonderful. Thank you!'

'My pleasure.'

After the chat, Ellen had a yearning to share her mother's letter with Jean. It would be so comforting to talk to someone who had known Betty but who wasn't family. To tell Jean where the information in the letter was taking her.

Ellen turned to her notes, relieved she now had the material needed for the email. All she had left to do was find some way of letting Peter Fraser know he was her father. Diplomatically.

* * *

'I see what you mean.'

Alex was sitting opposite Ellen in her flat that afternoon, reading her attempts at breaking the news to Fraser.

'The bit about your mum's work and what happened to her is fine, and about you and Kate. You can start with all that, no problem, but the part where you give Peter your news ...' He screwed up his face. 'None of that works.'

Alex was enjoying this too much for Ellen's liking. The pleasure he was getting at not just assuming control but also underlining her shortcomings rankled. Swallowing her annoyance was painful.

'I think we have to be direct, but in a vaguely roundabout way,' he announced.

Ellen bristled at his use of 'we' but kept silent.

'And we have to be careful about how you come across to Peter. If you sound too certain he's your father, then that could really scare him off. You need to come across as more tentative. Instead of telling Peter that your mother wrote in the letter that he was your father, how about saying your mum hinted at the idea he might be, but obviously she had no evidence to prove it. And you don't either, right?'

Ellen gave a slight nod.

'Let's see then, you could say – and you apologise to him at this point in case you seem to be taking liberties or whatever – that you would love to know if it was possible. That's all you want. You would have no claim on him or anything. Correct?' The question demanded her response.

'Yes, of course.'

'Good. Oh, and you'd better not mention that Hugh knows about him. It would just complicate matters.'

'No, obviously.' Ellen wouldn't have been surprised if there had been actual teeth marks across her tongue as she tried not to react to Alex's officiousness.

'Then let's type that and see what it looks like.' He had his hands poised on the keyboard. Ellen reached out and swivelled her laptop round and pulled it close. 'I'll write it, Alex.'

'Well, you're the boss.'

Ellen didn't look at him. She typed slowly, stopping now and again to think, to shake her head, to delete words. Alex became restless, leaning forward, his elbows on the table, hands cupping his chin then stretching back in his seat, humming to himself. He got up, walked round the table and stood behind her. Was he reading over her shoulder? His quick intake of breath was the tipping point.

'Could you get me a mug of tea, please?' she said.

With an exaggerated sigh he disappeared into the kitchen, made tea and set a mug down beside her without a word. He sat on the sofa and played silently with his phone. Engrossed in her work, the tea remained untouched. Finally she looked up.

'What do you think?' she asked. As he hurried over to the table, she said tersely, 'Don't even think of clicking *Send*. That's my job.'

He raised one eyebrow, then began to read aloud.

> Dear Peter,
> Thank you for telling me about the genuine admiration and love you and your colleagues had for my mother, and how much her loss has touched you.

Alex stopped reading. 'Hmm,' he murmured, shaking his head. 'Not too sure about *love*. A bit full on, I reckon.' He moved the cursor so it hovered over the word.

'No!' Ellen shouted. 'Don't change a thing. Just read it, please.'

Alex shrugged and continued.

I do appreciate everything you wrote about her.

You asked about her life after she returned to Northern Ireland. She worked for BBC Radio Ulster, first as a researcher and later as a producer and never lost her passion for politics and current affairs, which were the main areas she worked in. She also championed people's rights and produced programmes which really made a difference and brought her praise and awards. She kept working right up until she received the diagnosis that the cancer had spread and resigned only when she was unable to commit a hundred per cent to her work. She received the most wonderful care in the hospice and we were able to be with her when she died.

Sadly, my parents divorced when Kate and I were in our teens, but they remained on good terms. Kate owns an art shop and gallery in Belfast and is married to Alex, an accountant. They have an adorable six-year-old daughter. I'm an ESL teacher and single. I lived and worked in London for several years and loved it, but I came back to help care for my mum. I am thinking of moving back to London.

That is our potted history.

Alex paused. 'Are you not mentioning Sanjay?' he asked.
'No,' Ellen replied, 'there's nothing to tell yet.'
Alex went on reading.

Now I come to a very delicate matter. I feel compelled to write about this and I hope sincerely that you will not take offence. After my mother died, I received a letter written by her. In it she hinted that Hugh was not my natural father. The news has been very challenging for me to deal with.

Mum mentioned in the same letter that you and she were very close. Might you be my natural father? I would have been conceived in the autumn of 1984 while they were living in Durban. They returned to Northern Ireland immediately after and I was born in Belfast.

I'm sure my question has shocked you. Please forgive me for asking it, but if you feel able to give me an answer, whatever it might be, that would mean a great deal to me. It's not that I want anything from you, but as I'm sure you can imagine, I do need answers. I hope you understand why I must ask and are not angry with my mother for her openness with me.

With my warmest regards,
Ellen

'Well, yes, it reads pretty well. It does need to be tweaked though,' Alex said, stroking his chin.

But by this time Ellen was silently weeping. He leaned towards her, but she stood up immediately and, raising her hand, turned and walked into the bathroom, locking the door behind her.

After a few minutes sobbing quietly to herself, Ellen heard the front door close. Coming out of the bathroom, she spotted a note left on the table beside her open laptop.

Sorry, have to go & pick up Sophie. Don't delay, send the email. Now!!

Minutes passed without her moving, as if she was deprived of the ability or even the desire to. Finally, she stirred enough to save the email and close the lid of her laptop. The action lit a tiny spark. She would not be told to 'send the email now' with or without exclamation marks.

She needed to get out of the flat; it was as if Alex was still in it, hovering behind her, telling her what she must do. She grabbed her bag and her jacket, lifted her car keys, then set them down. Walking had always helped clear her head. She pulled the door closed behind her and turned in the direction of her mother's apartment.

It was that time on a Friday afternoon when everyone was impatient to begin the weekend as soon as possible. The roads were clogged with traffic; the decision to walk had been a good one. Still, having to pass a school entailed muscling her way through the gaggle of children juggling a full week's collection of artwork, and parents trying in vain to steer them rapidly along the pavement.

The more pleasant stretches of the walk came as she neared Betty's apartment. But when she arrived at the door, she couldn't go in. Ellen had thought she wanted to be close to her mother to imagine what she might have said to her about the situation with Peter, but the apartment suddenly seemed too depressing for the setting of what struck Ellen as a kind of séance. She shuddered and turned away quickly, crossed the busy main road and stopped at the towering gates of Stormont, letting some of the tension in her body go with a long, deep sigh. She had often been in the estate as a child, learning to cycle and roller skate along the main drive lined with ranks of lime trees marching up towards the Parliament Buildings.

Ellen's mind flitted back to more recent times; to the autumn day six months ago when she and her mother had walked slowly along the avenue of fiery red and gold-leafed trees. The weather had been kind that day, with a low sun still holding the heat and warming her mother's tired, thin body. Now on this breezy spring day, Ellen strode up the steep drive, oblivious to the dog walkers and joggers, the running children and the gawping visitors, her mother's voice ringing in her head.

'I asked you, for Hugh's sake, not to tell him that you knew the truth.'

Betty's words floated into her head and Ellen did not chase them out.

'You only wrote *ask*,' she replied silently.

'I was trying to be considerate to you.'

'So I didn't have to do it then.'

161

'Now you're nit-picking. I was pleading with you to do the right thing. If I'd known you would take the attitude of a quarrelsome child, I'd have made my wishes even clearer. But it's too late now. You chose to ignore my request.'

'It was too much to ask. I've the right to find my natural father.'

'Yes, you have the right,' her mother replied more kindly, 'but it's come at a cost to Hugh, the man who loved you as his own. Can you not see how devastated he is?'

'I'm not abandoning him for ever, but I can't forgive him for keeping it a secret from me.'

'You must find it in your heart to let your anger go. Otherwise, it'll poison you. I know.'

Ellen leaned against a bench. 'I've found Peter Fraser. I'm ready to tell *him* the truth. Should I?'

It took a long time for Ellen to hear Betty's answer.

'This man, your natural father, what do you want from him?' Betty eventually said coldly.

'Nothing,' Ellen replied, 'and everything.'

Her phone pinged. She ignored it, desperate to hear her mother's answer, but Betty had gone. Maybe it was a text from Sanjay. The flutter of hope turned to frustration as she saw the sender was Alex.

Has email gone?

Ellen kept on walking uphill, wanting to shut out the conflicting thoughts that were causing nothing but stalemate. The parliament building was ahead of her, but she chose a quiet path that branched off the main drive. It wound past swathes of tired, brown-tipped daffodils and budding shrubs.

She was weary of being told what to do and what not to do. She was well aware of everyone else's stance. She had swayed from one side to the other until she was giddy with confusion. It was a habit that had exasperated her mother. 'Analysis paralysis' had been Betty's mocking diagnosis. Could she blank out all their advice? Stop weighing up the pros and cons?

Ellen glanced around. The path had changed to a soft earth track. It no longer led past shrubs and flower beds. The strong sunlight had gone; she was in dark woodland with the trees tightly packed. How did she get here? Disorientated, she retraced her steps, arriving with relief back at the fork in the path she hadn't even noticed. How could she have missed it? The path should have taken her to the small valley where the bluebells coloured the banks. She remembered the route from her childhood.

She sat on a bench, letting her heartbeat slow and her mind empty. Minutes passed. She focused on nothing around her – the tourist buses stopping on the drive below her, the shrieks of children running helter-skelter down the grass slope, even the couple walking past her whose 'hello' went unanswered. Finally she got up and headed for home.

Back in the flat she deleted yet another demanding text from Alex, then opened the lid of her laptop. The email was in front of her, sharp and bright on the screen. 'Press *Delete* or press *Send*,' she told herself. It's not a game show, she thought wryly. Hitting *Send* could change her life. Hitting *Delete* would be a relief to Hugh and Kate and make life so much easier.

'Okay, no more messing about,' she told herself sharply and she pressed *Send*.

When she heard the gentle whoosh of the email's flight, she shut down the laptop and sat staring at the lifeless screen.

Her phone pinged again. She began shaking uncontrollably.

Chapter 22

The next morning, Ellen awoke to a pounding head, a dry mouth and a distinct intolerance to bright lights. It had been quite some time since she'd suffered such a hangover.

The previous night was a blur, mostly because of the copious amounts of mediocre wine she had consumed before, during and after a delivered takeaway. After the first glass she had texted two words to Alex: *Email's gone*. She couldn't cope with any more pestering from him. She ignored his excited reply and request that she keep in touch.

Dry toast and several glasses of water along with two painkillers for breakfast did little to dispel the muzziness and the throbbing, but they did help to revive her memory. The late evening phone call to Sanjay made its way into her head, and she winced with embarrassment. He had wanted her to come to London in a week's time, but she wouldn't commit, using the old excuse of her students' exams. Sanjay hadn't been fooled. She'd heard from Peter Fraser, hadn't she? What had he said? Had she replied? She couldn't recall how she'd answered him, but she remembered that Sanjay had sounded worried and frustrated all at once and his last words were 'book a flight. Please.'

Through the fog in her brain came a sudden memory of inviting Sinead for dinner that evening. What had possessed her to do that? She groaned. The very idea of preparing food made her queasy. She would have to go to the supermarket. A couple of light, ready-made dishes would be perfect, and a bunch of flowers to brighten the flat. She'd better get a bottle of wine too, although drinking wine was the last thing she felt like doing. A better quality one might help this time.

She decided to go to an upmarket shopping centre a little further away from home. A wise choice, as it turned out, for it was relatively quiet, lacking the noisy kids and bands of teenagers that usually roamed her local centre on a Saturday. There was plenty of space to park too, which saved her having to reverse anywhere, something she didn't feel up to in her delicate state. She made a mental note to go to the coast later on, if she felt better, and walk away the remains of her hangover in the sunshine.

It was almost pleasant wandering along the wide walkways of the shopping mall, its glass ceilings casting panels of light onto pristine tiles and potted plants. The pleasure ended as her stomach churned at the sight of the fresh meat and fish counters in the supermarket. She'd have to cancel dinner with Sinead; she couldn't face it. But as she was so close to the drinks section, she might as well replenish her wine stock.

She walked into the aisle and stopped dead. A familiar figure stood at the end, holding two bottles aloft, apparently studying the colour of their contents. Ellen ducked behind a tall display stand, rattling the bottles of gin stacked behind it. She grabbed a bottle and kept her head down.

'Good heavens, is that you, Ellen?' boomed Malcolm, peeping round the stand. 'It is indeed!'

Ellen put the bottle back on the shelf and forced a cheerful greeting. 'Hello, Malcolm.'

'Can't give you a hug I'm afraid, my hands are full.' He thrust the two bottles of wine in front of him as evidence. 'I didn't know you were a gin-loving girl. Having a party?'

'Just reading the label. How are you?' she added, trying to sound upbeat.

'Oh, I keep going, though bending the old elbow isn't as easy as it used to be,' he said with a loud chuckle. Then a frown creased his forehead and he lowered his voice to what he probably imagined was a whisper. 'But I'm very worried about your father.'

'Why, what's wrong with him?' Ellen asked, a wave of nausea gripping her.

'He's not himself at all. He doesn't understand why you and he can't get together to sort things out. Nor can I, frankly,' Malcolm said sternly.

Ellen felt like a naughty school child in front of the principal. 'Well, it's a sensitive situation, and to be honest, Malcolm' – she took a deep breath – 'it's a private one.'

'It's hardly private when I was the one who blabbed the secret, is it?' Malcolm said.

Now it was Ellen's turn to frown. 'But you didn't blab it. I told Dad—' It was then she remembered about the money that Hugh had given Kate for the gallery.

'I take full responsibility,' Malcolm said sharply, raising his voice again. 'But I believed that you, of all people, would have understood and forgiven Hugh. I'm sure you know how much he regrets not telling you about the gift. He's suffering so much because of it. All this upset over money.' He tut-tutted and stepped closer. 'Shame on you, my dear,' he added in a stage-whisper.

Ellen found herself backed up against the wall of bottles. She couldn't move. Her heart raced as the two of them stood face to face while Malcolm gave her a lecture on the evils of money. She should have known that Hugh would never tell even his closest friend the secret he had kept for almost thirty years. And to think that she'd been seconds away from divulging it! Her stomach lurched. She opened her mouth, then shut it as she saw, past Malcolm's shoulder, Hugh walking towards them, basket in hand, his eyes roving from one side of the aisle to the other.

Malcolm noticed the direction of Ellen's gaze and turned round. 'Hugh!' he exclaimed loudly. 'Look who's here.'

Hugh and Ellen froze.

Malcolm tried to usher them together. 'Imagine us bumping into each other. How's that for timing!'

Malcolm's prattling gave Ellen a chance to study Hugh. She was shocked to see how much he'd changed since they'd last seen each other three weeks ago. His usually straight back was slack and his shoulders drooped as if all the confidence had been sucked out of him. He had obviously skipped shaving that day, something he never did, and he looked as if he'd been living in his clothes for a week. He inched forward and attempted a smile, but his lips quivered and the smile died.

For once Malcolm read the situation correctly. 'Well, I'm sure you want to chat to each other, so I'll go and pay for these,' he said, wiggling the two bottles of wine. 'Goodbye, my dear.' He kissed Ellen's cheek. 'And don't forget what we talked about.' As he walked away, he called back over his shoulder, 'I'll be in the car, Hugh. No rush, take your time.'

Hugh faced Ellen, leaning almost drunkenly towards her. Finally, he took the initiative and spoke.

'You're looking tired. Are you all right?' he asked tentatively. For a man who had a limited range of facial expressions, he was displaying most of them in one go.

'I had a late night, that's all. Really.' Ellen became suddenly aware that her mouth was dry. 'I should have called round to see you, it's just I've—'

'You've been so busy, I know,' he finished, nodding and looking at the floor.

From the corner of her eye, Ellen noticed a woman leave her trolley and head in their direction.

'We're in the way here,' Ellen said to Hugh, stepping a little to one side, hoping he would follow her.

The woman edged around them, trying to look at the bottles of wine stacked in a pyramid behind Hugh, but he ignored her.

'Have you found Fraser?' he demanded, taking hold of Ellen's arm. His eyes were fixed on hers, boring into them.

'Let me go,' Ellen whispered fiercely.

The woman turned to observe them.

'You've found him, haven't you? You're going to contact him, aren't you?' He was still gripping Ellen's arm.

'You're hurting me,' she cried.

'Let her go!' the woman said unexpectedly.

At the same time, Ellen pushed him away with her free hand.

He stumbled backwards and knocked the woman aside as he tried to steady himself; then he collided with the pyramid of bottles. The bottles swayed in a slow wave from top to bottom, then toppled, smashing onto the floor. The woman shrieked. There were broken bottles everywhere and red wine coursed across the floor like trails of blood. Ellen put her arm around the woman's shoulders, checking she was unhurt, speaking calming words in a tremulous voice. Hugh stood dazed and shaking. Other shoppers circled around to watch. An assistant rushed towards them.

'Is anyone hurt?' she asked.

'No, no, I don't think so,' Ellen said. 'It was an accident. We're so—'

She turned to speak to Hugh but he had gone.

Chapter 23

Sophie's cheery temperament and the bright morning sunshine mirrored Kate's good mood. Zoe had been enthusiastic about the idea of another exhibition at the gallery, and while Kate had yet to approach the artist, she was already imagining his work hanging on the gallery's walls. She glanced out of the kitchen window at her daughter sitting on a rug under the climbing frame, surrounded by cuddly toys that were propped up with books in their outstretched paws and toy food at their feet.

Sunshine backlit the late spring flowers crammed into pots sheltering by the wall. Kate felt the pull to go outside, to talk to Sophie and briefly enter her world. She saw herself in that self-contained part of her daughter. It was others – Alex, Ellen, Betty, even Hugh at times – who brought out the fun and the impishness in Sophie. Not her. That pained her. She wanted there and then to make Sophie smile, to hear her giggle, to see her eyes dance with mischief. Suddenly Alex put his hands on her shoulders, making her jump. She swung round.

He laughed. 'I fancy a coffee,' he said, beaming.

'I'll join you.' She leapt up and went to the cupboard, keen to put some space between them. 'You sound cheerful this morning,' she remarked as she poured a glass of juice for Sophie.

'It's great to all be together again,' he said, taking a step towards her.

She turned to open the fridge door and lift out the container of milk. 'That's good. Can you bring the drinks?'

She hurried outside and sat down on the only available space on the rug. Sophie immediately regaled her with stories of which cuddly toys were well-behaved and which were naughty. Kate smiled, but without paying much attention.

Alex brought Sophie her juice and a few biscuits.

'Could you bring me my coffee, Alex?' Kate said. 'I'm hearing all about the picnic guests here. Isn't that right, Sophie?'

Sophie's head bobbed enthusiastically. Alex handed Kate her mug and sat at the garden table, looking like a friendless child.

Kate had expected to feel some relief, even pleasure at what should have been a return to normality, but she wasn't experiencing that at all. His chirpiness was annoying her for no logical reason, and she was almost repelled by his physical closeness.

The previous night Kate had suggested that they take turns doing things with Sophie.

'Not all of us together?' Alex had asked, his mouth tightening. It was the same expression Sophie made when she didn't get her own way.

'Well yes, together too, of course,' Kate said. 'But we need to get some sort of balance. Having separate time with her will help us all.'

'I might as well go back to the apartment,' he'd muttered.

Alex finished his coffee and announced he was going for a run along the towpath. A wave of relief washed through Kate. She asked Sophie if she'd like to go to the adventure playground.

Sophie said that Daddy had promised to take her to the playground after lunch.

'He might have told me,' Kate said under her breath. 'So much for co-operation.'

She was not going to change her plans, so she offered Sophie the chance of two playground visits in one day, which was accepted with a shout of joy. They were about to set off when the doorbell rang.

When Kate opened the door, Hugh was standing on the doorstep, looking haggard and dishevelled. His usually well-brushed hair stood upright in tufts. Kate brought him into the living room.

'I don't want to intrude if you're busy,' he said. He glanced distractedly at Sophie and patted her on the head.

'We're not busy, Dad,' Kate said. 'Why don't you take off your jacket and sit down.'

'Mummy, the playground,' Sophie said, tugging Kate's sleeve.

'I've come at a bad time,' Hugh said. 'I'll leave it for another day.'

'No, no, stay,' Kate said, more sharply than she intended. She hunkered down in front of Sophie.

'We'll go to the playground another time, sweetheart. I need to speak to Papa for a wee while. Sure you'll get to go with Daddy after lunch.' Seeing Sophie's mouth turn down, she added, 'Go and watch one of your programmes in the meantime.'

Sophie dragged her feet all the way to the breakfast room, making sure her mum knew how displeased she was.

'Sit down, Dad, please,' Kate said to Hugh. 'I'll make us some coffee.'

'No thanks. Listen, I'll go and let you get out with Sophie.'

'No,' Kate said firmly, 'you're staying.'

She helped him slip off his jacket and draped it over the back of a chair. He sat down, his head lowered.

'What's wrong? Is it about Ellen?' she asked.

Hugh looked at her vacantly. 'I saw her yesterday.'

'That's good.'

'It was by accident, in the shopping centre,' Hugh continued in a dull monotone. 'We only spoke for a minute or two. She's found him. I know she has.'

'Did Ellen tell you that?' Kate asked.

'She didn't need to.'

He lowered his eyes. 'I got cross. The woman thought I was hurting Ellen.' There were tears in his eyes.

Kate reached out her hand and Hugh took it in his. She couldn't remember ever having seen him cry, not even when their mother died.

'You wouldn't hurt anyone,' she said. 'But let's back up a bit. What woman?'

'I'd gone to the shopping centre with Malcolm. He came across Ellen in the drinks aisle. Then I came along and Malcolm left us to talk.'

'And this woman, where does she fit in?' Kate asked.

'She was standing near us.'

'But what did you actually do?'

'Nothing really. I took hold of Ellen's arm. Maybe I gripped it too tightly. I wanted to know the truth, that's all.' He shook his head. 'But Ellen pushed me away.'

'So Ellen didn't actually say "I found him"?' Kate asked.

'She didn't need to. I knew. I'm certain I'm going to lose her. I don't know what to do.'

'We won't lose her, Dad. But it might take some time. As long as she knows we're here for her—'

Sophie burst in from the breakfast room. 'It's finished. Can we go now, Mummy?'

'I'll leave,' Hugh announced, standing up and looking around for his jacket.

'You don't have to. Sophie can wait a while longer.'

'I want to go now, Mummy,' Sophie protested. 'You can come too, Papa. We're going to the playground. Daddy's taking me to another one this afternoon. He's back home now.'

Hugh peered down at the child and in that moment Kate saw the Hugh of old – sharp and inquisitive.

'Was Daddy away somewhere?' Hugh asked.

'Yes, he was guarding Nana's flat,' Sophie said proudly.

Kate told Sophie to go to the toilet before they went out and Sophie skipped out of the room.

'Alex was *guarding* your mother's apartment,' Hugh said to Kate. 'Why?'

'We needed a bit of space from each other to sort things out, so we told Sophie he was protecting the apartment because it was empty. We've been getting on each other's nerves lately.'

'I'm sorry you didn't feel you could talk to me about this,' Hugh said a little tetchily.

'He only stayed in it for a few nights, and he's back home now. I didn't want you to have another worry on top of all Ellen is piling on you.'

Sophie rushed back into the room, eager to go, diverting their attention again. Kate asked her to fetch the bag of food and cartons of juice from the fridge. Sophie stomped off impatiently.

Hugh looked closely at Kate. 'Has Alex found someone else?'

'No,' Kate said, then added 'and nor have I.' She contrived a laugh. 'I don't have time.'

'Well, I'm glad. I never considered Alex good enough for you. He hasn't your drive or—'

Kate held up her hand. 'Please, don't say any more, Dad. It doesn't help. I'm well aware of his shortcomings.'

Hugh looked hurt and lost and it scared Kate. She stepped closer to him just as Sophie rushed into the room, waving her backpack.

'Got them!' Sophie called out in a sing-song voice. She ran up to Hugh. 'Please come, Papa. I've got juice for you and an apple. You can see me coming down the biggest slide in the world.' She waited. 'Papa,' she said more loudly. She touched his hand.

Hugh cleared his throat but didn't speak. Sophie's face fell.

'I'm upsetting her,' Hugh said to Kate. 'Don't fret, Sophie. I'm going now.' He absent-mindedly patted her on the head again. Sophie went and stood behind Kate.

Hugh lifted his jacket from the back of the chair. Kate followed him into the hallway with Sophie in tow.

'I'll go and see Ellen tomorrow, find out what's going on. I promise,' Kate said, touching his arm.

Hugh glanced down at her hand. 'I hate you having to act as a go-between.'

'Let me tell her what you've told me. She'll come round.'

'Thank you,' he said without raising his head as he left.

Chapter 24

Ellen felt trapped inside the flat and inside her own head. Sunday was a day for families. Sophie was the only relative she missed, but she came with parents who Ellen wished to avoid. She hadn't responded to the text from Alex telling her he was out for a run. What kind of a reply did he expect? If you're running near here come on in? The shuttling between hope and despair over Peter was bad enough without having to deal with Alex's inane messages.

She could phone Sanjay, but she didn't trust herself. In this mood she could easily snap at him if he began questioning her again and wondering why she didn't confide in him. She would then feel obliged to tell him about her encounter with Hugh in the drinks aisle, but she couldn't face reliving it.

It was Hugh's reaction that disturbed her most. First, him tightly gripping her arm. She had bruises as proof. Then him fleeing the scene before checking if she and the woman were all right. Not a single word of apology. Not even an offer to pay for the broken bottles. It was so out of character. He rarely lost his temper with them when they were young and had never physically chastised them. But maybe her mother had seen a different side to him; worse still, perhaps she'd experienced it.

She had to get out, go somewhere, anywhere. She had wanted to go to the coast the day before but the incident with her father in the supermarket put paid to that. Helen's Bay would be the perfect place to clear her head now. But just as she reached the front door, her phone pinged. *If that's Alex again*, she fumed and pulled the phone out of her bag. The screen lit up; it was an email from Peter.

She put down the car keys and walked back into the living room, setting the phone on the table as if it were a hot brick. One touch of the screen and the email would be there to read, but she dreaded what she'd find. A memory sprang to mind. She was holding a thin brown envelope in her hand, while her parents waited impatiently for her to open it, to find out if she had got the results that would take her to university.

Taking a deep breath, she picked up her phone again, tapped the screen and, after skimming over the opening pleasantries, started reading.

> *I was, I admit, taken aback by your mother hinting that Hugh might not be your real father. Such a shock for you to process. Let me assure you that I am not offended by you asking if I might be your father, and I am certainly not angry with you or your mother. It is a natural question to ask, as Betty and I did indeed become very close at that time, when she and Hugh were far from being a happy couple.*
>
> *I feel it is crucial for us to meet. We have a great deal to talk about and I would like to get to know you better. I am attending a conference in Geneva on Wednesday and Thursday of this coming week and can rearrange my flight home, overnighting in Dublin on the Friday. Could you meet me on Saturday? I know it is short notice, but I think you would agree that this is an opportunity we should not miss.*

> *Obviously I feel it best not to travel to Belfast to see you.*
> *I know you will be discreet about any arrangements we make*
> *and the reason why we are meeting.*
>
> *If you are indeed willing and able to see me in Dublin, can*
> *you please let me know as soon as possible? I can then adjust*
> *my travel plans. I do hope it suits you. It is such an important*
> *step for us both.*
>
> *Affectionately,*
> *Peter*

Fizzing with excitement, she reread the email, her fingers hovering over the words on the screen. Before she replied to Peter she simply had to share this news with someone who she knew would understand her sense of elation.

Alex answered on the first ring. 'Well?'

'Peter's replied. He wants to see me,' Ellen said, the words tumbling out in a rush.

'Wow! That's amazing. So he accepts that he's your father?'

Ellen nodded enthusiastically, forgetting that Alex couldn't see her. 'He said it must have been a shock for me to deal with, finding out that Hugh wasn't my real dad. He's flying into Dublin this Friday and wants us to meet on Saturday.' She had tears in her eyes as she laughed.

'You mean next weekend?'

'Yes!' Ellen shouted.

'No way! He's coming all that distance to meet you?'

'Well, not exactly,' Ellen said, a little annoyed at having to explain that Peter was fitting her in. 'He's rearranging his journey home so we can meet. He said it was *crucial* that we met.'

'There you are then,' Alex said cheerily. 'I can drive you down to Dublin, no problem.'

'What? No, no. But thanks, Alex. That's not why I'm calling. I'll take the bus down on my own.'

'If you're sure.'

She could hear how disappointed he was, but she was adamant. 'Yes, absolutely.'

'I guess it's your call.'

There was an awkward silence.

'Bye, Alex.'

'I'm here if you need me, day or night.'

'You've done enough already, but thank you.'

'I enjoyed every minute.'

'Sure, I'll let you know how it goes.'

'Blow by blow account? You've a habit of not answering my texts and calls, Ellen Anderson.'

'I'll keep you informed, Alex McCandless,' she replied, forcing brightness into her voice.

Should she make a quick call to Sanjay? She brought up his number on the screen then paused. Peter first. She didn't want Sanjay's reservations to spoil the moment. She typed her reply to Peter's email, laughing at the trembling of her hands.

> *Dear Peter,*
>
> *Thank you so much for offering to meet me and for rearranging your travel plans. I will keep all my questions for when we meet. I'm really looking forward to it!*

How should she sign off? Would 'With love, Ellen' be too much? How about 'Ellen x'? Maybe not yet. 'Yours, Ellen'? Yes, that would do.

* * *

Alex and Sophie spilled through the door in the late afternoon, giggling and joshing with each other. It clashed spectacularly with Kate's mood. In the silence of the empty house, Kate had felt restless and troubled. She hadn't been able to settle either to work or relax. The change in her father filled every part of her mind.

Sophie launched into elaborate detail about the differences between the two playgrounds – which had the faster slide, the higher climbing nets, the better ice-cream van. Alex was talking excitedly over her, his voice dominating hers.

'I've been thinking, I could really do with a high-vis lightweight jacket for running and a waist pack.'

'What?' she asked, struggling to follow either of the conversations.

'A waist pack,' he answered, emphasising both syllables. 'It's pretty obvious. A bit like a bumbag but I hear these new ones are better.'

Kate ignored him, trying to focus on Sophie's chat, but Alex hadn't finished.

'And I definitely need a fitness tracker. Essential bit of kit. State of the art and—'

'For God's sake, Alex, would you shut up!' Kate shouted.

They all froze, then Alex hurried over to Sophie. 'No need for that, Kate,' he said, putting his arm around his daughter's shoulder and drawing her near.

'My dad came when you were out and he was very upset,' Kate said to Alex. She hunkered down in front of Sophie. 'I'm sorry I shouted, sweetheart. Mummy's a bit worried about Papa.' She stretched out her arms towards Sophie but the child huddled even closer to Alex.

'About Papa falling out with Ellen in the supermarket?' Sophie asked quietly.

'Let's go outside, Soph, while Mummy gets the dinner ready,' Alex said hurriedly and the two of them, as if joined at the hip, strode out of the room in step. Alex gave Kate a scathing glance over his shoulder before they left.

The meal was a strained affair. There was no communication between Alex and Kate. They took it in turns to direct their chat towards their daughter. Sophie was quiet too, reluctant to be drawn out and she didn't protest about going to bed. Kate hugged her, feeling Sophie's body stiffen against her. Alex was the one she requested for the bedtime story reading.

Kate busied herself clearing the table and stacking the dishwasher. It didn't do much to blank out the image of Sophie's rejection. She slammed the dishwasher door shut. If only Alex hadn't riled her. If only she hadn't let him get to her. She started preparing Sophie's packed lunch for the next day, criss-crossing the kitchen as she fetched and forgot items.

Alex appeared. 'She wants you,' he said flatly.

Kate turned and walked towards the open door but he closed it before she got there.

'I have a question first,' he said.

'Go on,' Kate said, warily.

'How come you told Sophie about Hugh and Ellen *falling out at the supermarket* but you didn't bother telling me? Why the hell did you load that onto Sophie anyway? She's only six. She's a sensitive child and she worries about things.'

'I know my own child,' Kate retorted.

'Our child,' Alex hit back.

'What was I supposed to tell her when she asked me if her Papa was going to die? Dad looked awful when he called round this morning and Sophie thought he was ill, like her Nana. What would you have said?'

Alex kept glaring at her.

'I explained to her how we all fall out with friends or family but after a while we make up again,' Kate continued. 'Sophie understood. She can cope with a lot more than you give her credit for. If she isn't told the truth, she imagines far worse things.'

Alex took a step towards Kate. 'Well, because of you telling her *the truth*, our daughter is crying upstairs,' he said, stabbing a finger at her. 'She asked if we had fallen out too. She's really scared. She asked, "does Mummy not love you, Daddy?"' Alex's voice broke as he said the word 'Daddy'.

'What did you say?' Kate asked quietly.

'The truth would have been "I don't think she does love me any more, Soph". I couldn't tell her that, so I said, "Mummy just lost her temper. Nothing to worry about". But of course, we know there's plenty to worry about, don't we?'

'I'll talk to her,' Kate said coldly. 'Credit me with some sensitivity. I won't say anything to make her more upset or scared. Now let me go to her.'

They stared at each other for several seconds before Alex stepped aside.

Kate took time outside Sophie's bedroom to calm herself. Alex hadn't quizzed her about what happened in the supermarket. She could imagine his over-heated reaction if she had explained. Relief swept through her as she pushed open the bedroom door.

Sophie was sitting on her bed with the contents of her favourite trinket box spread across the duvet. Kate sat down beside her and lifted the box, a treasured gift from Betty. It was made of dark, ancient-looking wood adorned with carvings of small elephants. But it was the gleaming brass key in the lock that had delighted Sophie the most. The box held Sophie's prized collection of gemstones and shells, feathers and seed cases. At one time, her nana had been the only privileged viewer of its contents. When Betty came to visit, Kate would often linger outside Sophie's room, listening to them happily discussing each item until Sophie declared quite solemnly that it was time to lock them away.

The irony of the gift didn't escape Kate now. The beautiful box for cherished, secret things given by Betty, who had kept her life under lock and key, well hidden from her own daughters. It soured the sweet memory and saddened Kate.

* * *

Ellen steeled herself to tell Sanjay about the invitation she'd received from Peter. Sanjay would probably issue dire warnings once he heard about the arrangement to meet in Dublin. But she didn't want to keep it to herself. Maybe he would be pleased for her. And with that faintest of hopes, she rang him.

After a few minutes, Sanjay suggested switching to Skype. Ellen tried to stay calm – she knew her facial expressions would give away more than her words – but it didn't last, and she delivered her account of Peter's email and the Dublin meeting in one breath. She took another, ready to continue, but Sanjay held up both hands.

'Hold on! Tell me it all again, slowly.'

She went through it all again.

'So did you actually tell him you were his daughter?' Sanjay asked when she had finished.

'Well, no, not exactly. I told him Mum had hinted that Hugh wasn't my biological father and I asked Peter if it was possible that he was my natural father.' She attempted an encouraging smile.

'Hang on,' Sanjay said, solemn-faced. 'So he wrote back saying *yes, I am*? He admitted paternity?'

Ellen bridled at his courtroom manner. 'Well, not exactly. But I'm sure that's why he wants us to meet. He'd prefer to tell me that in person. He said it was an important step for us both.'

'But that's not enough, Ellen. It's far too vague. Do you want me to go with you? I don't mean to meet him, just to be around if you need me.'

'I don't need a bodyguard,' Ellen retorted. 'I'm going into this with my eyes open. I'm not a fool.'

'I'm not saying you are. But I'm worried you're getting your hopes up, and if he doesn't accept that he's your father—'

'He will.'

Sanjay shrugged his shoulders. 'So you'll meet him anyway, regardless of the consequences?'

'Yes.'

'I don't mean just the consequences for Peter Fraser. I mean for Kate and Hugh as well.'

Ellen didn't react.

'You're risking losing both of them. Is it worth that?' Sanjay pressed.

'Yes,' she replied without hesitation. 'If they really love me, they'll let me do this. That goes for you too.'

He studied her for a long time and she returned his gaze without flinching.

'I don't want you to get hurt,' he said softly. 'But I can see you won't change your mind. Will you call me next week and tell me how it goes? I really hope it all works out.'

Ellen, relieved to have Sanjay's tacit support, assured him that she'd phone as soon as she could on Saturday and they said their goodbyes. But she sat on afterwards, mulling over their conversation and trying to ignore the niggling feeling that Sanjay might just be right.

Chapter 25

No one in the McCandless family had overslept on Monday morning, but there was an urgency to leave the house which suggested they had. The outcome was that Kate avoided having to spend much time with Alex. She needed that undemanding start to her day. She was on her own in the gallery and had two things to do, one a great deal more taxing than the other.

She tackled the easy task first. It involved a phone call to the artist Dermot Caven, putting forward the idea of an autumn exhibition of his work. Yes, he replied, he was very interested in her offer, flattered too. He asked her to email him all the details and then they'd arrange a meeting.

Kate was thrilled, and it boosted her confidence for her other task: to hopefully confront Ellen at lunchtime. But as midday approached, her eagerness to ambush her sister seeped away. Kate hadn't spoken to Ellen since Sanjay had been over a week ago and she felt uneasy as she put a notice on the door to let any potential customers know the gallery would re-open at two o'clock.

Kate had overheard Ellen telling Sanjay that she often went for lunch at The Dock, a recently-opened donation café by the waterfront and close to the college. It was a gamble that Ellen would go there today, but one worth taking.

Kate parked the car, walked to the open waterfront and spotted the café. A shower of rain made her dart towards the door.

The chairs and sofas, even deckchairs, had obviously been donated. The exposed brick walls displayed a few prints, some original artwork, too, which impressed Kate, and a couple of interesting artefacts from the Titanic. She'd expected a basic, student-style café with clientele to match, but was surprised that the customers also ranged from office workers still wearing their lanyards to retirees meeting for a chat.

As she sat down beside a window, she tried to focus on possible venues for her meeting with Dermot Caven, but found it almost impossible not to slip into a rehearsal of what she wanted to say to Ellen. She checked her watch and glanced out of the window, anxious to spot her sister yet hoping now she wouldn't appear.

'What are you doing here? I wouldn't have thought it was your style.'

Kate swung round to find Ellen hovering over her, looking far from pleased.

'I heard you mentioning this place and I thought I might catch you for lunch. It's been ages since we spoke,' Kate said tentatively.

Ellen draped her jacket over a chair, ran her fingers through her damp hair and sat opposite Kate. Her expression gave nothing away.

'Is Dad going to walk through the door too?' Ellen asked, her words dripping with sarcasm.

'No, I wouldn't do that.' Kate kept her tone level.

They avoided eye contact, looking everywhere except at each other, feigning interest in their surroundings. It was Ellen who finally spoke.

'I'm sorry, I shouldn't have jumped down your throat. It was just such a surprise to see you here.'

'I wanted to speak face to face, not on the phone,' Kate said. 'They have soup, it's the only hot thing they seem to serve. Would you like some?'

'Yes, thanks. I usually bring a sandwich too.'

'Do they not sell sandwiches?' Kate asked.

Ellen gave a little laugh. 'It's the way they do it here. You can bring in your own food if you want. It lets those with little money, like students, have somewhere to hang out. I usually get tea and something sweet and put money into the donation box.'

Kate raised her eyebrows.

'It's not revolutionary,' Ellen said with a shrug. 'Lots of places in London do the same. It's a good community thing.'

Kate prickled at the patronising explanation but said nothing. She fetched two bowls of soup, drinks and biscuits from the counter, and posted a couple of notes through the slit in the donation box.

They didn't talk while they had their soup. The silence, at first disconcerting, gradually became an acceptable stillness. When Kate saw Ellen glance at her watch it spurred her to try to start a conversation.

'Dad called round yesterday unannounced. He was distraught,' she said.

Ellen swallowed a mouthful of tea and leaned forward. '*He* was distraught?' she hissed. 'Did he tell you about Saturday? Losing his temper in the supermarket, grabbing my arm, gripping it until it hurt? You should see the bruises.'

Kate was stunned into silence.

'So I gather he didn't tell you he hurt me,' Ellen said, almost triumphantly. 'I bet he skipped the bit about him stumbling into a display, sending bottles smashing to the ground and knocking a woman out of the way. And I'm pretty sure he didn't tell you about fleeing the scene. I haven't heard a word from him since. Nothing. He frightened me. I've never seen that side of him.'

'He is sorry. He was in tears,' Kate whispered.

'So his messenger says,' Ellen scoffed.

'Well, you won't go and see him in person. Anyway, Dad didn't ask me to come.'

Kate caught a glimpse of her sister's face behind the curtain of hair that had fallen over it. Her cheeks were burning.

'He desperately wants to talk to you,' Kate went on. 'He's convinced you've found Peter Fraser and he's frightened you've already turned your back on him.'

'Last week I didn't know where I was going,' Ellen said, looking up. 'I had no idea what I was going to do with my life.' Her face was still flushed and her eyes wide and bright. 'Now I have plans and' – she laughed – 'maybe not dreams, but real hopes.'

'Did you hear what I just told you? Dad's on the verge of a breakdown. All he wants—'

'All he wants is for me to stop looking for my father. Well, he's too late. I'm going to meet Peter this Saturday,' Ellen declared.

Kate stared at her and read the look of elation on Ellen's face as her sister continued talking. She heard Ellen's voice, but it was muffled and distant. She caught some of the words and tried to make sense of them.

'Conference ... Geneva ... not going straight home ... meet in Dublin. And ...' Ellen leaned towards Kate, her eyes still glowing, 'his first email to me, after I told him about Mum, was beautiful.'

Kate sat transfixed, horrified by Ellen's total obsession with this stranger.

'I'd love you to read it. You'd understand then,' Ellen enthused. 'He wanted to know about Mum's life after she left Durban, and about us ... and you too. He's such an important man and so well known. He's done really great work for people with AIDS. And he—'

'For heaven's sake Ellen!' Kate's raised voice brought curious glances from people close by. 'Did you hear a single word I said about Dad?' she said more quietly.

'Yes, of course I did,' Ellen snapped. 'And I *will* talk to him, but I can't get past the fact that he was never going to tell me about Peter. He ordered Mum not to tell me. Ordered her. How do you think that makes me feel?'

'Dad believed he was doing the right thing,' Kate said.

'For himself, not me.'

'Well, I'm sure it was more about keeping us together. All he wants is to know that you're not ending everything with him, or with us.'

'I'll talk to him when I'm ready,' Ellen retorted.

'Hi, Ellen.'

The cheery greeting came from behind Kate. She swung round. A tall, lanky young man carrying a steaming mug of coffee was standing smiling at Ellen. He glanced at the empty seat beside her and grinned.

Ellen, her face still flaming, rushed an introduction.

'Can we catch up later, Dave? Kate and I have family stuff to discuss,' Ellen said with a false laugh.

'No problem,' he said with a weak smile. He raised a hand as he moved away.

'Have I spoilt your chances?' Kate couldn't resist saying.

'No, no way. He's interested in Sinead. I reckon he was going to pump me for information.'

Dave's interruption defused some of the tension between them, and Kate felt more at ease about asking Ellen what role Alex had played in finding Peter Fraser.

'He's been a huge help. I wouldn't have got this far without him,' Ellen admitted with an uneasy laugh. 'But he's a bit overeager at times.'

'I bet he is,' Kate said flatly.

'I want you to be happy for me,' Ellen said, suddenly bright again. 'I want to be able to share it all with you.' She reached across the table and touched Kate's hand lightly. 'I don't want to lose you. You're my sister. But I have to do this. I have to meet him. I'm going ahead with it whether you like it or not.'

Kate fixed her eyes on Ellen's hand lying on top of hers. 'Phone Dad tonight, Ellen,' she said, slowly raising her head. 'Phone him and tell him what you're planning to do.'

Ellen withdrew her hand abruptly and stood up, lifting her coat off the back of the chair. She glanced out the window. 'At least it's stopped raining,' she said without looking at Kate.

'Ellen!' Kate said sharply.

Ellen faced Kate. 'I'll phone him tonight, okay?'

Kate stood up and took a step towards Ellen. They hugged but it had no warmth. A token gesture. Kate was about to step back, but Ellen gripped her for an unsettling moment longer.

'Be happy for me,' she whispered fiercely before hurrying out of the café.

Kate, fighting back tears, watched her leave.

Chapter 26

When Ellen got home that evening, there it was: the email arranging a time and place to meet.

> *My dear Ellen,*
> *It will be wonderful to meet you. I will be staying at Buswells Hotel, near St Stephen's Green. Could we meet in the hotel lounge at 11.15 on Saturday morning? That should give you enough time to travel from Belfast without too early a start. I assume you will be on your own. My flight to Durban is not until the evening so we will have plenty of time to get to know each other. I will be very interested to see if you look like your mother. I'm looking forward to our meeting very much.*
> *Affectionately*
> > *Peter*

In her eager first read-through she had missed the 'My dear Ellen'. If only Kate and Sanjay could see that; then they would believe that Peter Fraser accepted her as his daughter. And he had said it would be 'wonderful' to meet her. She couldn't have been more thrilled.

Ellen checked the bus timetables. The coach was cheaper than the train and should get her to the city centre well before the meeting time. She sent Peter a brief reply confirming everything. Then she contacted her flatmates in London and was happy to learn that her old room would still be available for her to use for a weekend.

She tried to get Sanjay, but his phone went directly to voicemail. She found herself getting straight to the point.

'I still want to come over to see you in London. Would the weekend of the 25th suit you? Not this weekend but next? My old room is free and I'm ready to book my flights. Bye.'

She was happy until she remembered the promise she'd made to Kate at lunchtime. She phoned Hugh.

'Is this a bad time to ring?' she asked when he picked up.

'It's never a bad time for you to call me, Ellen. I'm so glad you did. I wanted to phone you but you asked for space. I'm sorry if I ... I'm sorry I frightened you in the supermarket. I shouldn't have left you with all that mess either. I'll cover any costs for the damage. And I'm sorry I grabbed your arm. I didn't mean to hurt—'

'Kate thought I should let you know that I'm meeting Peter Fraser this Saturday,' Ellen said in a rush.

There was a long silence before Hugh said, 'I see.'

'Is that all you can say?' she asked crossly, then instantly regretted it. 'Sorry, I'm not handling this very well.'

'It can't be easy for you.'

Ellen needed more of a reaction from him. Anger, sorrow, anything would do. She couldn't bear his compassion. 'I know this must have come as a shock to you.'

'No, I assumed it would happen eventually,' he said tonelessly.

'Why aren't you angry with me?' She was shaking.

'There's no point. I can't say or do anything to change your mind. It's your choice.'

'You've been an important part of my life, but—'

'I was your father from the day you were born.' Ellen heard a tone of defiance creep into Hugh's voice for the first time.

'You acted as my father, but you denied me the chance to know my real father. I'm taking that chance now.'

Hugh sighed. 'Maybe I did make mistakes, Ellen, but every decision I made, every action I took was to protect our family. My big mistake was to give Kate money without telling you and without offering the same amount to you. So I'd like to rectify that now, if I may, and give you twenty thousand pounds too.'

Ellen gasped. 'You want to ease your conscience by paying me off? You think that makes everything right? *Maybe* you made mistakes? If it hadn't been for Mum's letter, I'd never have known the truth. You were never going to tell me. I was the mistake and it was you who insisted on covering it up. Do you know how that feels?' Ellen started to pace the room. 'Every memory I have of growing up with you and Mum is spoiled. Everything I was certain of, that I took for granted, is a lie. You talk about losing me? I've already lost you, the father I thought I had. Now I'm losing my sister because she sides with you. None of this is my fault. I don't want your money. Give it to a charity if it makes you feel better. Meanwhile, I'm going to meet the father who never knew about me but who's ready to welcome me into his life.'

Ellen's heart was hammering and her head pounding. She was drained.

'Take your anger out on me, but please don't let it cause a rift between you and Kate,' Hugh said firmly. 'You need each other. You've made your decision to meet Fraser and I sincerely hope you get the outcome you want. But just know that I will *never* turn my back on you, no matter what. You will always be my daughter, Ellen.'

And with that he hung up.

Hugh's call replayed endlessly in Ellen's head afterwards. Only when her old flatmates got in touch later that evening did her mood lift. She had to rein in their excitement about her planned trip to London, explaining that she was simply making a flying visit. They plied her for information about Sanjay and teased her about her guarded replies. Ellen found their enthusiasm infectious. It was fun. She had missed that.

Five days to get through until she met Peter. She needed to book flights. Perhaps it would do no harm to check job opportunities in London too. Her phone rang again. It was Sanjay.

'Hi, Ellen, I can't really talk right now. We're out wining and dining one of our clients. That weekend suits me fine. I just wanted to run an idea past you. Have you booked your flights yet?'

'No, I was about to do that.'

'Well, could you come over earlier on the Friday? I'd love to introduce you to everyone after work and let you get to know them.'

Ellen laughed. 'Yes, I should be able to leave here around lunchtime. But listen, while you're here, I got an email from Peter arranging to meet this weekend. He called me, *my dear Ellen*. Isn't that wonderful? He not only accepts me as his daughter, he also wants me to know how much I mean to him.'

Silence.

'Sanjay?'

'I'll call you later in the week. I can't talk right now.'

'There's nothing to talk about. I just wanted you to know that he accepts me.'

Ellen could hear laughter in the background. 'I'll speak to you later,' Sanjay said.

'Go back to your wining and dining,' she snapped and ended the call.

* * *

Kate stared out of the kitchen window, seeing nothing. What an evening it had been. First, Hugh had called to tell her about Ellen's rant. His words still echoed in her head: '*How do I compete against Peter Fraser? What can I offer her?*' Before they'd hung up, Hugh had pleaded, ' Don't let the rift between you and Ellen get any wider.' Kate had mumbled a promise to patch things up with her sister. 'Write a letter to her, Dad,' she'd added. 'Tell her you love her and explain why you did what you did.'

Then she'd had yet another row with Alex. She'd intended to talk to him about taking some decisive action about their marriage, but couldn't stop herself from having a go at him for helping Ellen find Peter Fraser.

Alex had laughed at her. 'You make it sound like a crime. Yes, I helped her find Peter, and I'm really happy for her. She's now this close' – he measured a tiny space with his finger and thumb – 'to meeting her real father and I got her there.'

'It's all about you, Alex, isn't it?' she'd retorted. 'It doesn't matter who gets hurt as long as you get your ego stroked.'

'Don't you dare blame me!' Alex shouted. 'It was her choice to go ahead with it all and she needed help.'

'Have you any idea what this has done to my dad? Ellen's turning away from him, and I reckon from me too. You don't care about him or me.'

'I care about your sister,' Alex had blurted out and stomped off through the house towards the front door.

That was thirty minutes ago. He wouldn't be away for long; Kate was sure of that. He hadn't taken the car and he hadn't changed into his running gear. She turned the lights off in the kitchen and went upstairs. After checking that Sophie was still asleep, she went into her bedroom and closed the door.

That Alex should harbour any kind of feelings for Ellen was too disturbing for her to contemplate. Ellen seemed keen to get back together with Sanjay. So if there was any attraction, it would be completely one-sided. Alex was just flattered by Ellen's attention and revelled in her reliance on him. Kate could imagine how much his leech-like persistence would irritate Ellen. Just before Betty had gone into the hospice, she had warned her daughter about him. 'He's a needy person and always will be,' she'd said. 'He wants to be important and indispensable, to be valued. And if he doesn't feel valued, he'll go looking for it elsewhere.' Kate shuddered.

She wondered if Alex would now consider separation too or if he was still set on saving their failing marriage. It was time to push him in one direction or the other. Rain spattered the window as she found a link to the Relate website and texted it to him with a brief explanation: *I think we need help now, for Sophie's sake at least.*

Ten minutes later, as she was settling down to sleep, she heard Alex come home and slip into the spare room.

The next morning after breakfast, he bent down to pick up Sophie's schoolbag.

'Okay,' he said to Kate without looking at her. 'We'll try Relate. See if they can get us back on track. You make the appointment. My time's more flexible than yours.'

Then he walked away, calling Sophie to hurry up.

Kate could cope with that. It was an acceptance, delivered without argument. That's what mattered. She left Sophie off at school, parked her car in a street near the gallery and rang Zoe.

'It'll be about half an hour before I get in. I've to pick something up. You can catch me on my mobile if there's anything urgent.'

She needed some time alone, away from Zoe's harmless, everyday chat.

She started walking in the opposite direction to the gallery, heading to the park. Stopping at a café, she bought a coffee to go. The warmth of the drink in her hand was comforting and she slowed her pace, sipping her drink as she walked. The park was busier than she expected. Dog walkers were already gathering in twos and threes to chat and mums were holding onto toddlers straining to run free. The occasional jogger and cyclist sped past.

Finding an empty bench, Kate sat down to finish her coffee and watch everyday life go by. She wished she could do this more often – let other people live their lives without worrying or feeling the need to interfere. 'Stop trying to fix everything,' her mother used to say to her. 'It gets you nowhere.' She knew what Betty would have advised about Alex: 'Leave him. Walk away.'

And she could, without too much hesitation or remorse. She longed to walk away from the mess, to make a clean break. Yes, marriage was meant to last, to grow stronger, especially when children were involved. And they'd made sincere promises to each other as they exchanged rings. But they were more like aspirations, Kate mused.

Divorce would be a kind of bereavement, she supposed. Another one on top of her mother's death. And the baby that had never been born. Kate's thoughts took her along a path she neither expected nor wanted. Down came the heavy curtain of guilt again, the self-blame that Kate could never will away, all because she hadn't been happy to discover she was pregnant. It had got worse with Sophie, when an added layer of self-judgement for failing to be a good mother had almost crushed her. Now she lived with the ever-present fear of failing in everything else.

She stood up, stretched and tossed the empty cup into the bin beside the bench. She would head to the gallery and phone Relate to make an appointment. Her marriage was collapsing. Time to let someone help *her*.

Chapter 27

'Excuse me, please. Is it "he has a lot of money" or "he has much money"?'

Ellen glanced up from the page that she had been staring at vacantly and smiled at the earnest young man who had posed the question.

'It's "he has a lot of money", Jakub.'

He beamed and resumed writing.

An easy question to answer, thankfully. She should explain why it was she corrected him, give grammatical examples and check that everyone else in the class understood, but instead she surrendered to the other concerns that filled her head. Wondering about all that lay ahead of her on Saturday in Dublin and what it might lead to, but dwelling more on the worry that she would not live up to the expectations of her renowned father. Would she measure up to his high-achieving daughter, Kirsten? Would he hope to see the qualities he had loved in Betty mirrored in their daughter? Ellen didn't have Betty's drive and charisma. She thought of herself as scatty and idealistic, naïve and easily swayed. Well, both her mother and Kate had told her that often enough. She had no dazzling career, nor did she have the confidence and poise that Kate possessed.

Trying to dispel the conviction that she would be a bitter disappointment to Peter, Ellen took the mental leap beyond the meeting and conjured up the dream of him inviting her to South Africa and a joyous get-together with her half-siblings. She left his wife, Diane, out of the picture. Peter's affair with Betty had happened almost thirty years ago. Diane would undoubtedly forgive him in time and at least accept, if not openly welcome, this new stepdaughter. After that, well, Ellen would surely win Diane over.

'Please, how much words do we write?' Jakub asked.

Ellen jumped as a chorus of voices rang out around the classroom, 'Many words!'

The South African dream disappeared as everyone laughed. But back in the flat after work, her doubts resurfaced. In the photographs she'd seen, the gifted, successful women in Peter's life appeared sophisticated and stylish. Peter had no idea what Ellen looked like. Maybe it would be better to send him a photo so that he'd recognise her. She began scrolling through the photos on her phone, looking for one she could send. Any recent pictures were selfies with Sinead, mostly in pubs with cocktail or wine glasses on the table in front of them. She couldn't even crop Sinead out of any half-decent shots as their heads were invariably jammed together.

She had older selfies but they all had Sanjay in them. Old holiday photos showed her only as a speck in the distance. Ellen hated to stand in front of the view or the building that was the purpose of the snap. There was nothing else for it but to take a selfie especially for him.

What kind of expression would she adopt? What impression did she want to make? Cool, confident, composed? But that was Kate, not her. Deciding on warm and friendly with an open smile,

Ellen dashed into her bedroom to get changed into something appropriate for a photo. There was a full-length mirror on the inside of the wardrobe door and she stood far enough back to see her reflection from head to toe. This was what Peter Fraser would see approaching him. She turned sideways. Was it obvious she was pulling in her tummy? Relaxing her muscles, she saw the bulge appear above the top of her jeans. How much could she lose in a day? Ditching a tight top was the only alternative. She swung back in front of the mirror again, stepping in close. Her face seemed fuller than the last time she'd looked closely, the eyes bleary from spending too much time looking at her laptop screen, and her make-up was blotchy. Her hair had grown long and unruly. She bent forward, then straightened, tossing her hair back. She glanced in the mirror and gave a panicky laugh. It was a scary bad hair-day look.

There was no time to mess about. The first priority was to find a decent top to wear for the photo. She wanted to appear more mature than her usual laid-back, older student look implied. So, the selection was important. Rifling her way through the hangers in her wardrobe, she finally returned to a top Kate had bought her. It was loose, silky soft with a delicate leaf pattern in jade and turquoise. It emphasised the blue of Ellen's eyes, Kate had said. She should be doing this with me, Ellen thought with a surge of sadness, which quickly turned to anger.

She tore off her t-shirt and slipped on the top, tugged a brush through her tangled hair and repaired her make-up. Holding the phone at arm's length, she smiled and snapped. Ellen studied the result. The blouse looked well, but she appeared as inane as she had done in the photos with Sinead, only there was no alcohol excuse this time. She was never going to look natural in a selfie. It was too close, too distorted, as if she was leering round a corner. Definitely not the kind of image you wanted to send to your new-found father.

She could ask Sinead to take a photograph but that would come at a cost. She would have to tell Sinead about Peter, the meeting, everything. Sinead was a good friend but she loved gossip, and Ellen had quickly learned to share private matters with her on a need-to-know basis only. Ellen would have to edit her story. Peter could simply be a friend of her mother's. That would surely avoid any intrusive questions from Sinead. She picked up her phone.

'Any chance we could meet in town tomorrow lunchtime?' Ellen asked her.

'Yes, sure. I need to get a birthday present for my mum in any case. You can inspire me.'

'Will you be on your own?'

'Yes, but why does that matter?'

Ellen winced at the sharp, inquisitive tone in Sinead's voice and almost changed her mind. But she took a deep breath.

'Well, I've a favour to ask. Could you take a photo of me? A proper one, you know, that makes me look good. Selfies look like ... selfies.'

'God, you've got me really interested now. What's this all about?'

'I'll explain when I see you tomorrow.'

* * *

'That's mad,' said Sinead when she heard Ellen's account of how a previously unknown South African man wanted to meet her. 'It's like an episode of that TV programme where people meet long-lost relatives and cry their eyes out.'

'Except he's not a relative,' Ellen added quickly. 'He's just an old friend of Mum's.'

Sinead narrowed her eyes. *Just* an old friend? Mmm, methinks the lady doth protest too much.' She laughed.

'Can you take the photo now, please?' Ellen asked, anxious to change tack. 'I want to send it to him as soon as possible.'

'Sure. Will I take it here? Let me move the mugs and things out of the way,' Sinead said, already clearing the café table.

'Yes, it's fine.'

Sinead leaned across the table. 'Just let me fix that bit of hair.' She scrutinised Ellen. 'There, that's better. Now give me your phone.'

Ellen handed it to Sinead, then sat up straight.

'Relax or it'll look like a mug shot.'

Ellen giggled.

'Good. Now, think about Sanjay.'

Ellen could feel herself softening.

'That's more like it,' Sinead said. She peered round the phone to look directly at Ellen. 'Why is this Peter not coming to Belfast to meet you?'

'I suggested that, but he's busy with meetings in Dublin, so it's easier for me to go to him. Now, does this look okay?' Ellen forced a smile.

'Too tight-lipped. Try smiling with your mouth open.'

Ellen bared her teeth and snarled, then laughed. In that moment Sinead managed to get the perfect photo to send to Peter Fraser – a laughing, self-assured, fun-loving daughter.

While Sinead went to the counter to join the queue for refills, Ellen composed a short email to Peter on her phone, attaching the photo. She found it hard to think straight in the busy café while keeping one eye on Sinead. After several abandoned openings and a brief reflection on Peter's possible response, she looked up from the screen. Sinead was returning, mugs in hand. Ellen glanced at the email and hesitated a moment over the closing line, then pressed *Send* just as Sinead reached the table.

'So what's so special about this guy?' Sinead asked as she sat down again.

'But we have to decide what to get your mum,' Ellen said, desperate to change the subject.

'Oh, don't worry, I'll grab a scarf for her. Your need is far more important. And far more fun too. Do you not think your mum and this Peter might have been more than friends if he's making this much effort?' Sinead's eyes widened with relish and an appetite for more.

'No ... no, I don't think so,' Ellen stammered, wishing she had made Peter a distant relative rather than a friend. 'He was interested in politics and so was my mum. Lots of their university friends were at that time.'

'Aye, right,' Sinead said. 'So why so much fuss over the photo then?'

Ellen wanted her phone to ring. Or the fire alarm to sound. Or someone to have a heart attack. 'It's to help him recognise me,' she said eventually. 'We've never met before. I know what *he* looks like.'

Sinead pounced on the revelation. 'Did he send you a photo? Can I see?'

Ellen had saved a photo of Peter to her phone, and she brought up the image and showed it to Sinead. It felt like a betrayal somehow.

'Wow, a silver fox *and* he's got style. I bet they did fancy each other. If I was into older men, I wouldn't mind having him as a sugar daddy.'

Ellen shuddered.

Sinead leaned forward. 'So what are you going to wear? Do you need my help?' She nodded encouragingly.

Ellen relaxed a little. 'Yes please! I think this man's high up in whatever his business is,' she said, 'and the place we're meeting is quite posh. I want to wear something that's a bit better than the charity shop things I usually buy.' She laughed.

'Great! It's about time we got you sorted,' Sinead declared. 'Forget about your mum's friend. Do it for you. Let's hit the shops.'

It took them an hour or so, racing around the stores, in and out of changing rooms, to find a couple of dresses that Sinead approved of. Having a choice was always better, Sinead maintained. Then, of course, Ellen would definitely need a pair of classy sandals, no matter which dress was chosen. Ellen bemoaned the amount of money she was spending.

'Sure, you're only going to keep one of the dresses. You can return the other,' was Sinead's justification. 'Anyway, the dress I think suits you best was in the sale, so what are you worrying about? And you need a decent pair of shoes no matter what. What about a jacket?'

'Oh, I've got one that'll go with either dress,' Ellen said, totting up the price of the whole outfit in her head and ignoring Sinead's sceptical expression.

Later that evening, back at the flat, Ellen looked at the high-heeled sandals and the discounted dress that lay over the back of the sofa. She would never have considered buying anything so sophisticated. It was an indulgence, but nothing else she tried on had given her such a confidence boost. It was a striking print dress in bolder colours than she usually wore. It clung more to her body than she would have liked too, but Sinead had told her it was sexy and sharp. Yes, she would keep it; Sanjay would love it too, but what impression would it have on Peter? For a split second she considered getting Kate's opinion. It was a split second that hurt.

* * *

When Ellen returned from work on Friday afternoon, a letter was waiting for her in the post box. She immediately recognised Hugh's handwriting on the envelope. He was the only person in the family to send her cards in the post. Ellen opened her bag and slipped it inside. She knew what it would say; not the exact wording, of course, but the sentiment, and she was too pre-occupied with her trip to Dublin the next day. Hugh would keep.

Chapter 28

Ellen stepped off the coach in O'Connell Street and took a few moments to look around her. It appeared far grander than she recalled. Her experience of Dublin was limited to two visits – one as a young child, with memories only of the zoo, and then as a teenager, again with her parents and Kate, doing the obligatory city sightseeing.

Before she left Belfast she had checked her route from the coach stop in O'Connell Street to Buswells Hotel and had calculated the time it would take to walk there, leaving nothing to chance. She had scrutinised the hotel on every website possible. If asked, she would have had no trouble describing it: *an elegant boutique hotel in a group of Georgian townhouses, the atmosphere cosy and relaxed, with an old-world charm.* A hotel that oozed history appealed to Ellen.

Her glowing introduction to Dublin faded as she began walking towards O'Connell Bridge, passing a disappointing number of fast-food outlets and mouthy groups of lads still recovering from the night before.

Now, as she hurried along, Ellen felt inappropriately dressed. Saturday morning in a slinky dress and tottering in high-heeled sandals: she must look like she'd never made it home from a nightclub. And her old beloved jacket spoilt the whole effect she wanted to create: the sophistication, the composure. On the coach from Belfast she had rehearsed greeting Peter, what she would say, how she would act, but all she could envisage was that it would be a disaster and everyone would say 'I told you so'. Now, as she tottered past Trinity, what little remained of her confidence seeped away. The urge to flee, to get the next coach back to Belfast, was alarmingly strong.

Her mobile pinged. She stopped in the middle of the crowded pavement to read the text. Her hand shook. It was from Sanjay, saying that he hoped she wouldn't be disappointed by the meeting with Peter Fraser, and wishing he was with her. Sanjay was not telling her to walk away. She had his support. That was a vindication of her decision to continue, and the urge to flee left her.

A quiver of excitement propelled her along the pavement. In less than half an hour she would meet Peter, her father. There was more than enough time to make it to the hotel, but she wanted to be sure of its location first, then take a wander through St Stephen's Green before they were due to meet at a quarter past eleven.

Her pulse quickened as she walked up Kildare Street and spotted Buswells Hotel on the corner ahead of her. Keeping her head down, she hurried past, making straight for St Stephen's Green. Maybe Peter was looking out, as anxious for the meeting as she was.

She thought the park would be a refuge, somewhere to draw breath and prepare herself, but as she approached the park gates, that idea receded. Her feet were throbbing with the strappy sandals cutting into them at every step. What had possessed her to wear new shoes when she had so much walking to do? She should have known better.

The sun vanished behind low, massing clouds that threatened rain. For all her planning she hadn't thought to check the weather. She had no umbrella, no raincoat. She turned. She had to get back to the hotel, but she badly needed to find a loo. The image of greeting Peter and excusing herself to go to the ladies was too awful. She had to find somewhere, quick. Scuttling back as fast as her sore feet would allow along Kildare Street past the hotel corner again, she scanned the elegant buildings gathered there and spotted the National Library. Please let it have public toilets, she thought, and it did. A hurried visit, a fix of her hair and make-up and another check of her watch.

Then she retraced her steps. She was far more nervous than she thought she would be. Her heart was hammering and her legs almost gave way as she climbed the steps to the hotel. All she could hear was her heels click-clacking as she crossed the lobby's gleaming tiled floor. She made for the nearest rug. Leaning against a marbled pillar, away from the glittering chandeliers, she slowed her breathing and looked around.

The photos on the hotel website had prepared her for a period drawing room, not a conventional hotel lobby, but the reality was much more impressive; heavy drapes and damask wallpaper, with brocaded armchairs and couches near an open fire. There was a surprising cosiness and a stillness too, exuding what she imagined to be the intimacy of a gentleman's club. An elderly couple reading newspapers; a woman flicking through a magazine; a man standing at the reception desk, his back to her, the receptionist talking to him. Ellen willed him to turn round. Surely people could hear her heart thumping. He turned. It wasn't Peter Fraser. There was no resemblance at all. She took a deep breath.

She slipped off her jacket and draped it over one arm, then smoothed the dress down over her hips, pulling in her stomach. Her mouth was dry; she tried to swallow. She glanced to her left where a glass partition separated the lobby from a lounge and bar. That surely was where he would be. She left her pillar, stepped from one island rug to another and ventured in. A rapid, sweeping look took in people sitting on sofas and chairs around small coffee tables. All so normal, so calm.

She felt light-headed. A member of staff was approaching, ready to help. But then she heard someone behind her quietly call her name. She swung round.

At the deserted end of the room, Peter Fraser stood beside a table, looking directly at her, his head tilted to one side, as if asking a question. He was immediately recognisable from his photographs. Not as tall as she had imagined but more tanned. She managed to take in his pale blue linen jacket, white shirt and navy chinos. Casual but classy as well. Ellen wondered what first impression she was making. Did she look ready for evening cocktails rather than a morning cup of coffee? Too late to put her jacket on and wrap it tightly around her.

The smile he gave her, tentative at first, broadened as she smiled back and walked towards him. She didn't know whether to extend her hand to shake or attempt a hug. He moved closer to her and, putting his hand lightly on her arm, guided her to a chair at his table. He took her jacket and draped it over the back of a chair. Then he sat opposite her, a low coffee table separating them.

'Ellen,' he said. 'Ellen.'

She could feel herself blushing. She lowered her head, unable to think of anything sensible to say.

'This must be overwhelming for you,' Peter said. 'It certainly is for me.'

'Yes, it is,' she murmured gratefully.

They exchanged shy, awkward smiles.

'How was your trip from Belfast? Any trouble finding the hotel?' he asked.

She warmed to his voice. It was pitched low and he spoke his words distinctly, his accent less clipped than Hendrik's and her mother's; mellow, like a quality wine. She told him about the trip down and made him laugh by describing her initial recce of the hotel, whizzing past so as not to be seen.

A waiter approached their table, halting their conversation. 'Are you ready to order now, Doctor Fraser?'

'Yes indeed, Stefan. I'll have an Americano please. Ellen, what would you like?'

'Tea, please,' she said. 'You've been here before then.'

'Yes, I've made a couple of visits to Dublin for work. I found Buswells on my first visit and it suits me perfectly. There's a lot of excellent research work being done at Trinity College that's relevant to the work of my AIDS organisation.' He stopped to look intently at her. 'I can't believe we're sitting here and I'm talking about work.' He shook his head. 'I gather it's only a few months since Betty died. It must have been such a painful time for you.'

'Yes, just three months ago. She was ill for a long time before she died. She was only sixty-four.' Ellen lowered her head.

'That's far too young,' Peter said gently. 'Betty was in her thirties when we met and that's how she's fixed in my memory.'

Ellen looked up. 'I've some recent photos of her on my phone, if you'd like to see them.'

'Thank you,' he said.

But before she could get out her phone, he pressed the tips of his fingers together and held them, prayer-like, to his lips while studying her face. Ellen's heart missed a beat; that was the way she often sat. Her blush deepened.

'You look exactly like your mother,' he said, giving her a faintly lopsided smile that somehow seemed familiar. 'The way you tilt your head as you listen. You're doing it now.' His smile vanished. He looked away for a few moments, then back to face her. 'Betty was very special. She was so full of life, ready to take on the world.'

He talked about the community newspapers they had worked for and the strength of Betty's commitment to giving a voice to ordinary people.

'She was fearless,' he said, his eyes shining. 'She inspired me.' He mentioned the places Betty took him to in Durban, the ones she had loved in her youth. It was almost as if he was reliving it all, as if he'd forgotten Ellen was across the table from him. His eyes were bright but fixed on something in the distance. Ellen lost concentration. Tiredness and hunger overwhelmed her. She recalled her skipped breakfast. His sentences came in snatches to her. And then she heard him say that no amount of emails could replace this unbelievable face to face with her.

'So do you accept that I'm your daughter?' she blurted out.

He reeled back, halting mid-sentence, taking a moment to reply. 'Goodness, that's a bit like being cross-examined in court.'

'Sorry ... I'm sorry,' Ellen stammered. 'I didn't mean to be so blunt.'

'It's okay,' Peter said quickly. 'None of this is easy. But yes, if Betty told you that I'm your father, then of course I accept you, with open arms.'

Ellen closed her eyes for a moment. If only Sanjay and Kate could hear his words, see the biggest of smiles he had given her. When she opened her eyes again, Peter was looking at her with concern. He patted her hand as their drinks arrived. Stefan, the waiter, stared at Ellen for a few moments, then glanced at Peter and hurried back to the counter.

They sat in comfortable silence sipping their drinks. Ellen sighed. Peter squeezed her hand and she returned the gesture; it was a far cry from Hugh's reticence. They held each other's gaze for a few moments until Peter's chuckle finally broke the spell.

'You have my wonky smile!' he exclaimed.

Ellen laughed and her hand flew immediately to her mouth.

'It's all right. Apparently it's one of my more endearing features, thank goodness. And you've got your mother's laugh,' he added softly.

'I guess I have.'

'I'm so glad we've found each other,' he said. 'A lot to take on board, of course, but I couldn't be happier. How did you manage to find me? How much did Betty tell you about us in her letter?'

Ellen explained all the online research she had done.

'I'm very impressed. And very grateful too,' he said.

'Mum didn't really tell me a lot about your relationship in her letter. She was more concerned with telling me what had happened between her and Dad – Hugh. When she found out she was pregnant, Hugh made her promise that no one else would ever know he wasn't my father. That's why they left Durban so quickly. But Mum decided I had to know the truth in the end.'

'It's been traumatic for you. Does Hugh know you've found me? Does he know we're meeting?'

'Yes,' she murmured. 'He's scared he'll lose me.' She fingered the teaspoon on the saucer, avoiding eye contact. 'Mum didn't want me to tell him that I knew everything, but I couldn't help it. I hate secrets.'

They relaxed back into silence which was suddenly interrupted by Peter exclaiming, 'I'm so sorry, Ellen. I didn't order the best scones in Dublin. You must be hungry after your journey. Can you manage a couple?'

'That would be lovely. Thank you.'

He beckoned Stefan over and gave him the order.

'I'll bring a selection and top up your drinks,' the waiter said.

Stefan returned with small dishes of butter, jam and cream,

which he set on the table along with an enormous plate of scones in a variety of flavours.

Peter suddenly grasped Ellen's hand. 'Stefan, this is my daughter, Ellen. She has travelled down from Belfast to spend some time with me.'

Ellen beamed at the waiter and felt her face flooding with colour. It was the first public acknowledgement of their relationship.

'Lovely to meet you,' Stefan said, smiling broadly at them both as he backed away.

'I feel honoured and proud to be able to say "my daughter",' Peter said, leaning towards her.

Ellen sipped her tea and buttered a scone

'Just one small thing,' he said with the flicker of a frown and his fingertips raised again to his lips. 'You remember I asked you to always use my personal email address and not my business address?' Ellen nodded. 'Unfortunately, you forgot when you sent your last email and its content was ... well, a little indiscreet.'

She sat back, bewildered. 'I'm sorry about sending it to the wrong address, but what was so indiscreet about it? I know it wasn't a great photo.'

'The photo was lovely, my dear, but the message that came with it – *I can't wait till we meet*, signed *love Ellen* and with a kiss – well, that sort of thing can easily be misconstrued. Do you see what I mean?' He nodded, inviting her to agree.

She mumbled a second apology and, to give her time to compose herself, took a bite of the scone. It turned to sawdust in her mouth.

'Don't worry about it anymore. No one else saw the email,' he said. 'But even here, in a hotel, people see a lovely young woman all dressed up with a much older man and jump to the wrong conclusions,' he said. 'I think Stefan was doing just that, poor man.'

He gave another nod and Ellen mirrored it vigorously. Her face was on fire. How could she have been so stupid?

Peter took a drink of his coffee. 'Now, you were going to show me some photographs of your mum. I'd love to see them.'

Ellen gave him her phone so he could flick through the images at his own speed, but he held the phone at an angle, inviting her to study them with him. She leaned in, delighted by his thoughtfulness.

Peter remarked how little Betty had changed from when they met. He commented again on the similarities between Betty and Ellen, but thought that Kate was more like Hugh.

'They're alike in many ways,' Ellen quipped.

They came to photos of Betty when she was older and Peter lingered over one in particular.

'That was taken at Kate's wedding,' Ellen said.

'She's beautiful,' he remarked in a wistful tone. 'So composed, so at ease with herself, as if she's left behind the rebellious, fiery young woman I once knew.'

'Oh, she still had that in her,' Ellen said with a grin. 'She never lost the love of arguing with us all, telling us exactly what we should be thinking.' Peter smiled too. 'Mum wrote that you loved each other.'

'That's absolutely right,' he said. 'It wasn't a fling. It was serious for those couple of years we had in Durban.'

'But she wrote that you couldn't have a future together,' Ellen added tentatively.

'Did she elaborate?'

'No, that was all she said.'

'It wasn't possible,' Peter said, 'no matter how much we might have wanted it. There were too many other commitments to honour and too many obstacles. It was hard for us both, but it must have been much harder for your mum.' He fell silent, staring at his cup.

'I've read some bits and pieces about your work but I'd love to hear more,' Ellen said, hoping to lift the mood. 'I'm sure it'll be far better than Wikipedia.'

He gave a deep throaty chuckle that made Ellen laugh too and went on to speak of the work of his AIDS organisation, of his recent retirement and his desire to continue supporting it in a different capacity.

Ellen listened and studied him at the same time. He was obviously a self-assured, assertive man in his professional life, leading from the front like a tour guide, sure of his facts and his followers. But he was also giving her glimpses of a caring and emotional side, and another shared trait – his desire to be of help to others, although on a vast scale compared to hers. He spoke with passion about his work. This charisma that he carried so lightly was in complete contrast to Hugh's buttoned-up indifference. It was no wonder Betty had been unable to resist.

'Now, let me hear more about you,' Peter said. 'You wrote that you're an English language teacher. Do you love it?'

She appreciated his use of 'love' rather than 'like'. 'Yes, I do,' she replied, her head raised high. 'I want to work more with refugees and asylum seekers, not only with language but also addressing all the practical and cultural issues they find difficult when settling in the UK.'

'I can see you're passionate about it. Good for you. A lot of people would support that idea, but you want to do something practical about it. For me, that's what life should be about. I've been very fortunate to be able to set up my organisation. Maybe I could help you in some way if you want to make a real impact with your work.'

'It would be great to get your advice. Just having your interest in what I want to do means a lot.'

He gave her a broad grin. 'Well, there's no doubt about you being my daughter.' He raised his coffee cup in salute and Ellen chinked it with her tea cup. They laughed.

'And is there anyone special in your life at the moment?' he asked.

'It's a bit complicated,' Ellen replied, then she told him everything, from the first time she met Sanjay to the arrangement to see him in London the following weekend.

'I like the sound of him. I reckon you'll be moving back there,' Peter said with a wink. 'Maybe I'll get to meet him some day.'

They smiled at each other, less self-consciously now.

'I hope there will be lots of times we can meet in the future,' Peter said. 'I'd like us to really get to know each other as father and daughter.' He paused. 'But only if that's what you want as well?'

'Oh, yes please.'

'I'm so relieved. I was quite anxious about this meeting.'

'You were? I wouldn't have guessed.'

'An act, my dear. It comes easily after years of having to present a calm, confident face to the world. But to meet your daughter for the first time in nearly thirty years ...' His voice rose along with his eyebrows.

'Your *younger* daughter,' Ellen said.

He sat back in his chair and stared at her. Then the lopsided smile returned. 'Do you have any photos of you growing up?' he said. 'I'd love to see what I've missed all these years.'

Ellen pulled a sheaf of old photos from her bag. She'd hoped that Peter would ask that very question. He set each one down carefully on the table so they could both see them. He studied them closely – baby and toddler pictures, then school age – and commented on many. He came to a photo of Ellen, aged six or seven, holding a certificate aloft and grinning broadly.

'I was awarded it for designing a road safety poster,' she explained. 'I didn't win the competition, but I was so proud of coming second. Mum said—'

'—but everybody else came second too!' Peter laughed as he finished her sentence.

Ellen swung round to stare at him.

'Ah, Stefan,' Peter announced triumphantly as the waiter approached them with more coffee and a pot of tea.

Peter held out his cup for the offered refill. Ellen left the teapot sitting. She waited until Stefan had left the table.

'How could you have known that?' she asked eventually.

'Known what?' Peter asked, adding milk to his coffee.

'That Mum said "But everybody else came second too".' Ellen enunciated each word slowly.

Peter took a long drink of coffee. 'It's what happens at lots of kids' competitions so no one's disappointed. I can remember when my son—'

'Those were exactly the words Mum used.' Ellen stared at him.

Peter set the cup down with exaggerated care and brushed imaginary crumbs from his trousers.

'How do you know that?' Ellen asked, almost whispering.

'Well, this is a bit embarrassing.' He cleared his throat. 'This is very difficult for me. Let me explain.'

Ellen gripped her hands together under the table.

'I knew that Betty was pregnant with our child when she left Durban.'

'But ... but she said in her letter that she'd decided not to tell you she was pregnant,' Ellen's voice wavered. 'So she lied, even in her last message to me.'

'It depends on how you read it. Betty was good at wordplay. I'd guessed she was pregnant, so there was no need for her to tell me.'

Ellen laughed bitterly. 'How devious was that? But why did *you* not tell me?' she demanded. 'You never let on in your emails. Or mentioned, when we first met today, that you already knew about me. You've been stringing me along.' Ellen's voice cracked.

Peter reached out his hand, but she kept hers in her lap.

'Yes, I'm sorry about that,' he said. 'I couldn't put it in an email. I wanted to wait until we met. But you're right, I should have said something earlier.'

'I want the truth now,' Ellen said, striving to remain calm. 'No more playing games. There have been so many lies and secrets and ...' Her voice gave way and she covered her eyes with both hands.

Peter reached over and gently peeled her hands away.

'We could never be together, the three of us,' Peter said softly. 'My wife knew nothing about my relationship with your mother and I simply couldn't abandon my family. Betty told me she was agreeing to Hugh's conditions to ensure that you and Kate stayed together.'

'But that still doesn't explain how you knew what Mum said when I was six.'

Peter glanced at himself in the mirror behind her and dabbed his lips with a serviette. 'I needed a connection to you, and to Betty. You were *our* child, so your mother kept in touch with letters and emails and photos.' He gave Ellen a smile along with the now familiar nod that sought agreement. Ellen sat mute and immobile. 'I still have every photo of you,' he said. 'I got to hear about your milestones and achievements, your first steps, starting school, right up to your graduation and your teaching job in London.'

'And about coming second,' Ellen added in a scathing tone.

'I was always so proud of you and hungry for news. There had to be absolute secrecy with our correspondence. Hugh was unaware that I knew about the pregnancy and we had to keep it like that. We never wanted to hurt him or endanger your relationship with him or with Kate. Ellen ...' He waited for her to look at him. It took several seconds before she was able to. 'It broke our hearts that I couldn't meet you, that we couldn't tell you anything, but it would have torn our families apart if we had.' He leaned forward. 'I didn't know your mother was going to write that letter to you. It was entirely her decision. But you can't imagine how much it means to me to be meeting you today. I suppose her confession was a gift to me as well as to you.'

'I can't get my head around this,' Ellen said, struggling to keep her voice level. 'It's as if you were stalking me, spying on me, tracking every single event in my life.' She saw that Peter was about to interrupt and she raised her hand to stop him. 'But I can see you meant no harm. You did it out of love for my mother and, I guess, for me.'

Peter watched Ellen intently but said nothing.

'Ever since I got in touch with you,' Ellen continued, not daring to make eye contact, 'I've been going over and over what it would be like to meet you, imagining a trip to South Africa.'

He sighed. 'If it's to meet me there, I'm sorry, but that can't happen.'

'I had hoped that I might be welcomed into your family,' she said, with a note of desperation. 'That I might meet Kirsten and Benjamin, maybe even your wife.'

He sat upright. 'You've obviously been doing your homework,' he said sharply, silencing Ellen. Then his expression softened. 'There's nothing I want more than to continue this wonderful relationship, and we can, but I'm afraid it must remain a secret, as far as my family are concerned.'

'But why?' Ellen asked. 'It all happened decades ago. And Mum isn't alive anymore. If you explained everything, would Diane not understand?'

He started at hearing his wife's name. 'My wife was totally unaware of the relationship I had with your mother. Betty wasn't in our circle of friends those couple of years she was in Durban, and my time at the university was entirely separate from my home life. I'm sorry, Ellen, but I can never tell my wife and children about the affair or about you. It would devastate them, even though it was almost thirty years ago.' He paused, pressing his fingers to his temples. 'And for me, personally, there's too much at stake if all this became public. I'm well known for my work throughout South Africa, and prominent in every sector of the media. A renowned epidemiologist who has devoted his life to the treatment of AIDS, who advocated for family planning and birth control and who campaigned against unprotected sex.' He laughed sharply. 'Can you imagine the reaction? My reputation would be ruined and it would jeopardise the work I'm still doing. I'm sorry, but I can't risk losing that as well as my family.' He leaned forward, hands clasped. 'But please, Ellen, do let me remain a part of your life.'

As Peter had been speaking the blood rushed to Ellen's face. Now she stood up. 'As your dirty little secret?' Her voice rose to a shrill pitch.

Peter, frowning, put a finger to his lips to hush her.

She leaned towards him. 'You might care what people hear or think, but I don't. Not any more. I ...'

She watched Peter rummage in his jacket pocket and extract his wallet. He beckoned to Stefan.

'It wasn't just emails and photos, was it,' she said slowly as the truth started to register. She sat down again. 'You and Mum kept on meeting. Didn't you?'

His mouth was a tight line. 'Yes, Betty and I continued seeing each other.' He sat back in his chair as if that was all Ellen needed to hear.

'For how long?' She spotted Stefan coming towards them, then suddenly retreating as Peter raised his hand. 'Oh, God, you met Mum here and Stefan knows all about it.'

'We never stopped loving each other,' Peter murmured.

Ellen clenched her fists beneath the table. It would feel so good to let her temper fly, but she had to find out more.

'When did you see my mother again after my birth?' she demanded, slowly and precisely repeating it as Peter told her again how much he loved Betty.

'When she came back to Durban for her father's funeral in 1989 or '90. I can't remember exactly. We were sure Hendrik would tell Hugh.'

'So Hendrik *did* know about the two of you,' Ellen said loudly.

'Shush!' Peter scolded.

'Hendrik was aware from the start that Betty and I were friends. When she was back in Durban for the funeral, we met up and Hendrik saw us out together. He asked Betty about it and she confessed but told him it was only a fling.' Peter smiled at the memory. 'I don't think Hendrik knew I was your father.'

'And how many times did you and my mother meet after that?' Ellen asked, her voice cold and controlled.

'I don't know exactly.'

'Guess.'

'We met wherever and whenever we could. It wasn't some tawdry affair. We loved and respected each other. I know it's hard to understand, but I loved my wife too. I still do.'

Ellen gave a quick mocking laugh.

Peter sat up straighter in his chair. 'It's true. I loved them both. And I wanted them both because I couldn't believe how blessed I was. When your mother's cancer spread and we both understood there was no hope for her, I was devastated ...'

His voice became distant, the words muffled as the true extent of the deception dawned on Ellen. 'Did you visit my mother in the hospice?' she asked.

'No, I ... I couldn't.' He looked away. 'I wanted to, but I couldn't bring myself to.'

Ellen remained silent, forcing him to say more.

'I didn't want to risk bumping into Hugh,' Peter said, regaining his composure. 'I was careful to protect our secret, just as Hugh had done. You're very precious to me. You've always been a huge part of my life and—'

'But you've been nothing in mine,' Ellen cried out, her voice ringing in her ears.

'Ellen!' Peter said sharply.

'What people think of you, that's all you care about. How did I not see it?' There were shards of ice now in Ellen's voice. 'No one must ever know that I exist just so you can maintain your image of the perfect husband and father, some kind of hero with an unblemished medical career. You wanted it all, but not at the price of your own reputation. To hell with what it cost everyone else.'

'That's not true, Ellen.'

'It is,' she hissed. 'You've done everything to keep the truth from me. You were never going to admit that you knew about me all along. I was never, ever to know a thing.'

'I would have told you everything in time. Look, we've only just met. It would have been too much in one go. But now that you do know, nothing need be hidden anymore.'

Peter nodded, looking for her agreement, but it only intensified Ellen's anger and her harsh laugh rang out. 'Ha! But you want to hide me for the rest of my life!'

She stood up, her arms held rigid by her sides; she was swaying. Peter rose too, coming round the table, trying to steady her and shield her from the prying eyes of the guests at the tables further up the room. She brushed his hand from her elbow.

'I have one more question,' she declared. She took a deep breath. 'If my mother hadn't written that letter to me, would you ever have told me I was your daughter?' she asked quietly.

The blood pulsed in Ellen's head. She longed to sink into the chair, but she remained upright and calm.

Peter kept his head down. He licked his lips but said nothing.

'Would you?' She flung the words at him.

He didn't reply.

Ellen grabbed her jacket and her shoulder bag in a single clumsy movement, but he held on to the strap, whispering fiercely, pleading with her to stay, to talk to him, not to let it end like this. His hands were shaking. She tugged the strap out of his grip and the bag tumbled to the ground, falling open, like a mouth in shock. Out spewed its contents – brush, purse, make-up, tissues, the photos, the unopened letter from Hugh.

Peter and Ellen bent down, their heads almost touching, as they began cramming things back into the bag. Ellen snapped it shut, bundled it into her arms, snatched her phone off the table and lifted the jacket from the floor where it lay spread-eagled.

Stefan was standing by Peter's shoulder.

'Just a misunderstanding, Stefan,' Peter reassured him with a strained smile. 'Maybe you could bring us some more tea. Ellen, would you like tea? Ellen—?'

But Ellen did not turn round as she scurried through the hotel lobby towards the front doors.

Chapter 29

When Ellen stepped onto the pavement, her legs almost gave way. She steadied herself for a moment, but the idea of Peter following her into the street to try and coax her back into Buswells drove her on to put distance between herself and the hotel as quickly as she could. She kept glancing over her shoulder as she hurried along. It was only when she reached the end of the street that she realised that Peter had no intention of pursuing her. Turning the corner, she stopped abruptly. She didn't recognise any of the buildings and she had no idea where she was. This was not the way she had approached Buswells, but there was no way she was going to retrace her steps to the hotel.

To get on the coach back to Belfast was her only goal. She kept walking, using instinct alone to find her way back to O'Connell Street and shutting out any flashbacks that threatened to overwhelm her. Taking no notice of the light rain that had started to fall, she hurried as fast as her sandals would allow through quiet side streets until she reached bustling

Grafton Street. Ellen knew it by name. It was somewhere Kate went when she made trips to the Dublin art galleries.

She had to elbow her way through groups of onlookers, circle buskers and living statues, weave through the smartly dressed, strolling shoppers with their designer bag purchases, and step out past the flower stalls dotted along the street. The chatter, the laughter, the music – it all became one shrill, distorted jumble as she struggled along. A side street gave her a chance to escape, but it was nearly as busy. Small boutique shops proved magnets for would-be customers to gather and window-gaze, blocking her way.

The first flashback caught her unawares, stopped her dead. Like the searing pain of a burn, it made her gasp. Peter wrestling with her bag, pleading with her; Stefan's intervention. Only now she recalled the shocked and disapproving faces of the other people in the room. Did that all really happen?

Ellen glanced about, took another street, then another, each bringing fewer shops and fewer people. But now, in the comparative stillness, more recollections flooded her brain. The first, when Peter greeted her, when she recognised similarities in his mannerisms, when he introduced her to Stefan as his daughter. Those sweet memories now turned rancid. Ellen shivered. The images continued to pile into her head, leaving little room for logical thought.

Coming suddenly to a busy junction, she joined the jostling crowd at the crossing and was carried by them to the other side to more unfamiliar streets. Ellen stopped. Had she walked in a circle and arrived back in Grafton Street? No, there were cobblestones beneath her aching feet for a start. Wandering on, the street became tighter, busier; alleyways branching off on either side, shops crammed with tacky gifts for the tourists; pubs and bars galore, most of them proclaiming their Irishness with music and signs. More crowds, tourists this time, with cameras slung around their necks. She spotted a sign: Temple Bar. Ellen recalled Kate's unflattering remarks about the area, a place to avoid.

She pushed her way through the groups of drinkers who, oblivious to the drizzle, were downing their pints outside packed pubs. Turning a corner Ellen was confronted by a band of hen-party-goers clad in emerald green tutu skirts and tiaras, whose raucous banter seemed aggressive, not fun. On she went, head down, past waiters standing outside restaurants, their one-liners intended to entice her in but striking her as threatening. She was breathing heavily, as if she'd just run a race, and her heels were making her unsteady. She knew she must look drunk, wobbling all over the cobbles.

In an instant the drizzle turned into a downpour, catching everyone out. Umbrellas were hoisted and crowds ran laughing into the nearest pubs and restaurants, much to the waiting staff's delight. As people darted away, Ellen stood helpless and isolated, like a lost child in a supermarket. She shivered under the damp weight of her jacket. Her hair was plastered to her head and her dress clung to her legs, inching provocatively up at every step.

She spotted a gift shop two doors down and squeezed inside the already packed space. Ignoring the shelves of souvenirs, she found some umbrellas. They were all green and no doubt sported some inane slogan, but she didn't care. Shouldering her way to the till she spied chocolate bars for sale, reminding her that all she had eaten since leaving Belfast was a bite of a scone. She put a bar of chocolate alongside the umbrella on the counter and reached into her bag for her purse. But her hand found everything except it – tissues, make-up, brush, photos. She was trembling now and her heart was pounding. There were impatient grumbles from those in the queue behind her. Panic rising, she tipped out the contents of her bag onto the counter and rummaged frantically through the bits and pieces.

'Jesus, would you get a move on,' someone in the queue muttered.

But the purse wasn't there. Ellen glanced at the assistant and, close to tears, she shrugged and gestured to the items still spread out before her.

'Excuse me,' said the next customer, manoeuvring himself in front of Ellen, shoving her belongings aside and setting his purchases down.

The young assistant gave her an apologetic smile as Ellen scooped everything back into her bag and barged her way out of the shop. The rain bounced off the cobblestones as she splashed through the puddles. She pulled at her dress and hugged the sodden jacket tightly around her, desperate for respite from the rain so she could think clearly.

Had her bag been open or closed when she went into the shop? Easy pickings for someone in those jostling crowds. Or was the purse still lying on the floor of the lounge in Buswells? Everything grabbed in that rush to escape, everything but the purse. How could she have been so stupid! Her mind raced. What was in the purse? A few euros, a fiver in sterling and her credit card. She stopped dead in her tracks – her return coach ticket to Belfast! Losing a purse and some money she could cope with and she could sort out the credit card later, but no ticket home?

She fought back the panic and tears of self-pity and tried to think straight. There was no way she was going back to the hotel to look for the purse. She only had one option. She stumbled across the cobblestones to a covered entry and took out her mobile. When she saw how low the battery was, she almost cried. She hesitated for a moment before she brought the name onto her screen, and a few seconds passed before she tapped it.

The call went to voicemail. She stabbed at the screen to end the call and brought up the landline number. It was answered almost immediately.

'Hello? Kate?' Ellen said.

'Ellen? So how did it go?' Alex asked eagerly.

Ellen's heart sank and she slumped against the brick wall, unable to speak. Then she heard her sister's voice in the background.

'I need to speak to Kate, now!' Ellen shouted. She could hear the muffled sounds of a squabble.

'KATE!' Ellen yelled and a second later, Kate spoke.

'Ellen? Just a moment ...' Ellen heard Kate call out, 'She wants me, not you, Alex!' A door slammed. Then Kate was back. 'Sorry I didn't get to my mobile in time,' she said. 'What's wrong?'

Hearing the concern in Kate's voice was too much for Ellen and she began to sob.

'Take a deep breath and tell me what happened,' Kate said as calmly as she could.

Ellen laughed through her sobs. 'Oh Kate, you sound like you're talking to Sophie! I'm so glad to hear your voice.'

'Did it not go well?'

'I lost my purse when I ran out.'

'But what happened? Why are you crying?'

'I can't talk about it on the phone. Listen, I can't get home. My bus ticket was in the purse.'

'Right, don't worry, I'll come and get you.'

'Oh, thank you. I'm in Temple Bar.'

'Bring the map up on your phone and head for Dame Street. It's not far away. Find a nice café and—'

'But I haven't got any money.' Ellen's laugh was almost hysterical.

'Okaaaay ... so find Dame Street, then head up towards Dublin Castle. Look for signs for the Chester Beatty Library. It's more like a museum than a library and it's usually quiet. No money required. There's a beautiful roof garden too – perfect if it's dry.'

'It's pouring and I'm soaked. I didn't bring an umbrella.'

'Oh Ellen,' Kate said sympathetically. 'Right, I'm leaving now,' she added briskly. 'I'll phone you when I get parked, and I'll come and find you. Don't worry, everything will be alright.'

'Thank you so much.' Relief coursed through Ellen. 'The library sounds good, if they let a drowned rat in.'

'I have my keys in my hand,' she said. 'It'll take me about two hours to get there. It's a pity you can't go into the library café.'

'I had a scone at the hotel, so I won't need to raid any bins.'

It was good to banter back; even better to have her sister coming to rescue her.

Ellen found her way easily to Dame Street. The panic that gripped her earlier had lost its power and, with the reassurance that Kate was on her way, she felt foolish and exhausted. The rain had stopped, but her feet ached as she hobbled up the slight incline to the Castle. She followed the signs to the Chester Beattie Library and, once inside, took the lift to the top floor. There were bench seats in the corridor looking out on the rooftop garden, its plants still dripping after the downpour. She slumped down on a bench, kicking off her shoes, grateful no one else was there.

Her body seemed weighted down, her head too heavy to raise. Ellen longed to sleep, to sink into oblivion, but her mind wouldn't let her. Questions streamed into her head, queuing for answers. What was Peter doing now? Did he know what he had done to her with his lies and deceit? The sangoma had been right. All questions without answers. She dared not think of her mother's part in all of this. Not now.

Then her thoughts turned inwards, and she castigated herself for her naivety, her blind trust that the dreams would come true. She should have listened to Sanjay. The huge sense of loss flooded through her, making her gulp for air as if she was drowning. She buried her head in her hands.

'Excuse me, are you all right?'

Ellen jerked upright and swung round. A woman, fiftyish, smartly dressed, was standing in the doorway that led to the stairs. She approached Ellen.

'I ...' Ellen clasped her hands to her chest as if to dam any outpouring of emotions. 'Is it okay if I just sit here?'

'May I?' The woman gestured to the space beside Ellen on the bench. Ellen slid along the seat leaving a damp trail.

'I'm Deirdre. I work here,' she said with an encouraging smile, showing Ellen her identity badge.

'I'm Ellen.'

'Oh, goodness, you're soaking!'

Ellen glanced down at her dark rain-stained sandals, her limp, shapeless jacket and her dress, still clinging to her. She could only imagine the state of her hair and make-up.

'It's not too bad. I think I'm starting to dry out now.'

'Well, can I help in any way? You seem very upset.'

'I'm waiting for my sister. She's on her way from Belfast to collect me.'

'That'll take some time. Would you like me to take you to the café? You'd be more comfortable waiting there.'

'No, no, I can't.' Ellen saw the puzzled look on Deirdre's face. 'I've lost my purse. It had my return bus ticket in it too.' She tried a smile and a dismissive shrug, but the effort brought tears.

'You lost it here in the library? Have you told anyone?'

'No, I think I left it behind somewhere else and I don't want to ... I can't go back for it.'

For a split second Deirdre looked wary, but she repeated the offer to take Ellen to the café, assuring her of a drink and a bite to eat. 'Sure your sister can pay for it when she gets here.'

'You're very kind, thank you,' Ellen answered. 'She glanced out of the window; the sun had appeared. The very sight of it lifted Ellen's spirits a little. 'Maybe I'll go and see the roof garden first.' She turned back to Deirdre. 'Someone – a relative – upset me very much this morning.'

Deirdre patted Ellen's hand. 'Taking time in the garden would do you the power of good. It's an oasis of calm, we like to say. I'll reserve a quiet table in the corner of the café for you and explain to the staff. They'll get you whatever you want when you're ready.'

'Thank you,' Ellen said, her faith in human beings restored somewhat.

Ellen made her way out. Grey stones and bench seats of silver-bleached wood; planters filled with soft waving grass and rustling bamboo; glimpses of the Dublin skyline through airy trellises. The garden's restraint was somehow soothing. No wonder Kate loved this small garden with its pared-down simplicity and order. Ellen was surprised that she too found it beautiful. She usually preferred cottage gardens, crammed with plants of every possible colour. She wandered over to the low stone wall and studied the Castle garden below, the green sward with its swirling, inter-woven paths. Mythical serpents, Celtic knots – whatever you wanted to make of it.

The sun warmed her as she sat beside the grasses. She peeled off her jacket, draped it over the seat to dry and eased the damp dress from her legs. She ran her hand over the seed heads bowed down beside her. Opening her bag, she checked if anything else might have been lost along the way. She pulled out the contents again – hair brush, photos, tissues, make-up, the envelope addressed to her. She had completely forgotten about Hugh's letter. Sighing heavily, she slid her finger under the flap and removed the single sheet.

My dear Ellen, it began.

She bit her lip. The same term of address that had given her such joy when Peter had used it in his email.

I have had time to reflect on everything I did or didn't do, and it has been a painful experience. I am writing to tell you four things. The first is that I am utterly ashamed of my behaviour in the shop when I grabbed your arm and then abandoned you. I never apologised properly. That is unforgivable.

I also wronged you by not telling you years ago that I was not your biological father. You had the right to know and I denied you it. I should have trusted you and told you the truth, no matter what the consequences. I was too afraid of losing you, but I can see now that was selfishness on my part. I don't blame you for wanting to find Peter Fraser.

The third thing I want to tell you is that I am still sure that I took the right course of action in bringing you up as my own daughter. I saw no other way to keep our family together. That meant everything to me. I do believe, however, that I could have handled the whole issue with your mother much more sensitively. As she used to say, I am 'old school'. I saw myself back then as the head of the family and I imposed my values on her. I cannot apologise to her. I have left that too late but I hope you will be able to forgive me in time.

The last thing I want you to know is that I love you in just the same way as I love Kate. I admit it was not always easy at the start to set aside the circumstances of your conception. But I love you and always will, even if the precious bond we once had is gone. I fear that this declaration may have come too late. If so, I'll have to live with that, but I'd regret it for the rest of my life if I said nothing.

I wish you a happy, fulfilled life, my dear Ellen, and I hope you find what you're looking for. Whatever the outcome, know that you are loved.

Your loving father,
Hugh

Ellen leaned back against the stone wall as a tidal wave of relief washed over her. She longed to lie down on the bench, to have the blissful sleep of a child feeling safe in the knowledge of unconditional love. A gift from Hugh.

The letter's contents went far beyond anything she could have imagined. And the beautiful way he expressed his deepest feelings. Who would ever have believed that of the reticent Ulsterman?

Not many children would receive heartfelt letters from both parents, Ellen thought with a wry smile. Here was Hugh, open and honest, while Betty had rationed her letter to a few hand-picked details, denying Ellen the key to unlock her other secrets. Hugh was holding his hand up, admitting his faults, not expecting forgiveness, while Betty defended her secrecy and asked to be pardoned.

In that instant, she knew she had forgiven Hugh. The certainty surprised her. And her mother? Was there forgiveness for her too? The answer took longer. No, not yet. And then came the sickening, shocking awareness that she might never forgive her. With it came tears, shed for every emotion that coursed through her.

'That lady's crying. Why's she crying?'

Ellen jumped. She rubbed her eyes with her damp sleeve and glanced self-consciously over her shoulder. A family had entered the garden, the father holding a child aloft, the mother ushering two other children forward, steering them away from Ellen to the view of the Castle garden below. The boy, now perched on his father's shoulders, was pointing at Ellen.

'Why, Daddy?' he persisted, leaning over at a perilous angle to question his father, who hushed him and hurried away.

Ellen slipped the folded letter back into its envelope and into her bag. She left the bench, hurried back into the building and dashed into the toilets. Catching a glimpse of herself in the mirror, she laughed a little hysterically. The drowned-rat hair, the mascara smudges across her face, the party dress – it was no wonder the parents spirited the children away from her. She dragged a brush through her matted hair, reapplied a little make-up and angled her body at the hand dryer for a few minutes.

She reckoned it would take Kate just over an hour now to reach her. A few moments later and a little less damp, she was sitting at the table reserved for her in the café with a bowl of soup, a sizeable slice of warm wheaten bread, a pot of herbal tea and some biscuits. She devoured everything. It gave her a boost and a gritty determination to show she could cope.

Her phone pinged and she lifted it from her bag. It was Sanjay texting to see how she had got on. She stared at the message, feeling no sense of urgency to respond. She couldn't face the humiliation of having to admit the venture had been a disaster, that his earlier doubts had been justified.

But she needed to reply with something, just to hold him at bay for a while longer. A short and simple text: *It didn't go well with Peter. I'm ok now and Kate's coming for me. I'll call you as soon as I get back. E.* Rereading it, she deleted her initial and retyped *love Ellen xx.*

Chapter 30

Ellen left the café after promising the staff she'd be back to pay and lifted a leaflet about the library from a stand. She needed something to occupy her. Who was Chester Beatty anyway, and would 'one man's stunning collections of art and literature across three continents' do the trick? Worth a try.

Wandering through the galleries, she idly glanced at the ancient manuscripts, the miniature paintings, the rare books, admiring all, but superficially, unable to give them proper attention. The rooms were dark – to protect the precious articles, she supposed – and drifting through the galleries in the half-light with awe-struck visitors hovering over glass display cabinets did soothe her; she could understand why Kate liked to spend time here. But as occupied as Ellen tried to be, it was Peter Fraser, her mother, Hugh and Sanjay who began to clamour for attention.

The old question of Hugh favouring Kate slipped into Ellen's mind first, and answers followed surprisingly fast. Maybe it wasn't favouritism. Shared interests might have made his relationship with Kate stronger than with her. Kate loved the big natural garden of the family home, but not for climbing trees and making dens, the things that Ellen liked to do. No, Kate wanted to grow plants and Hugh responded eagerly. He taught her how to sow seeds and how to tend the seedlings, and the two of them had spent hours pottering in the garden.

Had Ellen been jealous of that relationship? She took a moment to reflect on that. No, no, she thought, it was Betty's attention she craved, not his. She could see why he hadn't responded to her as he had to Kate. He wasn't a dad who played silly games with his children or let them away with the odd tantrum or disobedience. Kate was five years older than Ellen and had been sensible and well-behaved. He had demanded good behaviour and Kate obeyed. Ellen hadn't. The things they were interested in Ellen found boring. She wanted to share Betty's bold, rebellious, off-the-wall approach to life and Betty let her. She had given Ellen the attention she wanted, but only when she was a child. So when had it changed? And why? Could it have been meeting Peter Fraser again? Was that the—

Kate's phone call cut through Ellen's soul-searching and she hurried out of the gallery to take the call.

'I've just parked.' Kate said. 'Stay there. I'll come and get you.'

Kate in her favourite double role, Ellen thought, of chief organiser and big sister. She was glad of it now.

She waited at the library entrance and spotted Kate hurrying towards her, the expression on her face cycling through anxiety as she searched for Ellen in the crowd, relief at seeing her and eagerness to console. They embraced, laughing and crying, as if reunited after years of separation.

'What on earth are you wearing?' Kate said.

'Don't go there,' Ellen replied with a quick laugh.

Kate gave Ellen a bag containing dry clothes and Ellen went to the toilets to change while Kate paid for the food she'd eaten in the café. They met up again ten minutes later in the lobby, then hurried through the crowded streets towards the car park, their flight hindered by the oversized borrowed trainers that threatened to trip Ellen up. She clung to Kate's arm and, laughing and linked together, they made it to the car. Catching Ellen's infectious desire to flee Dublin, Kate accelerated out of the car park.

Ellen was grateful that Kate didn't question her or talk much at all. And as the distance between them and Peter Fraser increased, Ellen gradually relaxed. She stretched out her legs, laid her head against the headrest and closed her eyes. Less than a quarter of an hour into the journey, she drifted asleep.

* * *

'So, you're not coming back here with Ellen?' The sound of Alex's voice on Bluetooth speaker woke Ellen some time later. 'You're going to stay on with Ellen at her flat and you won't need dinner.'

His plodding repetition of what Kate had told him drew some exaggerated eye-rolling from both sisters.

'Yes, Alex, there's some leftover lasagne in the fridge, enough for you and Sophie,' Kate said, matching his leaden tone. 'I shouldn't be too late.'

'Is Ellen all right?' Alex sounded quite deflated.

'Yes. I'll fill you in soon,' Kate replied.

'Yes, but did—?'

'Give Sophie a hug from me,' Kate said quickly. Then, noticing Ellen pointing at herself, added, 'And from Ellen. Listen, there's traffic slowing up ahead. I'd better go now. Bye.'

'That's strange,' remarked Ellen with a grin, 'there's hardly a car in sight.'

'Sometimes with Alex you have to be inventive. Anyway, you know what he's like. He'd try everything to get you to tell him all the details. He should have been a criminal investigator.'

Out of the corner of her eye Ellen watched Kate driving, her hands resting on the steering wheel, rather than gripping it, her eyes never leaving the road ahead. Being driven like this, carried safely and effortlessly along, past neat green fields and soft rolling hills was calming. It was good to let Kate take the lead and handle the situation. Dublin, with its fuss and noise and distressing memories, was slipping further from her mind with each passing mile.

* * *

'I'll hang up your dress and jacket in your bedroom. We can see what state they're in when they've dried out.' Kate announced. 'But I'm afraid the sandals look ruined.'

Ellen shrugged. 'It doesn't matter. They weren't me anyway. Just leave the clothes in the bag. I'll see to them later.'

Kate set the bag on the floor. The change in Ellen from car to flat was startling. Kate sat on the sofa and watched her pace the small living room, unable to stay still.

'Would you like a drink?' Ellen asked, turning towards the kitchen.

'A coffee would be good, thanks,' Kate replied, hoping it would encourage Ellen to sit with her.

'Not something stronger?'

'No, I'll be driving home soon,' Kate called out as Ellen disappeared.

A few minutes of noisy preparations passed before Ellen appeared with a large glass of wine in one hand and a mug of coffee in the other and sat facing Kate. As Ellen sipped her wine, her free hand played with a strand of hair, winding it constantly around her finger, a habit Kate remembered from Ellen's teenage years, especially around the time of their parents' divorce.

'I've been such a fool,' Ellen blurted out and took a gulp of wine. 'I'm so sorry. To think I turned my back on you and Dad.' She shook her head.

Kate's heart leapt with joy to hear Ellen refer to Hugh as Dad again. 'I must admit it was hard for us, and scary too. You were totally obsessed with Peter Fraser. I couldn't understand it at first but then I tried to put myself in your shoes. You were given the chance to find your biological father, and I guess you got swept up with the excitement of the search and suddenly nothing and no one else mattered.' Kate glanced at Ellen who was gripping her glass of wine with both hands. 'None of us dealt with it well,' Kate added. 'We all made mistakes.'

Ellen shuddered, then drained the glass. 'I've caused everyone so much pain.'

Kate reached across and squeezed Ellen's hand. 'We'll all mend. Look at us now.'

'Dad wrote me a letter,' Ellen said, her voice faltering. 'It was lovely, and so honest.'

'That's wonderful. I'm glad he did that.'

'It was humiliating, Kate, the way he treated me,' Ellen murmured.

Kate was stunned. 'What are you talking about!'

'It was all so wonderful at first in the hotel. He was warm and charming and really thoughtful.'

Kate breathed a sigh of relief. It was about Peter.

'I can understand why Mum fell for him. And when he told the waiter I was his daughter, I was over the moon. He said he was honoured and proud to be able to say that.' A shadow seemed to darken Ellen's face as she described what happened.

Kate listened in disbelief, then growing anger, to the sequence of confessions Peter was forced to make. She held back the acid comments about him that she longed to insert, allowing Ellen's account to flow uninterrupted. It gave Kate a sense of how Ellen's reactions that morning had moved from joy through shock to fury, and she imagined the sledgehammer blows that each revelation must have brought. But she could no longer contain her own anger when, finally, she heard that Peter admitted – by his silence – that he never intended to come clean about Ellen being his daughter.

'His plan to keep you a secret, his collusion with Mum. There was never any love in that,' Kate raged, as Ellen, her eyes enormous in her ashen face, stared at her. 'And him gleaning information about you from a distance! It was like you were some prize specimen they examined together. An insect under a stone that Mum lifted when he wanted to learn more about you. It's sick, it's depraved, it's—'

'No more, please!' Ellen cried. 'It hurts so much. Mum's role more than his.' She sat with her head in her hands. 'I can't bear to think about it. It's just too painful.' She shivered violently.

Kate put her arm around Ellen's shoulders and pulled her close.

'We were right about Hendrik and Rosa knowing about the affair,' Ellen said, sitting upright again. 'Hendrik saw them together after Mum had been to Grandad's funeral.'

'Did Peter say if Hendrik knew he was your father?'

'He didn't think so, but I'm certain Hendrik knew. Maybe I'll tell him what I know now.'

'Do you think that's wise?'

'I'm not going to let my life be dictated by Peter Fraser. He's a control freak,' Ellen declared with a new defiance. 'You would have been proud of me,' she continued. 'I stood up to him at the end when I made him tell me everything. I was shouting at him in the *oh so refined* lounge of Buswells Hotel. Can you believe it?' Ellen laughed. 'And when he tried to quieten me, I told him I didn't care what other people thought – unlike him. It felt so good.'

Kate grinned. 'I'd have been cheering you on. I didn't know you had it in you.'

Ellen jumped up, lifted her empty glass from the table and disappeared into the kitchen. Alarmed, Kate followed her.

'I didn't mean that I thought you were incapable of standing up for yourself.'

'No, it's not that,' Ellen answered quickly. 'I've just remembered I have to talk to Sanjay. I feel so stupid. He warned me and I didn't listen.' She began twisting the strand of hair again. 'I didn't listen to you either and I should have.'

'Just be honest with him, the way you've been with me. He's not the type to lecture or judge.'

Ellen refilled her empty wine glass.

'It's nearly seven,' Kate said quickly. 'How about I get us some food? Fancy some Indian? You can phone Sanjay without me hanging about.'

When Kate arrived back with a paper bag filled with foil containers and bagged naan bread, Ellen seemed much more upbeat.

'You were right. Sanjay was worried about me and there wasn't a hint of *I told you so*,' Ellen said, almost breathless with excitement. 'I'd forgotten to book my flights to London for next weekend, so I've just done that. Everything will be fine.'

'Is that not a bit rushed? I mean—'

But Ellen cut Kate short by snatching the takeaway bag out of her hand and carrying it into the kitchen. The silence continued as they ate.

'How are things with you and Alex?' Ellen asked eventually.

'Not good,' Kate said, setting down her fork, 'but we've an appointment with Relate on Tuesday evening. An assessment apparently.'

'That's something positive. I can look after Sophie if you like.'

'That would be great. Thanks'

'How do you feel about counselling?'

'I think we should separate,' Kate said, 'but Alex wants us to stay together, even if we're not getting on. The only thing we agree on is that Sophie is our priority.' Kate broke off a piece of naan and used it to mop up her korma.

A few minutes slipped by.

'Alex seems infatuated with you,' Kate said. The sentence hung in the air.

'If he is, then it's one-sided, I can assure you of that,' Ellen replied. 'I would never dream of it.'

Kate couldn't hold back a wry smile. 'He must have over-whelmed you at times. That's just him and he'll never change. Mum said Alex is like a child, always wanting to be valued. If he doesn't get enough attention from me, he'll try and find it somewhere else.'

'I'm so sorry, Kate. You've enough to deal with without my problems.'

'I'm coping with it better now so don't worry about me. Anyway, I've the exhibition to distract me.'

'You and Alex are great parents and you'll always do what's best for Sophie.'

'Yeah, Alex is a great dad and Sophie adores him,' Kate said. 'I think I'm getting better at the parenting bit as Sophie gets older. But I'm scared for her. Living the way we do now, exposed to our problems, it can't be good for her. We have to make the right decision. I never want to let her down again.'

'You can't blame yourself for what you went through after her birth,' Ellen said firmly. 'You had no control over it.'

'Alex still wants another child, but I won't risk it, ever.' Kate stared down at her empty plate. 'I envy you, you know. I always have.'

'Why would you ever envy me?' Ellen asked, wide-eyed. 'You have the looks, great taste, your own gallery, a lovely house and family. It's me who envies you.'

'But you're far better with people. You make friends easier than I do,' Kate said. 'I put on an act. I'm never that comfortable with people. I worry what they'll think of me … I sound like Peter Fraser!'

'You worry what people will think of you because you always try to have everything perfect. Peter Fraser worries because he's vain and pompous and totally self-centred. Honestly, if you'd seen him in the hotel, trying to impress everyone, and looking at himself in the mirrors. So no, there's no comparison between you and him.'

Kate laughed. 'All right, I'll give you that, but I know you'd make a much better mother than me. You're so natural with Sophie. You've a knack of choosing the right presents for her and knowing what she'd enjoy doing. You were always good with her.'

'I get the fun part of playing with her. I'm not the one bringing her up, you are. You have the best six-year-old I know.'

'You're a biased aunt,' Kate said, secretly pleased. She pushed her plate aside. 'Listen, do you want me to tell Alex about your meeting or would you rather do it? I don't think we'll get away with telling him nothing.'

Ellen lifted Kate's plate and took it into the kitchen. Through the open door, Kate watched her at the sink, gazing out of the window, the plate dangling from her hand.

'Will you tell him?' Ellen asked when she returned to the room. 'I don't think I could cope with all the questions he's bound to ask.'

'Okay, I'll tell Alex what you told me, but as simple facts, no opinions, and I'll get him to swear on pain of death that he says nothing to Dad.'

'Thanks.'

Kate began clearing the table, but Ellen put a hand on her arm. 'Go home now,' she said. 'Go and see Sophie before bedtime and give her a hug and a kiss from me. Being able to talk to you about it was exactly what I needed but I'm tired now.'

'It's what we both needed. I've missed us.'

'Me too. Are we okay?' Ellen asked shyly.

'We are.'

'You know, I thought I was getting a brother as well as another sister,' Ellen announced. 'I found out all about Kirsten but never got the chance to look for Benjamin.'

'No more looking, please,' Kate said.

'I've got you back and I don't need any other sibling.'

'Will you speak to Dad?' Kate asked tentatively as she slipped on her coat.

'I will. I'll go and see him tomorrow. I don't need to go into any details.'

'Let me know how it goes. And if you want me anytime—'

'I will, and I know. I promise.'

Kate pulled Ellen's front door behind her, feeling much more light-hearted, and got into the car to drive home.

* * *

The house was quiet when Kate got back. She found Alex and Sophie in the living room, sitting on cushions on the floor at the low coffee table. They faced each other over a game of Monopoly and were so involved that they didn't notice she was there. Kate waited until Sophie had demanded rent from Alex before coughing to announce her presence. Sophie jumped up and ran to her. Kate bent down to give her a hug.

'I've bankripped Daddy,' Sophie cried.

'Bankrupted,' Kate said, immediately regretting the correction. 'That's great.'

'Daddy said I'd be asleep when you got home.'

'I didn't want to miss our bedtime read. Ellen sends you a hug and a kiss, so here they are.' She held Sophie tight, nuzzling her neck and giving her noisy kisses, which made Sophie scream and giggle.

Kate glanced at Alex still sitting on the floor. He smiled at Sophie and then at Kate, which surprised her. It had been a long time since he'd smiled at her.

'Right, Sophie McCandless,' Kate announced, 'you race on upstairs and get ready for bed. Then you can choose a book.'

'Books, Mummy,' Sophie said with a grin.

'Cheeky imp,' Kate said, laughing and chasing her.

Sophie dashed to the door and bounded upstairs, laughing loudly.

Kate turned to Alex. 'I was able to leave earlier than I thought,' Kate said. 'Ellen needed time on her own.'

'I gather things didn't go well in Dublin.'

'No, they didn't,' Kate replied, braced for a barrage of questions.

'You must be shattered. That's a lot of driving for one day,' Alex said. 'Sure you can fill me in later.'

'Okay,' Kate said, surprised by his response.

'You've changed, Kate,' he said, standing up and gazing intently at her. 'With Sophie, I mean. You're so good with her now. It's lovely to watch.' He stepped close to her, unsettling her. 'And Sophie's loving it. She's much happier. You're a great mother to her and you could be again. I know you could.' He touched her shoulder, stroking it gently.

'No, Alex! What part of no don't you understand?' Kate backed away from him.

'Please, just think about it. Relate could get us back on track. You could discuss the depression you had after Sophie was born. We're good parents, and another wee one—'

'That's just not going to happen. Ever.'

Alex's face fell. He wasn't angry; he was utterly crushed.

'I mean it. I've told you so many times, I'm never going to take that risk. I couldn't cope if the depression hit me again, if I couldn't love the baby. Anyway, our relationship isn't working. Another baby won't fix that.'

He stared at her. 'Then is this the end of us? Because we can't agree on having another child?'

Kate swallowed the words *Because I don't love you any more. Because I recoil from your touch.* But she could sense how wounded Alex was.

'Let's just wait to see what happens at Relate,' she said. 'We know we need help to sort things out.'

'Mummy, I'm ready. Come up.'

'I'll be with you in a few minutes, Sophie,' Kate called out. She turned back to Alex. 'Our appointment's in a couple of days. That's not long to wait. Yes, we can talk about my depression, but I won't change my mind about another child. I want you to know that before we go. In the meantime, let's do our best to avoid any rows. Sophie's bound to feel the tension between us.'

He sighed loudly. 'All right,' he said.

As she left the room, Alex followed her into the hall.

'But I won't simply walk away from our marriage,' he said, striding past her and calling out, 'Daddy's coming to say goodnight, Soph. You'd better be ready for the big bear hug.'

Kate climbed the stairs after him, in no hurry to catch up.

Chapter 31

One more ring, then she would hang up. Ellen would not leave a message; she wanted to speak to him.

'Ellen, is that you?'

She jumped. 'Yes, it's me, Dad.'

There was silence, then 'Oh, Ellen ...'

And silence again.

'Can I come and see you tomorrow?' she said. 'In the morning?'

'Of course you can. Come as early as you like.'

She sensed he was smiling. 'I'll text you when I'm leaving,' she said, smiling back.

'No need. I'll be ready.'

* * *

The front door was opened before Ellen's finger reached the bell. Hugh, almost shyly, beckoned her in. He was pale and looked tired, but his smile was warm and genuine. He shut the door firmly behind her making her feel as if he was safeguarding her from the outside world. There was no emotional greeting, no embrace, no tears, and Ellen was grateful for that. Hugh ushered her into the kitchen where the sharp, nutty aroma of coffee filled the air.

'I'll get your tea,' Hugh said, lifting the kettle, showing no signs that this was anything other than a normal visit.

'I didn't sleep well last night, so could I have coffee this time, please?' she said. 'Good and strong with a big spoonful of sugar.'

Hugh smiled, pulled out a chair for her, then prepared the coffee.

Ellen couldn't help comparing him to Peter. They shared a natural air of self-assurance, but Hugh's was quiet and unassuming, whereas Peter's confidence was for others to see and admire. She wondered if Peter's demonstrative show of affection had also been for effect. She had only ever seen Hugh's emotions overflow once: when he believed she was abandoning him. Peter had let Ellen walk away from him, out of his life. He hadn't come after her, suggesting he had been more concerned about the commotion Ellen had caused at the hotel than losing his new-found daughter.

'I'll add milk, then?'

Ellen jumped. Hugh was hovering beside her, milk jug in hand.

'What? Oh, yes please, lots.'

She stirred furiously then drank quickly, disliking the bitterness that still sneaked through the sweetness of the sugar. Hugh watched her as he drank his coffee, a small frown creasing his brow. Ellen noticed his hand lying on top of an envelope. He slid it across the table towards her and took his mug over to the counter.

The envelope wasn't sealed. She removed its contents – a cheque with a handwritten note attached. The cheque was made out to her for twenty thousand pounds. She glanced at Hugh, standing at the coffee machine. Ellen read the note.

I should have given this cheque to you at the same time as I gave the cheque to Kate. I was responding to Kate's financial need at the time, but that is no excuse for ignoring you. I acted without thinking of the consequences. It's a flaw in my character as you have learned to your cost, and one I intend to correct.

My love for you was never meant to be any less than my love for Kate, and I hope that, apart from this appalling omission of mine, I showed no difference between the two of you.

With my love,
Hugh

'Please don't tear it up,' Hugh said, still with his back to her.

Ellen held the cheque lightly between finger and thumb, then set it on the table.

Hugh turned round. 'Are you keeping it?'

'Can we go for a walk? The sun's out now. It looks okay.'

'Yes, of course, whatever you like.' Hugh was flustered. 'A stroll around Stormont, maybe.'

'No, not there. Let's go to the coast,' Ellen suggested decisively. 'Crawfordsburn beach is nice.'

She got up and headed for the door, Hugh, bewildered, trailing after her.

Hugh did the driving while Ellen sat silently in the passenger seat. Twenty minutes later they pulled into the almost deserted car park.

They began walking along the coastal path that led to a rocky shoreline. Hugh said it was always a special walk for him. He loved spotting the cut-out hills and mountains of Scotland on the horizon and gazing back along the lough to Belfast Port with its cranes and docks.

'Scotland's close today,' he murmured.

They said nothing else as they strode out, watching a ferry pushing through the swelling waves and the birds spear-diving into the sea. A plane gently swayed above the lough, wheels lowered for landing.

'About the cheque,' Ellen said, breaking the silence. 'I'll be inheriting the apartment with Kate and we'll sell or rent it out, so I should be pretty comfortable. But I will accept it, thank you. I know how much you want to set things right and I think it would ease Kate's conscience too.'

'Thank you,' Hugh said.

'Well, with the mad cost of living in London, and as the work I want to do won't be highly paid, I'm very glad of anything I'm offered.'

'So you're definitely moving back to London then.'

'I'm going to give it a go. I can stay in my old flat, and if I get a job, I'll think about getting my own place. I'll see Sanjay, of course,' she added in a rush. 'It's ... well, we were apart for quite a while and it seemed like the end for us. But it was good when he came over here. We'll see how it goes.'

This was all so strange. She had never seen Hugh as someone to confide in or go to for advice. She wondered what had changed. Whatever had brought about this new kind of relationship, she welcomed it.

'I'll miss you,' he said, turning to look at her.

She stopped. 'You could come over anytime and I'll do the tour guide bit.'

They exchanged smiles and continued walking.

'You're right to go to London, both for your job prospects and to find out how you and Sanjay feel about each other,' Hugh said. 'It's good that you're staying with friends, too, rather than moving in with Sanjay straight away. That'll give the two of you a bit of space. He's a good man, but you still have to make sure he's right for you. You've been through such a lot. You need to have some fun again.'

Hugh's words touched Ellen. This was the most he had ever said about personal matters and it all made sense. Ellen moved a little closer to him as they continued walking.

'He ... Peter didn't really want me in his life,' Ellen said. She immediately sensed the tension in Hugh. 'Well, only if I remained a secret. I told him I wouldn't have that.' She spotted a bench ahead of them. 'Let's sit down,' she suggested.

Hugh needed no persuasion. He sat bent over, his hands clasped between his knees.

'So he was prepared to meet you and ... and admit that you were his daughter, but he wasn't prepared to tell his wife and his children – his other children – about you.' He glanced at Ellen.

She was used to his way of working methodically through events and situations, a trait she had often been impatient with over the years, but now found strangely comforting. 'Yes,' she said.

'So he had no intention of ever introducing you to his family, even though it had only been a fling with Betty all those years ago.' Hugh shook his head in disbelief.

Ellen sat rigid; she couldn't tell him the truth.

'Fraser was willing to lose you rather than risk his family finding out,' Hugh continued. 'That must have been so hurtful.'

'Yes, it was.'

'And after the shock of your mum's letter. You *have* been through the wringer.' There was a tremor in his voice. 'I have a bit of a confession to make.'

Ellen took a sudden deep breath.

'I never stopped worrying that your mother might break the promise I imposed on her and tell Fraser that you were his daughter. I was sure he'd come and whisk you away. That fear never left me.' His voice broke for a moment. 'But now that I know he was totally unaware of anything, well, I feel ashamed that I doubted your mother.'

Ellen's heart lurched. She hid her face from Hugh, staring blindly at the sea. There was so much she could disclose – that Peter not only knew of Ellen's existence but also every detail of her life, that Betty and Peter's relationship had continued for more than twenty years – but she wouldn't. She longed to tell Hugh just how deep her hurt ran. But now she'd have to keep secrets herself, the very thing she most despised, to spare Hugh the truth that Betty never stopped deceiving him. Such a cruel irony.

Ellen stood up. 'Let's go back now,' she said.

'We've only just got here. Are you sure?'

'Yes, Dad, I am.' Ellen heard his sharp intake of breath. Hugh got up and Ellen linked her arm through his. 'Have you got anything at home for lunch?'

Hugh straightened his back, raised his head and looked along the path towards the car park. 'I'm sure we'll be able to rustle up something together,' he said.

Ellen, tightening her grip on his arm, matched him stride for stride.

* * *

With Kate and Alex out for the night – a 'Relate date', Alex quipped – and with Sophie settled in bed, Ellen opened her laptop and resumed her search for work in London. She'd been in contact with her old flatmates and had suggested late June as a date for moving back in with them. There was an urgency now to her job hunt. She wanted to continue teaching English but specifically to asylum seekers and refugees. While she was hunched over the keyboard, navigating several open tabs in her browser, her phone rang.

'Hello, Ellen? It's Jean Mason. I hope I'm not disturbing you.'

Well, yes, actually, Ellen wanted to say. 'No, it's fine, Jean.'

'I wonder if we could meet.'

Ellen waited for Jean to add an explanation but none came.

'Is it about the tapes?' Ellen asked. 'The ones of Mum's programmes? You were going to look them out for me.'

'Yes, yes, those,' Jean said. 'And I want to have a chat with you about something else,' she added. 'I could call tomorrow evening.'

Jean was organising Ellen yet again and it irked her. 'I'm flying to London this weekend and the flat's a complete mess, so I'll come to you instead. Tomorrow evening suits me well. Can you give me your address? What time is best?'

Jean gave her the address and they arranged a time.

The sound of the car tyres crunching on the stone driveway prompted Ellen to shut the lid of her laptop. She was slipping it into her bag as Kate walked into the room, closing the door behind her. The earlier strained look had gone but Ellen could see she was weary.

'How was Sophie? Did she play up?' Kate asked.

'No, she was great, no problem at all. Where's Alex?'

'He's gone upstairs to see her and will probably disappear into his office. He doesn't want a post-mortem.'

'Are you up to telling me how it went tonight or would you rather not?' Ellen asked.

'There's not that much to tell, really. It went well enough, I suppose. The counsellor was nice but he mightn't be who we see next time.'

'But there will be a next time.'

'Yes, we both agreed we needed help,' Kate said, with a little more enthusiasm. 'It'll be a proper session then. This assessment was about discovering what our issues are, or what we think they are, and what outcome we're hoping for. That sort of thing.'

'Quite positive then.'

'Yes, but we have different goals.' Kate said. 'And the more I hear from Alex, the more I know we need to separate. With the help of Relate, we should be able to do that with less acrimony.'

'If Alex behaves.'

Kate responded with a tight smile and a nod. 'If Alex behaves.'

'I'll head on now,' Ellen said, lifting her bag. 'Oh, I nearly forgot, are you free tomorrow evening? I got a call from Jean Mason. She has Mum's tapes of her radio work for me but she also wants a chat. She didn't say what about. I'd love it if you could come too.'

'It's a bit cheeky for me to gate-crash,' Kate said, 'but I am curious about Jean. Is she coming to your flat?'

'No, I invited myself to her apartment.' Ellen giggled. 'I'm dying to see what it's like.'

'You're always so nosy,' Kate said, grinning.

'I'll pick you up about six thirty tomorrow evening, okay?' Ellen said.

They hugged and Ellen left, turning round to give her sister a quick wave as she walked up the driveway.

Chapter 32

Kate slid into the passenger seat and, as Ellen drove off, she looked back to blow a kiss to Sophie.

'I was thinking about you wanting to keep Dad in the dark about Mum and Peter continuing their affair,' Kate said when they stopped at traffic lights. 'You're probably right, but are you able to keep that to yourself? You hate secrets and this is a huge one.'

'There's no alternative. He must never know,' Ellen said firmly, accelerating away when the green light showed. 'It would destroy him.'

Ellen kept silent on the journey, staring straight ahead, her fingers gripping the steering wheel. She let Kate give the directions, acknowledging them with a nod.

'This is the road,' Kate announced.

Ellen swung into a broad avenue lined with trees and large, handsome Victorian houses, none exactly alike. The houses were set well back from the road and, judging by the numbers on gates, many had been divided into apartments. Ellen drove along slowly while Kate read out the numbers on the gateposts. Eventually, they found the house and parked the car.

Ellen put her head back against the headrest. 'Mum kept secrets all those years. We don't know her any more.'

'Let's ask Jean what Mum was like to work with,' Kate suggested. 'Maybe she can show us a different side of Mum, one we can feel more comfortable with.'

They walked up to the house and Ellen pressed the button for J. Mason. Instead of an intercom reply, the door opened, but Jean's smile fell away when she saw Kate there too.

'Ellen,' she said, 'and Kate too.' She inclined her head a fraction as if awaiting an explanation. 'Lovely to see you both,' she said and led them into her ground-floor apartment.

'What a gorgeous room,' Kate said, her tone reverential.

Jean invited them to sit and Ellen chose the large sea-green sofa. Kate remained standing, entranced by all around her. The offer of drinks brought requests for tea and coffee, and Jean disappeared to make them.

'Don't you love what she's done with the room?' Kate enthused, walking around it. 'All the original features balanced perfectly with a contemporary look. And this.' Kate hurried over to a tall turquoise vase. 'It's Japanese cloisonné! Early last century, the real—'

'Kate!' Ellen hissed.

Kate spun round. 'What?'

Ellen jabbed a finger at her own wrist.

'What's that supposed to mean?' Kate demanded.

Ellen put a finger to her lips and glanced furtively at the door Jean had disappeared through. She signalled for Kate to sit beside her.

'Her watch, did you see it?' Ellen whispered when Kate sat down.

'No.'

'It's Mum's. Remember, we couldn't find it when we were sorting through her things. The one with the turquoise strap.'

Just then, Jean returned, tray in hand. While she was busy setting down coasters, glasses of water and pure white porcelain cups and plates on the sleek black coffee table, the girls got a good look at her outstretched arm. Ellen nudged Kate gently and widened her eyes at her, then slid her gaze to a group of framed photographs on a small, exquisite desk in the corner of the room. They were photos of Jean and Betty at some formal events. Each one showed Betty holding an award while Jean stood either beside her or in the background.

Jean offered round the plate of biscuits and answered Kate's queries about the vase. She talked about her passion for antique markets and auctions, giving Ellen time to study their host.

She saw, as before, the perfectly groomed woman. Today, she was in slim black jeans and a rust-coloured, slash-necked top. But for all Jean's polished appearance, those fleeting glimpses of nervousness were still apparent. As Kate continued with her lavish praise, Ellen scanned the room for clues to Jean's life, trying to discover more about this woman who seemed to idolise her mother. It struck her as odd that Jean was almost a stranger to their family. She had a hazy recollection of meeting her at one of Betty's award ceremonies and of Betty making references to Jean. She also had a vague memory of passing Jean in the corridor of the hospice. And of course at the funeral. That was all Ellen could conjure up.

A small framed photograph sitting on a bookcase next to the fireplace caught Ellen's eye. A man, perhaps a few years older than Kate, was smiling the way Jean smiled, restrained, cautious. Jean's son, Ellen decided. She glanced back at Jean, taking in her wedding ring this time as well as Betty's watch.

Kate and Jean had moved on from talking about the vase to other artefacts that were dotted around the room.

'I'm really looking forward to hearing the tapes of Mum's programmes,' Ellen said, keen to move the conversation on from interior design.

'The tapes?' Jean looked puzzled and set down her empty mug. 'Oh, yes. Sorry, I still haven't sorted through them.'

'I thought that's why we were here,' Ellen said.

'Actually, no.' Jean went to the desk in the corner and opened a drawer. 'It was to give you this, Ellen,' she said, holding out a padded envelope with a shaking hand.

Ellen didn't move; she had been here before. Jean stretched her hand out further.

Ellen glanced at the envelope and saw Jean's name and address on the opened envelope. She took the envelope and turned it over. The sender's details were on the back. She cradled the envelope in her hands and stared at Jean.

'I know what's in it,' she said coldly, 'and who sent it. And you do too, don't you?'

'What is it?' Kate asked.

'My purse,' Ellen said, her eyes on Jean's bowed head.

'What, the purse you lost in Dublin? How did it get here?'

'The envelope has the Buswells Hotel address on it. Yes, how *did* it get here, Jean?' Ellen asked calmly, her eyes still fixed on Jean.

'Peter Fraser sent it,' Jean said, raising her head. 'There was a note in the envelope addressed to me asking me to give the smaller one to you. There was no explanation. I assume you managed to trace him and you met.'

'Oh yes, but I walked out on him.'

Jean looked startled, then relieved.

Ellen explained that she had told Hugh what Betty had revealed in her letters and he had inadvertently given her Peter's name. She then went on to tell Jean what she had discovered about Peter and her mother.

'But I gather you knew their whole story,' Ellen said, pinning her with a stare.

'I'll tell you all I know, but I want you to know that I wish I'd dealt with things differently.' Jean's eyes glistened with tears. 'I've known about Peter Fraser for twenty plus years,' she admitted, 'and you could say I was complicit in their affair.'

Kate gasped.

'I guessed right then,' Ellen said, leaning forward. 'We're waiting.'

Jean sank into a chair as if released from the burden she had been carrying. The tears still shone in her eyes but didn't fall.

'Your mother and I gelled right from when we met. She was the only person at work I confided in.' Jean paused, lowering her head for a moment before continuing. 'My husband died when our son, Daniel, was five. Clive had bipolar and deliberately drove his car at a wall. I told Daniel it was a terrible accident and asked friends and family to keep the truth to themselves. When Betty and I started working together, Daniel was an unhappy teenager and displaying bipolar symptoms too. He started asking me about his father's death and Betty advised me to tell him the truth. When I did tell him, he bitterly resented not being told before, when everyone around him seemed to know. It was a very upsetting time for me, and your mother helped me through it.'

Jean got up and lifted the photograph on the bookcase. 'This is Daniel. He lives in Toronto now. He still has issues but he copes. I go over to see him every year.' She set the photo gently down again, then turned to face the sisters.

'As regards your family,' she said, 'I presumed your mother was happily married with two lovely daughters and all was fine. I knew she was totally devoted to her work. It consumed her. But there was a change in Betty when she returned from a trip to Durban for a funeral.'

'Yes, our grandfather's,' Kate said.

'She became very withdrawn and showed little interest in her work after that. Not like her at all. I assumed she was grieving for her father. Then she became restless and impatient with everyone, including me. Betty was always feisty and didn't suffer fools.' Jean glanced away. 'But it became more extreme,' she added. 'One day she poured it all out, about her relationship with Peter and about you, Ellen. I was the only person she told. Betty said she could rely on my discretion.'

Ellen uttered a short bitter laugh.

'I was shocked, of course,' Jean went on, 'but she told me that she had to go on seeing Peter. She felt as if she was suffocating in her marriage. Her words.' Jean looked from Ellen to Kate. 'She loved you both, but her love for Peter was obsessive.'

'She loved him more than us,' Ellen said, leaning forward. 'It's as simple as that. She put him before us.'

'I'm sure she didn't intend to. Her judgement just went out the window where he was concerned. She thought she could hold on to everything and everyone as long as the secrets were kept.' Jean lifted a glass of water and took a few sips.

'But Mum needed help to keep those secrets,' Ellen said. 'We're still waiting to hear how big a part you played in that.'

'Betty liked to live life on the edge and she found the affair exciting, dangerous even. She was loving work again too, pushing the boundaries, especially in her investigative programmes. Working with Betty was a joy for me.' Jean's eyes glistened. 'I'd have done anything for her,' she added softly.

'You obviously did,' Ellen muttered.

'Yes, you're right. They met in whatever city Peter was visiting for work and I made the bookings for Betty's travel and the hotel rooms,' Jean explained. 'I was never out of pocket, of course. It didn't seem that much different to my normal work duties. I had my misgivings, but I let my loyalty, my admiration, my ... my attachment to Betty cloud my judgement.' She looked down at her hands gripped tightly in her lap.

'Your watch,' Ellen said. 'We recognise it. Did Mum give it to you?'

Jean glanced at her wrist and touched the watch face. 'Yes, she did,' she murmured. 'It was a present I chose for her. But she never knew that.'

Ellen frowned. 'What do you mean?'

'Peter often asked me to choose gifts for Betty on his behalf and I obliged. I knew she'd love this watch.' She glanced from Ellen to Kate. 'It should have gone to one of you.'

'I wouldn't have wanted it, not under those circumstances,' Ellen said. 'So you made the arrangements for them to meet, but that can't have been all. Come on, what else did you do?'

'I also made phone calls to Peter if there were any problems, like Betty's flight being delayed or if you girls took ill. They relied on me. They knew they could trust me.' Jean took another sip of water. 'It was mostly Peter who proposed these measures, not Betty,' Jean added hastily. 'I met him only once in person, in London.'

'What did you think of him?' Kate asked.

'Charming, confident, quick-witted, like Betty. They were in tune with each other. I could see why she was captivated by him. But after a while his charm seemed well-rehearsed, like an actor. On the phone I found him condescending, as if I was his PA. Everything was on his terms. He was the one in control.'

'Did you tell Mum how you felt about him?' Ellen asked.

'No, but I doubt she would have listened or cared what I thought of him.'

'He told me he didn't visit Mum in the hospice,' Ellen said. 'He never went to see the woman he apparently loved while she was dying. Is that right?'

'Yes.'

'Did Mum ask him to come?' Ellen asked, her voice breaking.

'Yes she did, repeatedly, but he refused. I'd have kept his visit secret if he'd wanted to come,' Jean said. 'I told him that. But he wouldn't take the risk, not even to grant her dying wish to see him. It was ... unforgivable.' The word was loaded with contempt. 'But your mother wouldn't hear a bad word said against him. Right to the end, she was certain he'd change his mind. She never gave up hope.' Jean's hands became fists. 'How could he have done that to her?' she said with vehemence.

Her words hung in the air for a few moments.

'Peter might not have said farewell to your mother but Hugh did,' Jean said a little more calmly. 'I bumped into him once in the hospice and he told me he'd been visiting her quite often when he knew no one else would be there. He said he liked to keep Betty company, even when she fell asleep. It was obvious he still loved her, and she seemed happy to have him there.' Jean leaned forward. 'I asked your mother to tell you the truth, Ellen, over and over again. I reminded her of the advice she had given me to tell my son what really happened to his father, but Betty said she couldn't tell you face to face.'

'I spent hours by Mum's bedside in the hospice,' Ellen said in a hushed voice. 'She recalled all the funny things I used to get up to and how defiant I was as a child. She asked about my hopes for the future and told me how proud she was of me.' Ellen's lip trembled. 'Why couldn't she have told me? We were so close then. Or I thought we were.' Ellen's voice broke but she kept talking. 'She never even hinted that there were secrets she was keeping from me. I'd have forgiven her, maybe even understood her, but she didn't give me that chance.'

'Betty was sure you would press her for information she wasn't able to give,' Jean said. 'I think she felt too weak by then to deal with any kind of confrontation. She told me she'd written a letter. Maybe that was the coward's way out, but I was relieved you were getting the truth one way or another.'

'So you knew what was in the letter,' Ellen said.

'Yes, Betty asked me to read it. She was worried that the strong painkillers she was taking might affect her mentally. She asked me to deliver it when you came home from Durban.'

She paused. 'Ellen, I ...' Jean closed her eyes for a few moments. 'I must tell you that, very close to the end, Betty asked me to destroy that letter.'

'What?' Ellen cried.

'Betty believed that if she kept her secret, the family would stay together and you and Hugh would remain close as father and daughter.' Jean's voice trembled. 'She was confident that Peter would never try to contact you, so your life would simply go on as before and so would his. Her final words about it were, "I've always stirred things up, but now I want to let things be".'

'But you obviously decided she was wrong,' Ellen said with ice in her voice.

'It seemed only right that you should know the truth and decide for yourself what to do,' Jean replied. 'It was what Betty had persuaded me to do with my son. But I never imagined you'd be able to trace Peter from the little information she gave. I ... I have so many regrets. If I'd thought you'd be able to find him, I'd have warned you what kind of man he was. I hope it hasn't jeopardised your relationship with Hugh and Kate. I sincerely apologise for my role in all this. I did what I believed was right at the time.'

'Was telling me the truth more important than obeying my mother's wishes?' Ellen demanded.

Jean was silent for a moment, then asked quietly, 'Did you not do the same?'

Ellen stared at her, unable to respond in any way. Suddenly weary, she bent over, cupping her head in her hands. Kate edged closer and Ellen put her head on her sister's shoulder. Kate stroked her hair. Jean sat silent, watching them.

Finally Ellen and Kate stood up. Jean rose too and all three walked to the door. They remained standing in self-conscious silence, like tongue-tied mourners at a funeral. Suddenly Jean hurried back to the table, picked up the envelope with the purse in it and handed it to Ellen.

'I'll contact you about those tapes,' she said. 'We can listen to them together.'

Ellen said nothing. She took the envelope almost reluctantly, and dropped it into her bag. Then the girls walked back up the driveway, got into the car and drove off.

Halfway along the tree-lined road Ellen braked and stared ahead through the windscreen, her hands welded to the steering wheel.

'How do I make sense of all this? That sangoma was right,' she said with a sardonic laugh. 'There are still "questions without answers" and there always will be.' She turned to Kate. 'It was my decision to track down Peter Fraser and meet him. Anyone in my position would have wanted to do the same. But I shouldn't have turned my back on you and Dad. I was as obsessed and as self-centred as Mum was. Thank goodness neither of you gave up on me. What's important now is that I'm closer than ever to you and Dad – my proper dad. Peter Fraser means nothing to me. I have both of you back and I'm perfectly content with that ...'

She gave a sharp sob. 'But Mum's disappeared. I've lost her in all the secrets and lies and deceit. I don't care what she did. I need to have her back too. I've forgotten all the good times.' She grabbed Kate's hand. 'I can't even picture her,' she whispered. 'Give me a good memory of Mum. Plant one in my brain.'

'Mmmm ... let me think ... It's as hard for me as—'

'Please, Kate, please.'

'Okay, here's one. All four of us on the beach in Donegal. We were making a huge sandcastle, but you ran down the beach into the sea with your sundress on, and your socks and sandals. You were jumping in the shallow bit.' Kate laughed, high-pitched.

'I can't remember. Tell me more.'

'You must have been about four or five. Mum and Dad shouted for you to come out but you were such a rascal. You just splashed about even more. So Mum marched to the water's edge, kicked off her shoes and walked straight in.'

Ellen turned to Kate, her face flushed. 'I do remember. I remember it,' she cried. 'Mum hoisted me under her arm and carried me back over the pebbles. We were laughing, both of us.'

'That's right. Mum's dress was soaked with all your splashing, but she didn't care. You made her laugh, you always did.'

'I could make her shout too,' Ellen said, with a trembling grin.

'Two of a kind.'

'There should be a photo from that day somewhere,' Ellen cried, suddenly distraught. 'I didn't see it in the album I had in the flat.'

'It must be in some other album.'

'Would Dad have it? It wouldn't have been thrown out, would it?' Ellen, so intense, so vulnerable.

'I don't think so. Sure we can ask him.'

'Let's call to see him now.'

'Okay, but' – Kate swivelled round and lifted Ellen's bag from the back seat – 'the envelope Jean gave you, are you not going to open it?'

Ellen's hands were shaking as she pulled away the tape, slid her hand inside and removed the small, beaded purse. She peered into the envelope, turned it upside down and shook it, tore it apart. But there was no note, nothing from the sender.

She unzipped the purse and removed her credit card, the five pound note, the euros and the return bus ticket. Then her fingers touched something else, tucked into the corner. She lifted out the little metal disc the sangoma had given her. Her hand tightened around it. Tightened until her knuckles went white.

Acknowledgements

My heartfelt thanks to all who helped over the years to make my dream of writing and publishing my novel come true.

I am hugely indebted to my editor and publishing consultant, Averill Buchanan, who painstakingly turned my manuscript into a book ready for publication. Averill's attention to detail has been exceptional and her 'pruning' skills masterly. Nothing escapes her. That level of perfection in everything she did was very reassuring. Thank you, Averill.

I am equally indebted to Siobhán Dignan who has, for years, skilfully helped develop the plots and characters. She knew my characters better than I did! She was my co-conspirator and stormed my brain with ideas. Siobhan was totally committed to seeing me through to the end. We will have to find another venture for the two of us.

I would never have got to this stage without both of you and I value your friendship greatly.

Thanks also go to my first editor, Marjorie Quarton, whose encouragement and belief in me set me on my way many years ago. And to Andrew Brown of Design for Writers for my much appreciated book cover.

I am very grateful to Brian Burke and Bob McKimm for their all-important research and guidance, and to my first readers Máire Callaghan, Glad Elliott, Carol McCaig, Margaret Smith and Geraldine Wilson for their valuable comments.

Local authors Bernie McGill and Helen Nicholl generously shared their knowledge and advice, and I am most appreciative.

My love and gratitude goes out to all my friends for their enthusiastic support.

Last in this list, but first in importance and affection, are my daughters Fiona and Claire and their extra special families who have always cheered me on. Above all, my ever-patient and supportive husband, Gordon, who has never complained about sharing our house with a fictional family for far too many years.

About the author

Belfast-born author Heather McConnell first developed a love of telling stories and capturing character as a singer-songwriter and portrait artist. She is fascinated by the undercurrents in complex family relationships. *Under the Stone* is her debut novel.

Printed in Great Britain
by Amazon

37253292R00158